The Note Played Next

Also by William M. Gould

Partners
A Little Score to Settle
Three Boys Like You

The Note Played Next

A Novel

William M. Gould

The Note Played Next

iUniverse books may be ordered through booksellers or by contacting:

iUniverse
1663 Liberty Drive
Bloomington, IN 47403
www.iuniverse.com
1-800-Authors (1-800-288-4677)

ISBN: 978-1-4917-4716-2 (sc)
ISBN: 978-1-4917-4715-5 (e)

Library of Congress Control Number: 2014917452

Printed in the United States of America.

iUniverse rev. date: 10/22/2014

Always, for Sue

"I always challenge myself. I get out in deep water and I always try to get back. But I get hung up. The audience never knows, but that's when I smile the most, when I show the most ivory."

Earl Hines

Before dawn on September 20, 1988, Ernst K_____ put his rowing shell in the bay at Redwood City. He was alone and it was his happiest time.

The sky, no longer opaque, had begun to fill with the soft light of earliest morning. He would set his course, but he held back, hunched over the oars for a moment, to enjoy the stillness. Then he gave the hood-string of his sweatshirt an extra tug, settled into the seat, and pulled.

The craft slipped out from the slough into open water, and he felt once again the near-religious sense of awe and connection with the physical world that had brought him back to rowing after such a long time. He was pleased that he'd mustered the self-discipline to keep at it. In college he had been on the crew, and now, forty years later, his neck muscles, and his back, and his shoulders and arms seemed to have precise memories of exactly how it was done.

Puffs of mild wind from the east pushed water against the bow, and he smiled, listening to the gentle slapping sounds.

A new day, the water, the sky, and his body—he, himself—all one. The immensity of this world.

What are we here for? What truly matters?

K_____ knew just one thing . . . if there were questions, this was the answer.

Far off to the north he glimpsed the bobbing lights of a solitary fishing boat heading up the bay toward San Francisco.

He existed only in the steady rhythm of smooth surges forward with each stroke, mesmerized by the dim whorls and wavelets of his receding wake.

The craft moved parallel to the shore, about thirty yards out, but he was aware of the border of sedge grass as he pulled along. Stroke . . . hover . . . stroke . . . hover . . .

He let it glide, listening for other sounds.

Nothing.

It had been three months since he'd taken up rowing again. There was nothing quite like it.

Alone.

A new breeze came from the north and he pulled harder.

Was he fighting an incoming tide? He hadn't checked the tables.

The craft rocked a little, and he saw that he'd inadvertently allowed himself to be pushed closer to the shore.

The sky had lightened even more and to check his bearings he turned to face the bow.

A large bird rose up from the sedge as he glided closer.

Another flapped up.

Then, a third.

Vultures?

There were no deer out here . . . maybe a dead fish.

He saw something white.

The craft nosed into the grass and came to a stop.

White . . .

Then he understood what lay there.

PART ONE

1951
Outrage

1

Even as they were happening, Josh Lowen knew he would never forget the details. The loud knocks of the campus police at his door; the sour smelling, vomit-stained shirt he'd pushed under the bed; and the questioning. They took him in a patrol car to the station, and the other guys were already there—Walt, Kenny, Zipper, and P.B. At that point it didn't seem bad. As long as they were all there together it would be okay.

The sergeant shoved a chair at Josh and then the five of them were sitting there, just waiting. They could hear another cop on the phone in the outer room.

"Okay, boys," the tall, thin sergeant said. He had a little pencil mustache, but he looked tired and wasn't smiling. "Start from the beginning."

"What's this all about?" Kenny asked.

The sergeant raised his eyebrows and shook his head. "I'm talking about the fight. You were in Vermont Hall. You fellows were pretty boozed up. Why'd you go there?"

They all spoke at once—half sentences—then sequentially, each telling a fraction of what had happened.

"Why'd you go there?"

They were silent.

"You attacked him."

"He did something we didn't like."

"He? You mean Tom Grillo?"

P.B. blurted it out. "He was wearing a varsity sweater. He's not on any varsity."

The sergeant shook his head again. The other cop came in and motioned to him. Both went into the outer room and the boys sat there looking at one another, and then staring at the floor. They could hear the cops talking in the hall, but they couldn't make anything out.

Then they heard, "Oh, Jesus."

It was 1951.

Tom Grillo was a returned veteran. In 1943, he had interrupted his education at Bartlett College to enlist in the United States Army. Initially, he was deployed to England, but because he knew Italian he was assigned to an intelligence unit and then transferred to Sicily from which the Germans were in full retreat. On January 23, 1944, he took part in the Allied landings at Anzio. One week later, he was wounded during a Luftwaffe strafing attack and evacuated home.

After recovery, he was reassigned to a clerical job at the Presidio in San Francisco. On July 17, 1944, not far from San Francisco, an enormous explosion occurred at the Port Chicago Naval Ammunition Depot. It killed 320 people, the majority of them black sailors who had been given no training at loading ammunition on to ships headed for the Pacific theatre. When fifty surviving black sailors refused to return to work that had proved so dangerous, a court martial for mutiny took place. The men were pronounced guilty, but there was a somewhat muted public outcry that the segregated military couldn't possibly have been fair in the judgment against them.

With the devastation he'd seen in Europe, and now with what he felt to be a travesty of justice for the Port Chicago 50, Tom Grillo was developing strong political feelings. After discharge he had worked on the docks in New York for several years before finally heading back to Bartlett College on the G.I. Bill.

Tom was a quiet man and spent most of his time in the library, but some younger students, especially the fraternity crowd, found him unfriendly and thought he should keep his left-wing opinions to himself. There was a feeling that he didn't fit in. And his name—Grillo—was an irritant, too.

Josh Lowen was one of only three Jewish Rho Iota Pi brothers. Because the three were athletes, and because the house wanted the best jocks on campus, the ongoing climate of not-so-subtle anti-Semitism was conveniently forgotten for the time being. The three were admired for their prowess in sports and made to feel welcome. Josh saw the brothers as a good bunch of friendly guys. He enjoyed the beer and the feeling that he was appreciated.

That night they'd had quite a few, but he'd finished all his class assignments, so he went along with the group. They started at the Rho house, and then went on to Theta Omicron where there was a lot of singing going on. By that time he was suggesting that they ought to call it a night, but the other brothers said they had one more thing to do and that he should go with them. There was some discussion about an "unfriendly" student and they wanted to teach him a lesson.

He felt a wave of nausea coming on and tried to slip away, but the others grabbed him and they all headed over to Vermont Hall.

Just outside the dorm he stopped to throw up in the shrubbery. Some of the mess got on his shirt and he wiped it off with his hand. The guys had already run in, but Josh headed for the bathroom where he vomited again into the toilet. He stared at himself in the mirror for a moment, blinking from the brightness of the solitary electric bulb above the sink. Then he heard the others and followed their voices to one of the rooms.

The door was open and this guy, Tom Grillo, was standing by his bed, facing Walt, Kenny, P.B., and Zipper. Grillo, who had been sleeping, was wearing a varsity sweater and Kenny had grabbed its sleeve.

"Take it off, fucker," Kenny said. "A pinko like you doesn't deserve to wear this."

Josh nudged Kenny. "C'mon, let's go," he mumbled.

"You creeps are real brave, aren't you?" Grillo said quietly. "Five against one?"

"Take the sweater off, Commie bastard." Kenny made a menacing motion with his other hand, but Grillo punched him in the stomach and Kenny fell back.

"Get out of my room, all of you," Grillo said. "Beat it."

Walt and Zipper moved quickly and threw themselves at him. Grillo stumbled, then recovered and tried to resist them, but they shoved him backwards and he tripped, falling and hitting his head on the end of the iron bed.

"Let's go," Walt said. "That's enough."

Josh watched the whole thing, and he had a sudden thought that seemed almost brilliant to him in his beery haze . . . if he had just come in a few moments sooner he might have been able to convince them that it was time to go to sleep. But he'd arrived too late. Whatever they had wanted to do was done.

"Okay, we're going," he said to no one in particular.

Grillo was rubbing the back of his head. "Get out," he said, even more quietly than the first time. "I despise you . . . you're scum, all of you."

The two cops returned.

"Can we go now?" Zipper asked, getting up from his chair.

"Sit down," the sergeant said. "You're not going anywhere tonight." He pulled out a ring of keys and waved them at the boys. "We have a nice comfy cell for you right here."

When Tom Grillo's roommate came back from the library he saw that Tom, still wearing the varsity sweater, was stretched out on his bed, rubbing his head. "Awful headache," he said.

"You okay?"

Tom began telling him what had happened, and then suddenly fell back, shaking uncontrollably. The roommate ran for help. Several students on the floor were still awake and they all managed to get Tom to the hospital. Within two hours neurosurgeons were evacuating the blood and clots that were pressing and pushing Tom's brain against the skull. But it was too late. Despite attempts at cardiac resuscitation, Tom Grillo died on the operating table.

Within three days Zipper, Kenny, Walt, P.B., and Josh were expelled from Bartlett College. In court, three months later, Kenny, Walt, and Zipper, who had all pleaded innocent to a charge of first-degree manslaughter, were allowed to change their plea from not guilty to no contest. The judge issued them sentences of one to two years in prison, which were immediately suspended, and a $500 fine for each. Josh and P.B. were considered to have been less aggressive in the attack against Grillo, but the judge lectured them separately, calling them "weak cowards" for doing nothing to stop the others, and they, too, paid $500 fines.

One week later a letter written to the judge by Tom Grillo's mother found its way into the newspapers.

"What an outrage. For killing my son they got a slap on the wrist. He served his country so that bigoted boys like that could go to college. There's been no justice done. A farce, but no justice."

2

The worst thing was his father's disdain. Getting kicked out of Bartlett was bad enough, but the embarrassment, disappointment, accusation, and shame in Sid Lowen's face was more than Josh could bear. He knew things would never return to the way they had been. Now there were just frantic moments sobbing, striking his fist into his stomach, and suffering constant headaches. Was it possible that what he felt about the pain he had caused his parents would never go away?

He knew the headaches were connected to the spasms of anger he felt toward the others, especially Kenny, Walt, and Zipper. On the other hand, how stupid he'd been, how weak and foolish to have gone with that bunch. How pathetic. Those bastards!

He and his parents had uncomfortable conversations about what he would do next, but nothing was settled. Besides the wasted money, there was the humiliation of having it all revealed.

"Dirty laundry" was what he kept thinking. Being a part of another student's death was not something that could ever be cleaned up.

"Take it off, fucker . . . you don't deserve to wear this."

"C'mon, let's go."

I said that, but I didn't raise my voice.

"Get out of my room."

That was Grillo.

"Take the sweater off."

That was Kenny. Grillo punched him and Kenny fell back.

"All of you, beat it."

That was Grillo again. Walt and Zipper moved, throwing themselves at him. Grillo stumbled . . . shoved backwards . . . tripped . . . hit his head on the iron bed.

Oh, God, what have I done?

"Let's go. That's enough."

Walt said that.

I got there too late. Why didn't I do something, anything? What—what could I have done?

"Okay, we're going."

That's all I said. Finally, I said something, but it was worthless. It was like saying nothing. And Grillo was just sitting there, rubbing his head.

"Get out . . . I despise you . . . you're scum, all of you."

3

December 2, 1951

Dear Josh,

I saw in the newspaper how it all came out. Those guys got off easily, but I'm sure it's terrible for you even now that it's over. Deep down I know it was just bad luck you happened to be with them. You know well enough the difficult stuff I've faced myself. It was a different sort, but I know how having a good friend helps. You were that good friend to me when my parents split up. So, keep in touch. I don't know what you plan to do now, but you can count on me. If you want to talk anytime I'm willing. Let me know. You'll get through it.

Larry

Josh read it and had to sit down on his bed. He was shaken, and embarrassed, too. They were still friends, but he'd never expected to hear from anyone—even Larry Gerst. All he wanted now was to hide. Being with people had always been comfortable, but that was all changed. And to get this letter . . . he didn't deserve it. What kind of a friend had he been for Larry back then when Abe and Betty Gerst's marriage had ended? The divorce had hurt Larry terribly, but Josh had been tongue-tied and awkward. Sure, they were younger then, but still . . . he could've tried more.

He opened a drawer and tucked the letter underneath some socks.

PART TWO

1933-1951
Brooklyn; Queens;
Bartlett College

4

For years the two families had been good friends, but Larry's parents' divorce had changed everything. There were no longer fond reminiscences about how two young couples had met during the darkest year of the Depression when spring had come so late to Brooklyn. Abe and Betty Gerst, and Sid and Mae Lowen had been grateful for the final arrival of mild and fragrant air. It was a perfect and congenial accompaniment to the births of their first children.

Lester Edwin Gerst, whom everyone would later call Larry, was born without a struggle in the last week of May. Joshua Mark Lowen, whom everyone would call Josh, was delivered by mid-forceps in the first week of June, and his parents felt especially blessed because Mae Lowen had had three prior miscarriages.

The couples were casual acquaintances, but brief stops to chat while pushing baby carriages along the sidewalks of Brighton Beach slowly began to take on the shape of a possible friendship.

A year later, when each little boy had almost mastered the art of walking, the two couples, quite separately and by chance, happened to move to the same neighborhood in Queens. Neither had mentioned to the other anything about leaving Brooklyn, but there it was, and everything suddenly seemed less strange. It would be easier to settle in, even comforting, knowing that friends were living close by. In fact, a shortcut through the few empty sandy lots that separated their new homes made paying visits effortless.

The two couples had some, but not all, things in common.

Baby Larry's father, Abe Gerst, had grown up in Berlin, but in 1927 he'd come to America, in part out of concern about the rising power of the Nazi party. His own middle-class Jewish family had gradually made a small fortune in the arbitrage of currency differentials between Berlin, London and Paris, but Abe's parents were alert to the sting of German anti-Semitism. "I don't think it will happen," his father told Abe. "But if Hitler, God forbid, comes to power, people like us may be in danger. You . . . you go to America. Then, if you get settled, perhaps we'll come later." There were distant Gerst cousins who had come to the United States right after the Franco-Prussian War, and they had done well. Perhaps Abe could work with them. Economically as well as socially, it might be a smart move.

Desiring a change, Abe sailed to New York—not just out of a more acute realism than that of his parents, but also from youthful curiosity and hopes for adventure. He wanted something new, something fresh. Upon arrival he took his cousins' advice, going to night school to become a CPA, and then found a job with a Wall Street firm doing exactly what the Gerst family had exploited in Europe—currency arbitrage. He was a quick study—diffident, yet brilliant—a person who rose higher and higher in the firm, never talking much about his work, but each year becoming more comfortable and demonstrably self-assured. In the hospital on the day of Larry's birth, the obstetrician gently placed the baby on Betty's chest. She looked up at Abe who, with tears in his eyes, was beaming. "Now," she told him proudly. "You have a true and living connection to your adopted country."

Little Josh's father, Sid Lowen, born poor in a Russian *shtetl*, had been brought to America at the age of three by his widowed mother, along with his two older brothers. Their deceased husband and father had preceded them and had started a successful dress business in lower

Manhattan, but eleven months after arriving at Ellis Island he had died of a burst appendix and peritonitis. Sid had a meager childhood, his mother supporting her three sons by designing and sewing clothes for wealthier ladies. She was a feisty, if uneducated, woman, and by thrift and determination eventually saved enough to buy a home. Quick to take offense, and always alert to possibilities in the local scene that might benefit her boys, it often surprised people that she could also show a tender side that revered music and took pleasure in beautiful things. If she had a guiding philosophy it was more a matter of instinct, and it emerged as frequent assurances to her offspring that they were as good as any other kids in Brooklyn and that they would not only be successful, but cultured gentlemen.

This made a particularly profound impression on her youngest son. Sid Lowen worked moderately hard as a salesman, but he also managed to fulfill the destiny that his mother's vision prophesied. There were high values to be pursued, and for Sid those included opera and concerts, and poetry readings, and long hours at the Metropolitan Museum. A happy man, he spoke beautiful Yiddish and was also completely at home in America. With the long hoped-for birth of Josh, he and Mae found it comforting to look at each other and one of them would always say, "Well, everything seems to be under control."

Although Russian and German Jews often carried preconceptions about one another and tended to stick to their own kind, Sid Lowen and Abe Gerst happened to join the same Reform synagogue in Queens, and each became active in its Men's Club. They discovered that they shared interests, particularly in art, literature and classical music, and it didn't take long for the two couples to become quite good friends. The Gersts and Lowens began to take short Saturday excursions into Manhattan together, most often to one of the museums. They would spend an hour or two at a new exhibit of paintings, and then recover their stamina and humor over a convivial and noisy meal at a Chinese restaurant. The little boys eventually came to anticipate and relish these outings, and they were beginning to feel rather special. By the time they were in kindergarten, and to their gleeful astonishment, both of them discovered that other kids had never even eaten chow mein and had no idea who Vincent Van Gogh might be.

The comfortable friendship between the Gersts and Lowens deepened with the years. They had special evenings of theater and opera, but there were even more times when they just played cards at home, talking about recent books and trying to make sense of current events both in the United States and beyond. Locally, the future was starting to look hopeful. They liked and trusted Roosevelt and felt he would lead the country out of chaos, but the ominous news from Europe hung over everything.

Abe Gerst had pleaded with his parents and two sisters to come to New York, but their life in Berlin, uncertain though it was, had a long history of successful enterprise and high culture, and America seemed a raw and crude place to them.

In December 1938, mere weeks after Kristallnacht, Abe received a smudged, water-stained letter that bore a German stamp. It was from a non-Jewish woman who had been his father's secretary, and she gently expressed regrets that his parents and two sisters had been deported. A month later there was one cryptic post-card signed by Abe's father, mailed from somewhere in Poland, with references to God's love and hopes for a reunion in the future. After that, there was only silence.

Young families with children were discovering Queens to be more attractive than some older, more crowded parts of New York City, and within a couple of years the Gersts and Lowens found themselves at the center of a group of amiable couples who seemed to enjoy similar things. The wives met regularly during afternoons and called themselves "the sewing circle." On weekends in warm weather there were cookouts, and card games—bridge for the ladies, pinochle and gin rummy for the men—that went on into the evening. The mood had always been convivial, but that changed one Saturday at the Gerst's home. The card games were finished, everyone else had left, and the Lowens were in the kitchen helping Betty and Abe clean up and put things away.

"I'm glad that's over," Abe said."

Sid was drying a large frying pan, and he looked up.

"Why? You didn't enjoy the day?

"It's always the same with this crowd," Abe said. "Same people, same ideas. Nothing interesting."

Mae and Betty were at the sink. They turned to face him, gave each other a look, and then quickly went back to the dishes.

"What do you mean, Abe?" Sid asked. "It was just friends talking . . . schmoozing. What's not to like?"

"They're not my friends," Abe said. "I'm not talking about you and Mae. But don't you think the conversation was dull?"

"It's what people talk about . . . politics, business, their kids, sports, gossip. What do you expect? Philosophy?"

"Yes, philosophy."

"Ah, c'mon."

"No, it's important. It's not trivial. These people . . . I don't like to say it, but they're not very bright."

Sid put the frying pan on the counter. Mae and Betty still had their backs turned, and the water in the sink was running.

"Abe's had a hard week," Betty said quietly.

"No, I haven't had a hard week, Betty. I'm sorry to upset you, but I'm tired of listening to mediocre people spouting off about things they've heard from other ignoramuses. Aren't there some big issues? Must we always rehash the same things over, and over, and over? Don't they read? Don't they wonder? The world is experiencing catastrophes and they're asleep."

"He's upset about his parents and sisters," Sid said as they walked home across the sandy lots. "A letter might come at any moment telling him the worst. I can't imagine what that's like. So, his anger comes out in this superior attitude."

"Betty begs him to unburden himself, but he gets furious and shouts at her."

"Remember how he used to be gentle, self-effacing, always avoiding contentious topics?"

"Maybe when you make a lot of money you get nasty."

"Having a nice bank balance doesn't make you crabby. It should do the opposite."

"It's terrible for Betty."

"People have their quirks. Wait and see. Abe will let us know when he wants to talk about it. I don't want him to think we're being nosy."

Mae agreed, but it lay heavily on them. How sad that a quiet, shy man now went out of his way to ridicule even what other people wore, or to scorn the poor taste in the decoration of their homes.

The Lowens continued to see Abe and Betty, and they tried to remain optimistic that things would get better. There were rare moments when Abe's remarks seemed gentler, but a shadow had come over their time—awkwardness and a consciousness of things not being right.

It wasn't until after the war that they would all know for certain that Abe Gerst's parents and two sisters had been murdered in Auschwitz.

5

"You cannot just give up on college," Josh's mother warned him. "There are plenty of other schools that aren't hard to get into; the main thing is to get through it and get the degree. It would be stupid to go through life without that."

Oh, God, that's all she wants to talk about, he thought, squirming. What about the whole story? What kind of person am I? Am I to think just about myself? Even if I was no better than they were . . . even if I went along with it?

Maybe he'd never overcome the shame of attacking a guy who had fought in the war, who'd been wounded, and who'd had the temerity to express political ideas that annoyed the frat guys. Courage? Did he even know what it was?

Bartlett College—he'd been so happy and proud when they accepted him, but life was over now . . . finished. He was expelled, stupid, spineless, and completely fucked up. Just a weak drunk.

How absolutely weird it was that Larry had introduced him to Bartlett College.

"Take a school like Bartlett, or Amherst," Larry had pronounced one day. "You graduate from either of those and you're set. Anyone knows that."

Josh knew absolutely nothing about colleges. Neither of his parents had gone beyond high school, although he knew there was an unspoken understanding that college was a certainty for him. On the other hand, Larry had cousins who had gone to Yale and Swarthmore.

Back at the start of 12th grade he and Larry had talked a lot about girls—mostly who had already put out, and who might—but Larry was also focused on college. He could characterize each institution in a few vivid words. Some were impossibly out of the question. Cornell was "Grind U." The University of Virginia was "smart" and "a party school." Vassar was "wug – world's ugliest girls." And then there were the select others that he spoke of confidently in awed tones—like Bartlett.

After his parents divorced Larry retreated into himself and didn't seem to care if he saw his classmates. He became morose, even bitter at times, but wanted to stay close to Josh. They spent plenty of time together, most often at the Lowen home, talking quietly in Josh's room or listening to records, but Larry didn't smile much anymore.

Still, he was always ready with supremely confident judgments about people, clothes, and especially colleges.

Eighteen was the legal drinking age in New York State, but the bar at Tommy's on Mill Road didn't mind serving boys who looked big. On Friday nights Josh and Larry would drop in and have a glass before they went on to a party at someone's house. It opened them up and they talked continuously for hours afterward.

Despite his cleverness, Larry's grades were mediocre and all the schools he worshipped turned him down. Late in the spring of senior year he was finally accepted at Lehigh, a university he'd never even mentioned.

"That's great," Josh reassured him. "Are you happy?"

"Yeah," Larry replied. "It's a good enough school. My father's disappointed and angry, and he won't talk about it, but Mom thinks it's fine."

When Josh's parents heard the news about Larry going to Lehigh, they smiled knowingly and nodded to each another with raised eyebrows. Later that evening Josh heard his father say something about "a bad influence." Larry had ceased being a favorite of theirs and they weren't sorry that he'd be out of sight for four years.

Josh's grades had continued better than ever and, besides doing exceptionally well in wrestling, he'd had several girlfriends in succession. He was accepted at three schools, all of them with the kind of prestige Larry worshipped, and he realized that his choice had been made long before. Bartlett College—medium sized, men only, emphasizing the liberal arts, and on a lovely campus in northern New England—was perfect. One of his interviews had been with the wrestling coach who had all but assured him that Bartlett College would be delighted to have him.

He would get credit for his first year at Bartlett, but the few months of his sophomore year that he completed before the expulsion would never count. It was now December and he didn't want to think about going to another school.

"I have to do something else for a while," he told his mother one afternoon. "I can't go back to school right now."

"You could work," she said. "Maybe until September, and then find another place."

He remained silent because he was thinking about something they would deprecate as irresponsible evasion. He nodded to her, went up to his room, shut the door, and lay back on his bed. His hand dropped over the side and he pulled out the map from underneath—the western half of the country. He unfolded it and stared for a long time at places where he'd never been. Then he closed his eyes.

It was dark when he woke up. He heard the clatter of pots downstairs. Onions were being sautéed. His mother was cooking dinner. He'd slept four hours. The map had fallen on the floor and he remembered something he wanted to check. He switched on the light and picked it up.

California. His finger traced over the cities, the National Parks, the coastal road from Los Angeles to San Francisco.

He heard his father come in downstairs. Muffled words.

But then everything flooded back.

"Take it off, fucker . . . you don't deserve to wear this."

"C'mon, let's go."

"Get out of my room."

"Take the sweater off."

"All of you, beat it."

"Let's go."

"That's enough."

"Okay, we're going."

"Get out . . . I despise you . . . you're scum, all of you."

"Josh! Josh! Dinner."

He washed his face and went down. His father glanced at him, tried to smile, but it was an effort and he quickly looked away. His mother brought out a stew and set it down.

"Well," she said.

They ate silently for a while.

"I've been thinking . . ."

They looked up at him.

"Yes?" His father raised his eyebrows. "What?"

Josh pushed his chair back. "I'd like to travel for the rest of the year."

"That's ridiculous," Sid Lowen sputtered. "You get yourself into this kind of mess and now you want to travel? What's the matter with you? You need to wake up. You've got to go back to school. Travel? You don't need a vacation. You need to get serious."

Josh couldn't respond. He'd never seen his father so angry.

"What were you thinking?" Mae Lowen asked.

He looked at his mother. "Maybe California . . ."

His father got up from the table, shook his head, shrugged, and walked out of the room.

6

Childhood had been creative, stimulating, and happy for Josh and Larry. Like the proximate placement of their homes, the boys grew up side by side, although the intervening empty sandy lots—a physical thing—made them understand that each had his own family, and that friends could also have their differences. It was hard to remember a time when they hadn't played together. Sometimes it even seemed to them that each had two mothers—Larry's mother for Josh, and Josh's for Larry. When they were older, both had memories of whispered chuckles between the parents about an infant nursing at the other mother's breast, but no one would ever confirm it. Maybe it was a playful joke, or even a dare in the shadowy past, but later, when they'd heard the tale of Romulus and Remus suckled by the she-wolf, that curious story had a special fascination for them.

Well, of course, it was only a fable. Those two hadn't been real . . . everyone knew that. Besides, they were twins.

The boys played street stickball, and in one of the empty lots they built a shack out of old boards that they called their clubhouse. Snowy days they roasted *mickeys* on sharpened sticks over a small open fire they set on a flat patch of sand under a sheltering tree. They even had their own little "museum" in a discarded cabinet at Larry's house where they placed a bird's nest, shells, and interesting rocks.

Josh was a secure and cheerful boy who did well in school without working very hard. He loved poring over maps of foreign countries, and began collecting stamps. He knew the capitals of all the states and most of the countries in Europe, Asia, and South America. His smile was engaging, he laughed easily, and he considered his world to be play. He read constantly, especially books for boys that told about dangers, far-off places, heroic acts, secrets, and treasures, and these stories fed his imagination. They were dreams, but seemed quite real to him . . . as real as his own street, his family's house, and his bedroom. And even if they were dreams (he knew they were), he didn't see any reason why life would exclude him from them. Things happened, and they might as well happen to him. Meanwhile, the make-believe games and adventures he played with Larry seemed real enough. For now, they occupied him and he was happy. Whatever actual future was destined for him presented itself as a vague thing and not even particularly interesting. He rarely thought about that.

Larry was a quiet boy with a serious disposition. He was friendly, but thoughtful and careful, and he had a straightforward approach to people. His smiles were shy, but he was not. He talked easily, and looked everyone in the eye. Some adults sensed a demeanor unusual for a boy. There was an element of scrutinizing in Larry's manner, a watchfulness in which he seemed to be searching for the real person behind any façade, but then he would suddenly loosen up and his bashful smile would reappear.

One cold December Sunday, when he was eight and a half, Larry came in from playing outside all afternoon. Allowed to ride their bikes only in the immediate neighborhood, he and Josh had been up and down the quiet streets and through the alleys between where each house had a garage. Two blocks away there was a park with a small frozen pond where some older kids were skating, and the two boys had sat on a bench talking and watching.

When Larry came into the kitchen he let the door slam and his mother looked at him, shaking her head.

"Sorry," he said.

She didn't reply. Then he saw his father standing in the doorway leading into the hall and he could tell that something had happened. The radio was on and he realized they were listening to the news.

"*. . . Japanese planes . . . Pearl Harbor . . . sneak attack . . . bombed . . . killed . . .*"

He started to ask something, but his father held up a finger.

"*. . . Four battleships sunk . . . over seventy airplanes destroyed . . . simultaneous attack in Singapore . . . hundreds of Americans killed . . .*"

"We're at war," Abe Gerst said.

Larry sat down. He was used to his parents talking about Hitler and Nazis, about France being taken over by German soldiers, and about the German army invading Russia, but this was much scarier. Hawaii was America—far away, but still America. A war that had seemed distant was much closer now. He was hungry, but only wanted to ask questions. What did it mean? Would they bomb here? Did they have to move away?

"It won't be just Japan," his father said. "We'll be at war with Germany, too."

Betty Gerst started moving around the kitchen, putting things on the table in preparation for supper. Later there were a lot of phone calls to and from friends and relatives, and the evening stretched on long past Larry's bedtime. When he finally crawled under the blankets, sleep didn't come immediately. How long did a war go on? It had been the Japanese who attacked America, but his father—who came from Germany—seemed more worried about Hitler. How was that connected? If his father was German, and America fought Germany, then what would happen to his father? Would he have to hide?

Everybody was nervous and upset; everything that Larry knew, everything that belonged to him—his home, his family, and his neighborhood—all looked different now. He was frightened, but excited, too, and he wondered if he'd suddenly grown up.

In the morning, Josh put on his warm jacket, cap, and mittens and met Larry at the corner to walk the half-mile to school.

"They're not going to bomb here," Larry said.

"Who?"

"The Japs."

"No, but the Germans might."

"How do you know?"

"They have submarines," said Josh. "They submerge and then come up, and can shoot torpedoes at us."

"I'm not scared."

"Me neither."

Abe Gerst and Sid Lowen were too old for the draft. Both volunteered for Civil Defense and became Air Raid Wardens. On night duty they wore white helmets and patrolled the streets to look for lights that might be seen by enemy bombers. Everybody had to have dark shades over their windows. Ration books were needed to buy butter and sugar. Tinfoil from the lining of cigarette packages was saved and rolled into balls for the war effort. Betty Gerst had a brother serving in the Navy as a pharmacist's mate. When he was promoted he got new insignia and Larry was given his old stripes to have sewn onto a shirt, and a real white sailor hat that he was taught to fold up in the proper way so that he could hang it on his belt. Josh's cousin was drafted into the Army and deployed to an anti-aircraft battery in Iceland. He gave Josh a red, white, and blue cloth arm patch reading *"AA"* and Mae Lowen sewed it onto Josh's windbreaker.

There were air raid drills at school where everybody had to march down to the basement, crouch on the floor, and put arms over heads as protection from flying boards or broken glass.

The boys talked a lot about German attacks.

"What if it happens when we're at home," Josh wondered. "What would you try to save?"

"My bike," said Larry. "It could come in handy. And books, too."

"I've got my Dad's old briefcase. I've already put four books in it. Just in case."

"Yeah, that's a good idea."

When it rained or snowed they stayed in and played war games with tin soldiers that Larry had gotten from an older cousin. After Pearl Harbor new toys were no longer made of metal. As a birthday present Josh received a box of flat cardboards that had pre-printed parts of military vehicles that you just pressed out and fitted together. Pretty soon you had a whole fleet of camouflaged tanks, jeeps, and half-tracks. He and Larry spent hours lying on the floor attacking and counter-attacking, mixing it up with whatever they heard every day about battles in the real war.

"If it keeps on until we get old enough, I would join the Navy," Josh said. "I wouldn't like the Army."

"Why not?"

"I'd want to be on a ship."

"You could get blown up and drown."

"In the Army you'd have to fight with your hands. You could get stabbed with a bayonet."

The conversation didn't get much deeper, but they loved playing together and when the weather was mild they spent most of their time outdoors. Each year they went a little farther afield. There were woods to explore, places to practicing shooting with a bow and arrows, a creek to splash around in, and other kids to challenge or befriend.

In their play and games, the ideas for new adventures often came from Larry, especially some of the more dangerous ones like creeping up an embankment to where the commuter trains ran so that they could place pennies on the tracks to get them flattened into thin discs.

The clubhouse in the empty lot didn't last long, succumbing eventually to destruction by weather and the depredations of other kids. By the time they were ten its ruins consisted of only two or three pieces of broken board scattered in the sand, but Josh and Larry still consciously saw themselves as having a special friendship. Impressed by a story they'd heard about the stoical heroism cultivated in ancient Sparta, they decided to make it official by calling themselves Spartans. Each had to prove worthy by undergoing a trial of courage and pain. Sliding down a ten-foot cement wall at the edge of the schoolyard and achieving scraped knees sufficed. Once they'd completed that requirement successfully they pricked their fingers with pins and touched the bleeding surfaces together. "Our blood is mingled," they agreed. "Now we're blood brothers."

7

Josh liked his name—Joshua Mark Lowen. It sounded distinguished to him, and sometimes he whispered the words just to remind him who he was. He'd never met another kid called Josh. Of course, his grandfather—his father's father—was Joshua, but even Sid Lowen had no memories of that near mythic figure who'd arrived penniless in America only to die before the rest of his family came over.

Larry absorbed his father's messages about taste. He never talked about it, but from a very early age he knew what constituted the right way to dress, to behave, to live. It was something in the background, something one didn't need to discuss, but he grasped its importance to his father and he accepted it. He also learned to evaluate things by how much they cost. Abe often talked to him about the big world of banks and finance, and by the time Larry was ten years old he knew a good deal about different kinds of investments, how interest rates were a determining factor in making decisions, and how smart people bought when other not-so-smart people were selling.

Betty Gerst painted. She had her studio down in the basement of their house and did mostly landscapes and street scenes of Long Island villages. She'd sold a few works to other friends and even to a couple of local restaurants, and she herself went to New York galleries and slowly acquired a collection of paintings by artists who were unsung at the time, but who later became celebrated. Sometimes Larry and Josh would sneak down the stairs to stand quietly watching her apply paint to a canvas. They were always charmed when she turned around smiling, and let them know that she didn't mind having admirers.

Both boys were conscious of the differences and frictions between their families, but neither of them said anything about them to the other. The comments they heard from their own parents were private, and for all the shared confidences between the two boys, some things were never said. At least on the surface nothing for them had changed. What they heard their parents talking about was only a hazy background to their days. They went dutifully to school, and dreamed their games of adventure.

Josh felt nothing discouraging or threatening about his family. Later, in fact, when he thought about his childhood, a smile often began to form. It was warmth and good times that he recalled. Mae Lowen was affectionate and responsive; Sid Lowen, interested and gentle. "Yes, my boy," had always been his beginning to any response to a question about how the world worked.

"What causes the Northern Lights?"

"How come the sea is salty?"

"Why does President Roosevelt use that long tubular thing when he smokes cigarettes?"

All questions were accepted. Sometimes Josh didn't completely understand Sid's answers, but he figured that would come later. In the meantime, he was introduced to science, encouraged to read books of history and adventure, and given piano lessons.

An upright, dark and heavy, stood in a corner of the dining room and the lessons began when he was eight. His first teacher was Miss Wertheimer, a refugee from Austria who believed in ear training. "Sing as you play," she told him. "Sing the note you play. Mastery follows."

What did she mean?

It took a while, but within the year he knew. Soon he was picking out tunes on his own, children's songs at first, but, later, even songs from the radio.

"I think he's playing by ear," his mother remarked one day. "He makes things up."

"Of course," Sid said. "He's a genius."

Inevitably there had been discipline, but it was carried out quickly and Josh was observant enough to see that perhaps there was truth in his parents' oft-repeated explanation that any punishment was more painful for them than for their erring son. Sometimes he'd look at them when they were busy with their activities around the house, and he would watch and wonder what they were really like. He could love them, yet have a cool objectivity, and still want very much to know things about them that he wasn't supposed to know.

In his earliest years he had been skinny. The smells of fish and of cooked broccoli were nauseating, so his mother surrendered and allowed him to follow his appetites for buttered bread, ice cream, roast chicken, and chocolate Mallomars. He had plenty of energy, but there were dark circles under his eyes and he spent his time reading and collecting nature specimens—the shed skin of a snake, pressed dried flowers and leaves, the skull of a squirrel, and moths and butterflies preserved in a picture frame behind glass. He showed no interest in sports.

Sid Lowen loved opera and symphonies. On Saturday afternoons music filled the house and Josh was taught how Bach preceded Mozart, how Mozart preceded Beethoven, and how Brahms came after that. One day, Sid set an armful of slightly damaged records on the kitchen table. There had been a fire at the local music store and the owner was about to throw them away.

"Some are burned at the edges," he said. "But you can still play them."

Among them were records by Fats Waller, Tommy Dorsey, and Louis Armstrong. They smelled of smoke, but had no visible damage and Josh put them on the Victrola, eventually playing them again and again. He liked his father's music, but this was something different—melodies that recurred over and over in his mind, almost as if he were actually hearing them again. He would softly whistle them for days afterward, and it wasn't long before he began to figure them out at the upright—*Handful of Keys; Song of India; Cornet Chop Suey.*

One day Josh heard on the radio that Fats Waller had died. He had seen photographs of the man—fat, of course, but jolly looking and always kidding around and saying funny things—and it was frightening to think what it must have been like to die on a train near Kansas City, alone and so far from home. He felt proud that he knew who Fats Waller was, but he was sad, too, because he would never really get to hear him play the piano or sing.

8

By thirteen Josh's body had begun to fill out and he was suddenly taller and bigger than his Junior High classmates. A friend who was a year ahead in school suggested that Josh and Larry try out for wrestling. After a few sessions of learning some basic positions and techniques, both boys were accepted into the wrestling team. They found that the struggles on the mat were not only enjoyable in themselves, but also that they were better at it than some other kids who had teased them only a couple of years before. Suddenly, they were admired, even popular. Girls talked to them, wanted to be with them, called them on the phone. It was surprising, but they certainly weren't going to reject it.

For Larry, the wrestling was a way to get his mind off the steadily increasing tension between his mother and father. Betty Gerst spent more and more time making art and talking to other painters. Introduced to a group of mostly gay artists who lived on Fire Island, she visited them often, and there were evenings when she didn't come home. Once she told her son and husband that she had met Jackson Pollock.

"Oh," Abe Gerst sniffed. "He's a thrower of paint. And you call him an artist?"

"Yes, I do, and a lot of astute observers would find your comment laughable," his wife responded disparagingly.

"Astute? What do you know about *astute*? I'll tell you who's astute. Rudi Nathanson is astute, but you've never heard of him."

"I can't say I know the name."

"No, you don't."

Betty Gerst looked away, and Abe turned to Larry. "An art dealer and a collector," he said. "They were from Berlin, but in 1938 they fled to Geneva. I think he's still alive, but I'm not sure. We've been out of touch. The Swiss didn't let in many Jews, but the Nathansons were lucky, and I know Rudi has quite a collection. Fine things. None of the psychotic daubs and splotches these self-styled artists peddle for the shock effect."

Larry wanted to walk away, but he had to listen. Something held him—some vestige of infantile omnipotence that told him he had to repair things, to make all the anger go away. He was very still. Only his eyes moved, jumping back and forth between his mother and father. He watched the adversaries, and judged them.

Suddenly, the conversation was over. The color had drained from Betty Gerst's face. She was dry-eyed, and staring hard at her husband.

"Fine," Abe muttered. "If this is the sort of life you want, Betty, it says only something about you. Far be it from me to interfere."

Larry held his breath. Something like a vise was compressing his chest, and he clenched his fists to keep his eyes from tearing up. At that moment he began to hate both of them.

In the following weeks there were evenings when Abe stayed in Manhattan overnight, but those were easily attributed to devotion to his financial calling.

Later came loud fights, screaming, and purple bruises on Betty Gerst's cheeks—and everything plunged rapidly toward divorce. It took a year, and then it was all over.

Abe moved to Connecticut with a new wife, Helen, a woman who worked with him on Wall Street. Betty kept the house in Queens, but began spending more time on Fire Island. Her usual before-dinner Scotch and soda moved to a before-lunch Scotch and soda with more to follow through the remaining hours. She painted all day long, but also cut off old friendships, including her longest with Mae and Sid.

Sometimes when Josh would play the piano—*On The Sunny Side of the Street* or *Oh, Lady Be Good*—Larry would listen respectfully, nodding approvingly. He himself had had no piano lessons, but he'd been with his father to jazz joints in Manhattan and could talk glibly about the differences between swing and Dixieland and the new jazz called bebop.

The divorce was the only one Josh knew of among all his friends' parents, and the acid of the conflict had etched toughness and cynicism into the only child. Larry had always seemed to know everything going on in the school, but now his conversation was limited to demeaning remarks and smug put-downs about teachers and other kids. Josh felt embarrassed, but he wanted to be loyal, so he laughed easily, willing to find amusement in the harsh, but seemingly apt and pithy observations. There was truth in such clever criticism, Josh told himself, and anyway Larry was good company and fun to be with. They were buddies.

Years later, when memories returned about that old vicarious aggression, Josh would feel discomfort and even the kind of shame that one doesn't talk about to others, but at the time the derogatory jokes just seemed funny and as long as Josh valued the friendship he went along with them. He even began imitating some of Larry's comments and grimaces, and sometimes his own parents seemed suitable targets for hostility. Sid Lowen's mild manner appeared out of touch and irritating, and Mae Lowen was dull and boring with her fixation on cleanliness and admonitions about Josh's friends. They had always praised him for being neat and orderly, but now they made him anxious with their own fears and he scorned their old-fashioned notions. They wanted to plan his life. It wasn't as if his studies were slipping. School was pretty easy for him, and no one else was complaining—certainly not his teachers. He excelled in math and in English. His papers were neat, and his handwriting meticulous and easy to read. He particularly loved Latin for the inherent logic of its grammar.

It was about that time that Josh's father read an article in *The New York Times* about a famous art historian living in Italy. "Look at this," he told Josh. "Here's a gentleman, a *litvak* like us, from the Old Country right near where I was born, and he's an internationally known art connoisseur." One photograph showed a slight, elderly man with a white goatee and fervent, but mournful eyes. He wore a three-piece suit and a fedora, and he was sitting on a folding chair in a garden with a tall hedge and marble sculptures in the background. He held a cane.

"I wish I could've done that," Sid Lowen said. He and Josh were sitting outside sipping cold grapefruit juice. It was a hot summer evening and the little cast iron walking tractor sprinkler was spinning, spritzing, creeping and clinking robotically across the grass along the track of the rubber hose.

Josh looked at the article. Another photograph showed the man inspecting a painting hanging on a wall. He was looking at it with a magnifying glass.

"What do you mean? Wish you could've done what?"

"Been . . . respectable."

"What are you talking about?"

"Ah, you don't know."

"You don't like what you do?" Josh asked his father. Sid Lowen sold lighting equipment, traveling all over the eastern seaboard showing individuals and companies how they could improve the lighting in their homes and businesses. "I thought you were happy in your work."

"Happy, yes. I've made a good living, but there's more."

Josh's mother came out. She sat down and Josh handed her the newspaper. "Dad wishes he was this guy."

She had already read the article. "Oh, yes. Why not? It's a wonderful story." She had read the man's book on Italian painters and she often went with Sid, or sometimes by herself, to the Metropolitan Museum on Fifth Avenue.

"He's not Jewish anymore," she added. "I read that he converted."

"I'm not talking about that," Sid said. "I'm talking about being interested in really fine things. Paintings, you know."

"Oh, sure, paintings," she agreed. "But some people are cut out for that. I don't think . . ."

Josh turned away. He didn't like the conversation.

In his senior year Josh found a new piano teacher. Herbie Campbell was a short man with greasy hair combed straight back, and fingernails that needed trimming as well as cleaning. His trio had a steady gig playing evenings at the Casa Granada in Valley Stream and he was teaching Josh how to use a fake book, to improvise, and to substitute more complicated chords to make a tune sound richer. "Just play," he repeated over and over. "Don't worry about mistakes. There are no wrong notes. Make them the beginning of something new, even something crazy." It was advice that Josh found freeing, and he realized he was playing better than ever.

One day, Larry came over and Josh played a few new songs he'd learned.

"You should try to make it sound more like bebop," Larry told him. "Dixieland is dead."

"You're crazy. I don't like bebop."

Larry said nothing more but retreated into a magazine he was flipping through.

The brief acerbic interchange stayed with Josh. He disliked confrontations, especially with a friend, but along with the smothered resentment he felt toward Larry, he also found himself wondering if Herbie Campbell's advice about "no wrong notes" was a hint that he should move toward the new style of jazz. He'd heard bebop records and couldn't figure how anyone would want to listen to the extreme, unmelodic sounds. How curious and annoying that Larry, who didn't play anything, had such a definite opinion about it.

Josh wouldn't get into arguments about his music. He was aware that his friend wasn't very happy these days.

9

In September 1950, Josh went up to Bartlett College on the train. His parents offered to drive him, but he thought his new classmates might see him as frightened or weak, so he traveled alone. The trip on the Boston and Maine was a long one and when he arrived at the campus the air under the elm trees at the edge of the College Green was sultry. Incoming students crowded around orientation tables, and in a pile of large white envelopes he found his name with a card assigning him to a triple room. He walked over to the brick, ivy-covered dorm and found that his two roommates had already arrived. He wanted to take a shower, but the three of them just sat around talking. They seemed okay. Skip was from Ohio and Gordie from a small town in Pennsylvania, but Josh knew right away that they were different, and he felt some tension immediately.

"From New York?" Skip said. "How come you didn't go to Columbia?"

Josh looked at him. "I wanted to come here."

"Columbia's a communist school," Gordie said.

Josh laughed. "I don't know anything about that."

"You going to join a fraternity?" Skip asked.

"Maybe . . . I guess so."

Classes began and Josh remembered what someone had advised.

Keep up. Don't get behind. There's a lot of reading. If you fall behind, you'll flunk out.

He took it seriously, and did all his assignments. He liked studying in the library and he was making new friends almost every day. All the freshmen ate in Commons and the scene there was noisy, but fun, too, with good-natured food fights and shooting the tubular paper covers of drinking straws dipped in gravy at each other.

The meals were pretty good, and you had to put your tray of dirty dishes on a conveyor belt that carried it back to the kitchen. One morning, a few classmates, including Josh, piled paper napkins on trays, set them on fire, and sent them down the belt. It wasn't appreciated.

"You are a privileged group," the Dean, a tall gray haired gentleman, told the involved students later that day. "Yet you've dishonored yourselves, the College, and your families."

He sat, but they stood, their backs toward bookshelves that lined an entire wall of his office. It was a sad group of eight boys who listened and shifted uncomfortably.

"I'm certain all your parents worked hard and sacrificed much to enable you to come to this place," he said. "We will not tolerate such shameful behavior."

A ray of afternoon sun glinted off objects on his oversized desk and Josh heard him announce their penance: a week in the kitchen scrubbing pots.

There was some grumbling, but the group knew it was a soft punishment, and they set themselves to the menial chores with more a feeling of camaraderie among sinners than disgrace.

Being a freshman was humiliating anyway. In those first months they were going through the hazing period. Wearing a beanie cap was required, and they were subject to arbitrary demands by upper classmen. They carried furniture; they were forced to run a gauntlet between two lines of the sophomores who took off their belts and lashed them as they raced by; and there were knocks on doors late at night when sophomore vigilantes made them come out into the cold to do calisthenics on the College Green. Life at Bartlett was defined by a set of traditions that went back a couple of centuries, and Josh found some of it halfway enjoyable. Whatever remained as terrifying and ugly he figured he'd get through soon enough. There were pep songs to be learned, and poignant melodies about alma mater and brothers standing heart to heart, and local lore, too.

Josh entered into all of it with good humor. The campus was beautiful, and, by October, on bracing sunny days, the sky was brilliant blue and the blowing, rustling tree leaves had turned to red, orange, and gold. He was happy he had come. It had been the right choice for him.

The ugly part had more to do with his roommates and some of his other classmates. He'd never come across guys like Skip and Gordie. They could be easy-going and likable at times, but there was an ongoing and intense political discussion that Josh decided he would put up with just for this first year and then he'd find new roommates.

Quite a few of his classmates were legacies. Their fathers had gone to Bartlett and they were a world apart, with negative attitudes about a lot of things that Josh took for granted. Gordie's crackbrained paranoia about Columbia University was an example, while Skip found Eleanor Roosevelt to his distaste.

"She's a nigger fucker."

Josh jumped up.

"What'd you say?"

He grabbed Skip's wrist, pulled him sharply to the right, spun him around and got him into a half nelson.

"Let go," Skip yelled. "Let go!"

Josh shoved him away in disgust. He was taller and stronger than both of them, but he didn't like pushing his advantage physically. "Don't ever talk like that again," he said. He knew he could take both of them in a fight, but he turned away and left the room, slamming the door. He could hear them laughing as he went down the hall.

Making the freshman wrestling team wasn't difficult, and it widened his circle of friends. He slept in his dorm room, but had very little to do with Skip and Gordie except to mumble a daily morning greeting. He stayed away from the room all day, preferring to study in the library, and he ate his meals with friends from wrestling or his classes. There was a piano in the dorm's common room that no one seemed to use, and several times a week he sat down and played a few tunes. He was beginning to get the hang of improvising, purposely hitting a wrong note, or even a dissonant chord, and then trying out different possibilities for getting back to the basic melody. He would play for fifteen minutes or a half hour, and he hoped someone would come in and appreciate what he was doing, but he was always alone there. It was a good way to unwind. He was taking chemistry, math, English, economics, and music appreciation. Many of his classmates were pre-med and he thought he might go in that direction, too.

Josh went home at Thanksgiving, and he and Larry spent some time together. They compared notes about college, but mainly what Josh would remember later was how subdued his friend seemed. Larry talked about earlier, calmer, happier days.

"That was long ago," he said. "I have pictures in my mind . . . brightly colored, jolly, vivid memories of my mother and father laughing, and the three of us going to the beach, or walking along with ice-cream cones on the boardwalk at Far Rockaway."

Josh listened and found it awkward and difficult to respond.

"I'd like the good memories to develop into reassuring blooms of tranquility," Larry said. "But they never do. They're just points of contrast to darkness and anxiety. My parents became so bitter, and they let it get to me. Those things should be private, but they didn't care."

He had overheard so many fights and accusations, and then came the divorce. Everything was changed. Life was never going to be the same.

"Sometimes I take my father's part, sometimes my mother's," he said.

Something primordial was pushing him to build a protective wall. He couldn't help himself, although he knew it kept more things out than he wished.

Josh asked him if he was looking forward to something new, and Larry said, "I'll survive. I'll take what I can salvage from each of them, like Robinson Crusoe after the shipwreck. Pick up what you can; maybe it'll come in handy."

Josh realized what he meant. From Abe Gerst, Larry was learning sharp cleverness, respect for the power of money, and the importance of taste and style. From Betty Gerst he was developing an appreciation for art and a worldview much broader than what other kids had. Including me, Josh understood. And along with all of that, Larry was acquiring a consuming hunger for status.

Larry told him that it was hurtful to see how his friends had dropped him. But then he said maybe it had been he who'd dropped them. He was always thinking about his classmates—which ones he feared, or respected, or hated. He admitted being very sensitive to any sort of slight, and kept a mental notebook of all of them.

"You're my oldest friend," Larry said.

Deep down, Josh thought, he judges me, too. Oldest friend, okay, but what he means is that I'm safe, and a little dense, a little immature . . . in fact, a puppy. He thinks I'm destined to hold on to those qualities, held prisoner by my own innocence. He can feel superior to me. If I need a teacher, he thinks he can be the one.

Later that year Josh pledged Rho Iota Pi, the "jock" fraternity at Bartlett. Several brothers had approached to assure him that he was the type of man who would fit in. "We know you play piano," they told him. "We like that because we have lots of parties, and besides we need a wrestler."

Their two colleges were over three hundred miles apart. Larry wrote Josh one short letter telling how he had joined a fraternity and that he was majoring in economics. He said the fraternity would advance him socially and he saw economics as a practical way of making sure he'd enter a high-income career. Josh sent him an even more perfunctory reply about his classes and wrestling. That exchange was the extent of their contact during the rest of that year. One thing was now pretty clear to both of them: two old friends were on different paths.

10

"Don't you read the papers?" Abe Gerst was disappointed. "Your friend, isn't he?"

"I'm under the impression that he—they, really—they're all, or they were, our family's friends," Larry said. "But yes, I still consider him a friend. And yes, of course I read the papers. What do you want me to say?"

"Well, how does something like that happen unless the person is stupid, or . . . maybe he's a psychopath or something."

"Pa, you know that's not what happened."

"How do you know what happened? He was with them; the young man was killed—a war veteran, for Pete's sake. And now he's kicked out of college. So, what are we supposed to think?"

Larry rubbed his eyes and yawned. These harangues tired him. It was the Christmas break and he was dividing his time—a week with his mother on Fire Island, and now a week with his father and Helen in Connecticut.

"Are you in touch with him?"

"Now and then."

"And what about you? You're passing everything?"

"Sure, what do you think?"

"You going to major in economics?"

"No."

"No? Why not?"

"I'm interested in art history."

"Oh, for Christ's sake. What are you talking about? Art history!"

Larry was getting A's in everything and he was taking lots of economics and government courses, but Art History 101 had been his mother's suggestion and he found the subject soothing, even relaxing, compared with the others which were interesting, but drier. The art professor's lectures were spellbinding, filled with all sorts of historical, theological, and even economic facts related to the beautiful things they were studying. Larry had always enjoyed trips to the Metropolitan with his mother, but now he found he really loved looking at paintings and could spend many minutes looking at each one, taking in the overall composition, the use of color, the brush strokes, and the particular quirks that separated one artist from another.

"Maybe I get it from Mom," he ventured.

"Ah, don't give me that." His father looked away.

Neither house was comfortable for Larry. His mother had sold the home in Queens and moved to Fire Island. Her new place, built on a small dune, had a wide view of the ocean. It was very modern, with odd angles and lots of unpainted wood, and the walls were full of pictures, many her own, but some by her friends, and a few of those were already well known. She had large shells, interesting looking driftwood, and colorful weavings placed around, all of which announced, "This is me, this is now my life." She was cheery and talkative most of the time, but Larry knew it was a deception. How happy could someone be, how fine could things be for a person who was blotto most of the time? Until late in the afternoon she was fairly clearheaded, even with the slow, steady intake that began with vodka in her breakfast orange juice; but by the time she and Larry, and perhaps another friend or two, sat down to dinner she was only half-coherent, and she knew it. When she gave

Larry and the others a little floppy wave and climbed the stairs up to bed, she did it with a sorrowful, apologetic look, and he and they saw the absence of happiness. At times, earlier in the day, there were artist friends around, smoking and talking, and Larry could relate to some of it, but he knew he was out of place. He had an inkling that one of the artists had been, or still was her lover, and that gave him a creepy feeling, but he tried hard to put it out of his mind. Indeed, it was her life. Anyway, what was he supposed to do?

Now he was in Connecticut, fending off Abe Gerst's carping, and pondering once again the story of Josh's undoing. The details in the papers were awful enough; his father's rant just made things worse. Something can suddenly come along, he saw, no matter how carefully you've planned, and it can completely ruin your life. Yes, it can happen to anyone . . .

But maybe not—maybe Josh could've been more aware, more careful about choosing his friends. Maybe he was so innocent and naïve that he was bound to stumble, to get involved in something through no actual conscious decision of his own. Stupid? No, you couldn't say that about Josh, certainly not. It was more like an inability, or maybe even a choice not to think clearly about what might loom ahead—a kind of laziness of mind. Yes, you had to think about the next move, to study people carefully, and to suspect. People could get you into trouble.

Larry was sure he himself had already learned that lesson. As upset as he'd been about what it must have been like for his friend, he hadn't had any trouble going on with his own semester. He'd written that letter to Josh, but when he didn't hear back he put it out of his mind. Not only was he not preoccupied by Josh's disastrous mistake; it had receded pretty much out of his thoughts until his father reminded him.

Now he was alone and bored, looking out the living room's bay window at snow on the lawn in the fading afternoon light. An open, paperback copy of Machiavelli's *The Prince* lay on a cushion alongside him. He'd been reading ahead for an upcoming government course, but the book was slow going.

Of mankind we may say in general they are fickle, hypocritical, and greedy of gain . . . One who deceives will always find those who allow themselves to be deceived.

He heard steps coming in from the kitchen.

"Well, Larry . . ."

Helen stood at the door. Tall and striking, his father's second wife was certainly not a beautiful woman, but she was someone who claimed more than a quick glance. She was made-up and perfumed, and her long, dark brown hair had reddish highlights. There was a sharp, angular look about her, something in the nose, or perhaps in the lower jaw that jutted forward in persistent assertion. Carefully dressed today in a close-fitting bright orange wool sweater and dark green slacks, she strode toward him, and Larry knew that the intimidation and annoyance he felt had a lot to do with how she was so sure of herself. There were mysteries behind her oversize tortoise rim glasses that Larry suspected might be unpleasant.

She had given up cigarettes, but her voice hadn't lost the rough quality.

"You don't look very happy," she said.

Larry shrugged. Her insincerity repelled him.

She came over and sat down too close to him. He saw how the powder she used was caked and failed to hide deep creases at the corners of her small eyes. "Oh, *The Prince*," she said. "I never got around to reading it. Should I?"

Larry observed her long, red nails as she picked up the book and turned a few pages. He edged away an inch. "It's fine," he said. "Interesting, especially if you want to be a leader, or if you're born into that role."

"Yes, ambition," she said. "Is that going to be you?"

"Everyone's ambitious. I think you are."

She pulled back. "All right," she allowed. "If you mean it in a positive way . . . a nice way."

He didn't want a long discussion with her. "Sure, in a nice way."

She smiled. Five years younger than Larry's mother, she nonetheless seemed older. Her mouth was wide, her lips just as red as her nails, and her chin dipped a tiny bit in acknowledgment of Larry's small retreat.

"I would like us to be friends," she said quietly.

He didn't want to look at her, but then he turned and acquiesced.

"Okay," he said.

"Larry, I didn't break up your family. Things happen, things no one plans."

He waited. If she were in the mood to talk, maybe he'd have to listen.

"Your Dad and I have worked together for a long time, but we didn't start dating until . . ."

"I don't want to talk about that."

"Why not?"

"It's between you and him." Then he stood, saying, "I'm going up to my room."

11

He was fed up—sick of having Helen in the house, and hurt by his father's outburst—but even as he kept coming back to it and getting angrier, he felt the cold, sickening realization that his father was right. Money was important. He'd already come to that conclusion, too, and he thought he knew the way—major in economics, and then go on to Wharton after graduation. And then make a ton of money—more than Abe Gerst ever had.

Once back at school he couldn't stop thinking about it. His father's way of putting people down destroyed them, but Larry saw how the technique achieved its purpose. Abe Gerst, harsh and unpleasant, had won the point.

Okay, first make money—lots of it. Art will be my hobby.

He buried himself in his courses. A particularly dull professor taught the government class, but the work wasn't difficult and he had no trouble getting a high grade on the mid-term. The best thing about the course actually turned out to be reading *The Prince*, not especially for the political interest, but much more because it led him into the Italian Renaissance. Machiavelli stimulated him to look at other books. The college library had an enormous collection devoted to the history and art of the period, and Larry found himself signing out one book after another, reading about Masaccio, Brunelleschi and Donatello instead of the mysteries and spy stories he'd always loved.

Florence in the *quattrocento* seemed especially fascinating in the way money, power and art were all intertwined, but he also saw the paradox in the weaving together of art and money. From his mother he was familiar with talk about the value of paintings, but for a long time he regarded that as not very interesting. Something in Machiavelli made him think again. *The Prince* was about how one can most effectively influence others, and not just 15th century Italian leaders. It applied to everyone.

One morning he woke up and realized he'd had a dream that made some connection between Machiavelli and paintings. He didn't quite get it, and it bothered him because he had a strong feeling it was important. For several days he turned it over and over in his mind, thinking about it while he walked to class, or while he was taking a shower.

Finally, it dawned on him that Machiavelli was talking about power, but power and money go together. So, that led to the monetary value of paintings. If one knew how, one might find a way of earning a living that way—even making quite a bit of money. Could he combine Machiavelli's tough pragmatism and an interest in art? Why not? He could go to Italy to see for himself. Especially Florence. Focus on the paintings. It would be a good way to begin.

He could be in the art world—a place where money might be made.

Just . . . how?

12

For Josh, finally, there was acceptance and forgiveness. Only a few evenings after the awkward and painful confrontation with his parents, things had moderated. Shame and embarrassment would never go away, but at least now he could feel gratitude, especially toward his father.

"Do you see that I can't go to school yet?" he implored. "It's too soon. I keep thinking about what I did. It's paralyzing me. And I don't want to stay here."

They watched his face and waited.

"I need to go away for a while; that's why I thought about California. I have to be on my own. I'll go back to school, but I want a few months."

He had it all figured out. If they would just give him enough for a month of living expenses, he could do it. Hitchhike; be on the West Coast in a week; find a job and a place to stay. Then he'd look into enrolling in one of the local colleges out there.

"What about the draft?" his father asked. "You have a student deferment, but you'll end up in Korea if you don't stay in college."

Josh knew. High school classmates who hadn't gone to college were serving in Korea now. One had already been killed in action.

"I went down to the draft board yesterday," he told them. "I explained that I was transferring to another school. They said I should just have the school send them a letter saying I'm enrolled."

"But you're not enrolled."

"I will be. I know I can get into a state school."

He didn't actually know how long the draft board would give him before he started back in school, but he was hopeful that he still had time.

"I just want a couple of months," he said. "As soon as I get to California I'll enroll. And a state school is much less expensive."

They listened quietly. Several times he watched his father's bushy eyebrows go up in skepticism, and then settle down again in a scowl, but by the time Josh had said what he wanted to say they were nodding in tentative agreement. It wasn't enthusiastic, but they had come around. They looked tired, and he suddenly realized that for their own reasons they wanted him out of the house. If he were far away in San Francisco, working, going to school, they'd be able to tell their friends that he was fine—that he was getting through the worst part of his ordeal. That would lift their terrible burden.

He left a week later. A classified ad in the paper asked for help driving to Chicago—share the driving, split the cost of gas. The guy sounded quiet, but intelligent, and Josh's parents acquiesced.

Saying goodbye was awful. His mother was tearful, but they hugged and she held him for a long moment, not saying anything. He kissed her cheek and went outside to wait while his father backed the car out. It was still dark and very cold. The light from the house barely illuminated the nearest patch of faded, frostbitten lawn.

He had the ride to Chicago, but what about beyond? Short hitchhikes around New England were one thing, but this would be different—long stretches of country, bleak terrain. Not like this. This was home. He looked up at the maple trees, their stark and leafless skeletons barely visible at this early hour. Small mounds of dirty snow lay along the curb, left over from a storm three weeks before.

It was a silent ten-minute drive to the station, and then the two stood on the platform waiting for the train to Penn Station. Josh glanced up and down the track, turning for brief moments to scan his father's face, but his father wasn't looking at him.

So be it—neither wanted an intense discussion.

"Where's he picking you up?"

"At the 34th Street side."

"You know anything about him?"

They were the only questions his father had asked since Josh announced how he'd arranged his own transportation as far as Chicago.

"He's a doctor. He's going to work in a hospital there."

"Oh?"

"An anesthesiologist."

The train was coming, and finally, they faced each other.

"All right," said Sid Lowen. "I guess this is it."

They embraced, held each other out, and embraced again.

"Call us when you get there. Call collect, but call us."

"Okay, Dad, I will. So long. Don't worry, I'll be okay."

13

"A blue Ford, four doors," the doctor had described the car. "I've got a beard and I wear glasses, but, don't worry, I don't bite."

He saw the car, waved, and the guy nodded.

"Hop in," he said, extending his hand. "George Parsons."

"I'm Josh. Thanks."

"No . . . thank you. I didn't want to do this drive alone."

He was a big, burly man with a wide smile; trim black beard and moustache, and thick eyeglasses in a red plastic frame.

It took a while getting out of the city, through the tunnel to the New Jersey Turnpike and then on into Pennsylvania. They didn't speak much at first, but every couple of hours they traded off and Josh enjoyed his share of the driving. Then George Parsons put his head back, seemed to feel more like talking, and gradually they shared their stories. Parsons was about forty, had worked at Coney Island Hospital in Brooklyn, but now was going to a better paying position at Cook County Hospital.

"So, how old are you, Josh?"

"Almost nineteen."

"You're not in school?"

"I was, but I had a little trouble."

"Where were you?"

Josh looked across at him. He was a doctor. He had an open face. Kind.

"Bartlett College."

"Really. Was it that . . .?"

"Yeah, I was involved in it, but I didn't do anything. We were all, you know, smashed. And I was just with them, so I was expelled, too."

"I read about it. He had a subdural hematoma. I've seen lots of those. Usually they make it, but not always."

"I hate thinking about it."

"I'm sure."

They sped along the winter landscape of gray hills splotched with white snowy patches. A light rain began to fall and Josh turned on the wipers. He talked about hitchhiking to the coast and getting a job.

"Eventually, I'll go back to school."

"What kind of job will you get?"

"Anything—clerk, gas-station, pick and shovel—I'll just have to see how it goes."

"What were you studying?"

"Pre-med."

"Ah . . ."

"I guess that's kaput."

"You never know. If you can get beyond this, go back to school, do well. I mean, get good grades. Who knows? Maybe you can do it eventually."

"But I'll always have this thing, this awful thing . . ."

The plan was to drive straight through to Chicago and they did it, each of them sleeping for a few hours at a stretch and then switching. They ate hamburgers near Pittsburgh and spaghetti in Ohio, and they kept the heater going all the way. By the time they got to Indiana it was even colder, and a light snow was falling.

They arrived in Chicago eighteen hours after they'd come through the Lincoln Tunnel and George Parsons dropped Josh off at a downtown YMCA. It was 2 a.m.

"Thanks for your help," Parsons said. "I'm glad to know you. I wish you well."

"Thanks. Thanks for the ride."

The Y had no vacancies, but they told him to go around the corner where there was a cheap hotel. It was a run-down neighborhood with garbage scattered on the sidewalks. The hotel was an old building, but seemed clean, and the reception clerk was pleasant.

"How many nights, Sir?"

"Just tonight."

"Seven dollars, please."

He went up to the room, brushed his teeth, and got into bed. Within moments after turning off the light he heard scurrying sounds on the floor and as he turned it on again three large cockroaches fled, rattling away to hide under the drapes and the chest of drawers. He closed his eyes, but kept the light on, and within ten minutes he was asleep.

In the morning he showered, took the elevator down, and handed the key to a new clerk. Outside the sky was clear, but it was bitter cold and the wind was fierce. Last night's snow had left a thin coating on everything, but traffic was moving normally. He found a cafeteria around the corner and sat at the counter for his roll with butter and coffee. The lady at the cash register told him where to get a local bus to take him to Des Plaines, a town on the city's outskirts.

He was standing at a crossroads: gas stations on two corners, a hamburger joint on another, and an empty lot on the fourth. The sign ahead said U.S. Route 20 and it was where he wanted to be. Cold, and lonesome, but not lost. His map showed the route going all the way into Wyoming, and that made him feel better.

Cars whizzed by and people stared at him, but he knew someone would eventually pick him up. He put his pack down and held out his thumb. Only yesterday he'd left New York, but it seemed long ago.

Maybe that's what travel did . . . moving through new territory . . . seeing people you don't know and who don't know you. It was a good feeling.

Was it possible that it kept the plague of thoughts about Bartlett and Tom Grillo away? No, not a chance. He had failed miserably. The Josh Lowen who had stood up to Skip for calling Eleanor Roosevelt a nigger fucker was ancient history. And Skip and Gordie? Those two assholes were still there in that old dorm. In a couple of years they would graduate—with clean, crisp parchment degrees written in Latin—from Bartlett College.

It took five more days to reach San Francisco. There were many hours of cold with brilliant sunshine, a few with freezing rain, and even a full day of light snow, but he was in luck all the way. The cars were warm and dry, and he loved the openness of the country. He spent nights in Sioux City, Iowa; Valentine, Nebraska; Rawlins, Wyoming; and finally Winnemucca, Nevada. The next day he got a ride in a semi-rig that took him to Lake Tahoe.

He'd met characters every day along the way: an intoxicated insurance salesman who was on his way to see his boss's wife and determined to "get a piece of that pussy."

And a silent old Nebraska rancher who smelled so bad that Josh kept opening the window on his side.

"What the hell's wrong with you, kid?" the guy complained. "It's fucking freezing out there."

Josh wanted to get out of the car, but it was the middle of nowhere and he stuck it out for the hour it took to get to Valentine where the rancher dropped him off.

In Utah, a young family picked him up—husband and wife, and two little boys.

"Where you headed?" the husband asked.

"San Francisco."

"Ooh, beautiful," the wife said. "Never been there, but he has." She looked at her man and smiled.

"Oh, sure," the husband said. "But too many people. Not a good place to raise kids."

"We're a Christian family," his wife said. "Are you a Christian?"

"Actually, no. I'm Jewish."

"Really," she said, her eyes widening. "He's Jewish," she repeated to her husband who nodded. No one spoke for a while. The little boys sat quietly next to Josh. One of them was falling asleep. Little blonde curls all along his forehead.

Much later he could conjure the whole trip, run the pictures through his brain, all the passing and perhaps meaningless glimpses he'd had of the broad land. One could read poetry about that, but the images that stayed with him of sweeping, extravagant views—blue and gold; white and purple; and, yes, small close-up emphases of orange and red and yellow—put poetry to shame. Everything seemed more alive and precious to him.

Des Plaines . . . Sioux City . . . Plainview . . . Valentine . . . the Sand Hills . . . Casper . . . Medicine Bow . . . Rawlins . . . Green River . . . Fort Bridger . . . Evanston . . . Salt Lake . . . Bonneville salt flats . . . Wendover . . . Elko . . . Battle Mountain . . . Winnemucca.

I'll never forget.

14

By the end of his first three full days in San Francisco Josh Lowen had found a place to stay, made a friend, and had two jobs. His head spun, but he was smiling. It seemed only hours before that he'd been barreling across the Nevada desert in the cab of the semi-rig. He couldn't get over how little traffic there was on such a major highway. From time to time, the driver, a tall, sun-tanned man wearing cowboy boots and wire-rim spectacles, rolled himself a Bull Durham smoke with one hand.

"Look-ee there," he pointed ahead with his cigarette.

In the distance a blue-gray shadow was rising on the horizon. As the miles fell away Josh saw the magnificent snowy peaks of the Sierra Nevada, and his skin tingled with a growing excitement.

The road turned and twisted, climbing higher and higher to where the air was pine-scented. When they finally began the descent, the turquoise blue of Lake Tahoe came into view and he knew he'd never seen anything so beautiful.

His ride ended at the lake and he got his final lift into San Francisco with a retired schoolteacher who was going to visit a daughter who had just delivered twin sons. "Two days ago I had no grandchildren," he said. "All of a sudden I've got two."

It was four o'clock by the time they crossed the Bay Bridge and Josh got out on Market Street. His dinner was a hot dog and Pepsi Cola, and he spent the night in another sleazy hotel.

The next morning he called home, assured his mother he was fine, and spent an hour reading classified ads in the *Examiner*. He cut one out and put it in his wallet.

Animal lab research assist. UCSF Hospital.

By mid-afternoon he had found a one room furnished apartment in the downtown area. It was grimy, but he was sure he could clean things up. The next morning he called about the animal lab job and was told to come for an interview the same afternoon. He'd seen a cafeteria down the block and he went in to have some breakfast. It was crowded and he squeezed into the one empty stool at the counter.

"What are you up to?" A tall, skinny kid with a big Adam's apple sat on the next stool. He held his cup of coffee and looked at Josh.

"I just got here." Josh said.

"Yeah? Where from?"

"Back east—New York."

"No shit? So, what are you doing?"

"I want to find a job."

"Yeah?"

"Maybe in a hospital. Or even a store, or an office."

"Good luck."

Josh thought he might as well keep the conversation going. "What do you do?"

"I'm a musician."

"Oh, really. You mean professional?"

"Well, I don't play for nothing."

"What instrument? I play piano."

"String bass."

They shook hands. "I'm Josh."

"Rich—Rich Mariani."

15

January 11, 1952

Dear Folks,

Thanks for giving Larry my address. He wrote me again. He says he's going to business school after college, but wants to go to Europe this summer. He says it was just bad luck for me - that I shouldn't feel guilty. Well, I do anyway. He's a character.

Sorry for not writing sooner; I've been busy. My apartment is small, but clean. I don't need anything. My job is in the animal lab at UCSF hospital. It's all about cancer research. The people are nice. I feel sorry for the animals, but it's a good cause.

I'm going to San Francisco State College. They're building a new campus in the southern end of the city. I'm officially enrolled. Luckily, I was allowed into one course right away although the semester had started - 20th Century British Prose. Writers like George Orwell, H.G. Wells, Virginia Wolff, Aldous Huxley, and E.M. Forster. I'm enjoying it, and I'm all set for next semester. They've already sent a letter to the draft board that I'm enrolled. So don't worry.

Some musicians are starting a jazz band and want me as their piano player. It's really fun and I'll fit it in. You can see I'm all set.

Love,

Josh

16

February 17, 1952

Dear Josh,

Thanks for writing back. Well, you lucky S.O.B., I'm envious. Frisco sounds like a blast. You're on your own, doing what you want. All that shit back there will fade. You won't have to think about it. Playing music with those guys must be great. Maybe you'll make a record sometime.

Europe is not going to happen. I'll work with my father this summer. He'll pay me and I'll learn a lot – currency exchange rates, a lot of stuff about investments. I'll be living in Connecticut. Not happy about that, but I'll go into NYC with him every day. Weekends I'll be with my Mom. Think you'll come home in the summer?

Larry

17

April 27, 1952

Dear Josh,

Your mother and I are very upset at your callous disregard for your obligations. We agreed to pay for your train fare home so that you could spend the summer here, and I can understand that you want to be self-sufficient, but the fact is that you're not self-sufficient. We have been sending you a check for $40 every month to help out and we've been paying your tuition. You may think it's smart to be on your own, but you're still only 18 years old and you don't know everything yet. Your idea of us coming out there is preposterous. I have a job and it's impossible for me to take a long vacation that includes hotel bills, restaurants, and two train fares across the country. So, suit yourself. We would like to see you.

Dad

18

It took him a while to decide, but by the middle of July Josh agreed to come home for two weeks in August. He was confident that he could manage indefinitely on his own, but he had to show his folks that he was fine and hadn't abandoned them. Maybe he even missed them. He would let them pay for a one-way train ticket, but he wanted to get to New York on his own. So, once again he shared the driving with someone he didn't know, this time an Air Force officer who was being transferred to Kansas.

The lieutenant dropped him in Salina on Route 24 and the hitchhike began there. Topeka, Kansas City, St. Louis, Indianapolis, Columbus, Pittsburgh, New York. It was scorching temperatures most of the way, but he saw a different part of the country and now his folks would see that he was grown up. He was feeling pretty proud of himself. That's how he wanted it to be.

The time in New York proved smart, maybe even essential, and it marked for him a departure from childhood. His folks were very kind and thoughtful, and Josh had a new appreciation for what he'd put them through, but he also saw that he couldn't be like them.

I've never realized how old they are, he thought. When you're a kid you're told that everyone eventually dies, but it's different when you see new lines in their faces, or how they stoop when they walk, or that they look more tired than before.

He was leaving them behind. If remembered images of San Francisco were sunlit and in brilliant colors, New York oppressed him with shadows, melancholy, and poignancy.

He was able to see Larry a few times during the two weeks and they had long talks about what had happened, what they were doing now, and what they hoped for.

"It's all a game," Larry said carelessly.

"What?"

"Life. If you win, you win; if you don't win, you lose. Do you see that?"

"What the hell are you talking about?"

"The real world, pal. I would think maybe you'd get that by now."

Josh looked at him. What was the point of this?

"Yeah, I get it, but I don't see it in those terms. I do what I need to do. I'm not competing with anybody."

"You may not think you're competing, but people are competing with you."

"Maybe so."

"Money," Larry said. "You can minimize it all you want, but it's the big thing."

"I don't know about that."

"You'd better learn. Money isn't everything, but being poor is stupid."

"I don't intend to be poor."

"You've got to have a plan."

"You have one?"

"Sure—the business world. Finance. Investments. I want to retire when I'm forty. Or fifty."

"Good luck."

"I mean it, pal. I'm serious and you should be, too."

How annoying this was getting. "Okay, let's change the subject," Josh muttered. "You still spending equal time with your Mom and Dad?"

"Sure, that's reality, too."

"How are they?"

"My father is impossible. My mother drinks too much."

"She's painting?"

"Yeah, she's painting, but going there is sad . . . very sad."

"That's awful. I'm sorry."

"Yeah, I feel like I'm becoming her parent. I'm more responsible than she is."

"How often do you see her?"

"Couple of weekends a month . . . sometimes three. But it's not pleasant. She's alone most of the time . . . alone with her booze, and her artist friends. I don't even know if they're really her friends. I don't trust them. She gets very touchy. I don't see how I can do anything to change things."

"And your Dad?

Larry told Josh about arguing with Abe Gerst.

"Arguing about what?"

"About everything. Even about you. One day he came in and wanted to know if I read the newspapers about you, about the whole Bartlett thing. How did it happen? But mostly why were you involved. He's very traditional. It was pretty disagreeable."

Josh listened, but he was already thinking about the train ride back to San Francisco.

PART THREE

1952-1953
Letters

19

October 3, 1952

Hey, pal –

I've been feeling awkward about this. The last time we talked when you were home I realized I came on pretty strong. If I hurt your feelings, I apologize. I know you don't see things the way I do. Maybe that's lucky for you, and unlucky for me. But I didn't mean to upset you. My ideas about life being competitive don't find agreement everywhere. When I think about it in relation to our friendship I guess I just wanted to warn you not to be naïve. That could be nervy of me. I know that.

Anyway, I hope things are okay with you. Please forgive my chutzpah. And keep me up to date on your doings.

Larry

20

January 20, 1953

Hi, Larry –

Sorry about the long delay. I was cleaning my room and found your letter from October. I have no excuse except laziness.

There was no need to apologize. I didn't take things that way. I've been able to keep my head above water. Being on my own in SF has been great. I've made some friends, and I'm pretty busy most of the time.

SF State has been good. I love the English courses, and when I finish next year I may go on for an M.A. The teachers are as good as those at Bartlett, and more encouraging. Most students are local and commute to school. No fraternities as far as I can tell.

I'm learning a lot from my musician friends. Some are fifteen or twenty years older, and have been playing in bands since the thirties. I've been on gigs with men who've played with Louis Armstrong, Sidney Bechet, Jack

Teagarden, Joe Sullivan, and Muggsy Spanier. Before the war there was a revival of traditional jazz here in San Francisco. When I play with these guys I feel I'm part of a timeline that began in New Orleans.

Let me know what you're up to.

Josh

21

April 30, 1953

Dear Josh,

The school year is almost over and I'm finally getting around to answering your last letter. I meant to respond right away and then got bogged down with an econ honors paper, but that's done now and I'm glad to say I got an A on it.

This summer I'll be working at Goldman Sachs in their research department. My father knows people there and thinks it'll be great experience for me. I'm especially looking forward to it because I'll be house-sitting an apartment on W 83rd for some people who spend the summer in Maine – good luck, that.

From the sound of your letter you're really enjoying SF. Do you think you'll stay out there after college? Do you miss NY at all?

Hope to see you one of these days.

Larry

22

August 15, 1953

Dear Larry,

I guess everyone's relieved that the Korean Armistice was signed two weeks ago. We've both been lucky. Let's hope things stay calm.

Your question about my staying out here made me laugh. If you only knew how great it is to live here. I think people move to California and leave behind some of the traditions they grew up with. They keep what they want, and discard what they think is dated or hurtful. This is the place for new ideas. I keep meeting interesting people. Sometimes they're strange and even difficult to decipher, but I listen to what they have to say, and then I find I'm even open to considering parts of their philosophies. I'm changing - - no question about it, and maybe it's the place itself. The city is spectacular - - I'm crazy about walking all over and continually discovering new spots, new views, new buildings, and new parks. The weather's wonderful.

Anyway, no, I don't miss New York. I talk to my folks on the phone. They're okay and I'll probably come home to see them sometime, but I'm not sure when.

Josh

23

September 30, 1953

Dear Josh,

My summer was busy, but I learned a ton. I can see how people make money in this world. I'm not getting cocky, but I think I'm right where I want to be. I'm definitely applying to Wharton, Harvard, and Columbia, but Wharton is my first choice. I like Philadelphia. Have you been there?

You mentioned meeting interesting people in SF. What about Marilyn Monroe and Joe DiMaggio? Sounds like they may get married.

What about you, pal? How's your love life?

Mine? Well, I won't go into that.

I hope you're saving some money for retirement. Someday I may be able to steer you into the right investments.

I guess I should come out to California and see what all the fuss is about.

Larry

PART FOUR

1967-1968
California

24

He was carefully making his way down a cracked sidewalk that led between tall modernistic buildings, some square and blocky, others curved and geometrically fashioned into complex shapes. What was their purpose?

No one was around. Suddenly, the quiet was broken by a loud, insistent signal.

The phone . . .

Josh bolted up in bed.

"Hello?"

Silence.

"Hello?"

"Hey, a voice from the past."

He couldn't place it.

"Who is this?"

Laughter on the other end.

"Who . . .? Larry? Larry Gerst?"

"None other."

"Jesus, you woke me up. Where are you, man?"

"In New York, but I'm coming out. I want to see you, Josh. It's been fifteen years."

"I can't believe it."

"I've got some business out there, and I hope you'll have a little free time."

"No problem. When?"

"In about a week or so. Matter of fact, I have a real estate deal out there and I'd like to tell you about it. It might be something you'd benefit from."

"Great. I'm not going anywhere."

"I'll let you know the exact dates. You're okay?"

"Sure, fine. And you?"

"The same . . . a few changes . . . but we can talk about that when I see you."

"You living in New York?"

"Part of the time, yes. And part of the time in Italy, but I'll tell you all about it. I have to run. I'll call you again and let you know exactly."

"Good. Thanks . . . thanks for calling."

"So long, buddy."

Josh rubbed his eyes. He loved the smell of cool ocean air that blew in through the half-opened window of his bedroom. What the hell time was it? Six-thirty—nine-thirty in New York.

He looked back at the phone he'd just hung up and shook his head. Images were spinning through his mind. Things from high school . . . beer at Teddy's . . . Larry's bitter jokes . . . and that bunch of annoying letters.

Could that really have been fifteen years ago? He'd tried to explain his enthusiasm for living in San Francisco in them, but there'd been something antagonistic and belittling in the tone of Larry's replies. Flip remarks about Joe DiMaggio and Marilyn Monroe, and unsubtle hints that New York was really the place to be.

Josh had delayed answering, but then one day started a long reply that waxed eloquent about California: hiking in the hills north of the Golden Gate; going to readings at pie-shaped City Lights Bookstore that sold only paperbacks and alternative newspapers and magazines; fishing happily, although unsuccessfully, from the jetty in Half Moon Bay; meeting poets and artists who were challenging old ideas; backpacking with a friend in Kings Canyon National Park.

But he never sent the letter. What he'd written seemed too much like trying to prove something. I don't need to do this, he had decided. He'd crumpled the paper and tossed it in the wastebasket.

It had given him a tiny pang of guilt for a day, but he quickly forgot about any more letter writing. Guilt was not something he wanted. If Larry had to needle and minimize, Josh certainly didn't need to respond. He was all too aware of the history of the Gersts' divorce and how it had affected Larry, but that was in the long-gone past and the world kept on spinning. Was it selfish to think that? He didn't care. I'm living my own life, he told himself. I have no intention of apologizing or feeling inadequate because my erstwhile friend needs to puff himself up. I get it. I know all about it. I understand the background, but I don't have to write back.

And now Larry was coming to visit him in San Francisco? Who was this person? He knew he himself was different, and Larry certainly must've changed, too.

Italy! Well . . . good for him!

1967. Christ! He went into the bathroom and looked in the mirror. His hair was down to his shoulders, and there was some gray there. Moustache. Beard. He checked his teeth. Yeah, it would all be okay. 1967. Tuesday, January 17, 1967. He was thirty-four years old, he had a gig at the Cormorant tonight, and it was a little hazy thinking back to what he was like ten, twelve, or fifteen years before.

So, what did his old friend want? Were they even still friends? Why would Larry want to see him? He always had his reasons. It might be uncomfortable, the two of them there . . . staring at each other. Larry was in some kind of business in New York. That's all Josh knew about him. He frowned. What the hell? Was he worried what Larry would think of him? Forget it.

He brushed his hair and tied it back. The ponytail wasn't new. He'd had it for a year and at times like this he smiled when he saw it. He knew it was a statement and he was proud of himself. Different world now. His world . . . not his parents' . . . or anyone of that generation. Probably he was a little too old for it himself, because it was the kids much younger who were really into it. Most of them were oblivious about the Depression and even about life during the War. He'd been a child then, too, but it'd been the big background to his growing up. Today, kids had their own ambience. Well, fine, but he was in this, too. It was a new age and even he embraced it. Yes, he did.

He made coffee and turned on the TV. They were still talking about that Saturday thing in Golden Gate Park, the Human Be-In—a happening. Big crowd . . . really, thousands must've been there. And he'd been one of them. Lots of kids, but older people, too; pot smoke everywhere you took a breath; people smooching; a girl in braids walking around with a basket of oranges, handing them out. *Peace, brother, peace.* A guy even parachuted into the park. Josh had seen it—the figure floating up there, descending, Levi's-clad legs waving a little like limp rags, gently, gently, then suddenly tumbling down onto the grass.

There had been music that day—not his kind, but it was okay. When it came to music, people went for the latest fad. Musical mediocrity would always win, hands down. Good taste? An appreciation for subtlety and elegance? Rare, very rare. When you found it you were pleased, but also amazed. It was like making a new friend.

He opened the front door. Pretty cold. Fog blurred the houses across the street. He could hear the surf pounding. Where's the sun? *Sunset District*—what a joke! His car was right there in front. Time to go. He grabbed his coat and locked the door.

The traffic wasn't bad. He drove over to Park Presidio and headed for the bridge. He'd be at the school in Marin in thirty minutes. Three and a half years he'd been teaching English at Los Arboles Country Day School—a steady, satisfying job that had all the trappings of respectability. Health insurance, and even a pension plan for the distant future. His musical life was erratic and uncertain, but something he'd never give up. Playing jazz constituted too much of his soul to even imagine living without it. If he were ever to get married and have a family the teaching job would make it all possible. It might not be what his parents had intended for him, but no matter. What he felt these days was accomplishment, fulfillment, and joy.

It had taken years to get to this point, and it hadn't been a smooth run. Even now there were unpredictable moments of terror . . . abrupt shameful memories of that awful evening. The unequal physical struggle of five against one; the sickening crack of Tom Grillo's head hitting the bed's iron frame; the look of disgust on the cop's face as he told them they were to spend the night in jail. He'd lost track of Walt, Kenny, Zipper, and P.B., but not completely. Over the years, and from a variety of sources, he'd gotten wind of the different paths they'd taken. Maybe it was natural to feel some curiosity about them. There was no way of forgetting that they'd all been in it together, but the curiosity was spoiled by a distinct unease. He was often depressed by the guilt brought on by wondering about those guys. It was better not to think about them. All he'd heard was that none of them had continued into anything that could be called interesting, not to mention elevated or distinguished.

No, he told himself. Put it out of your mind. Take life as it is now. Don't look back. Get on with it. Los Arboles Country Day was a good and happy fit. Many of the students came from wealthy families, but, especially for the handful of scholarship kids, Josh felt that he was stimulating every child to know worthwhile literature, to read carefully, to write clearly, and to think critically.

The school parking lot was packed when he arrived, but a Volvo station wagon was backing out of a tight space. He waited until the woman was ready to drive off, but she stopped and rolled down the window. She wore a white uniform and he recognized her as the mother of one of the younger kids, not one of his own students, but he'd never realized she was a nurse. Attractive . . . and about to say something.

"Hi," he said.

"Good morning," she flashed a smile back at him. He'd seen her a few times around the school, but was surprised that she would talk to him.

"Thanks for the spot," he said. "I was about to drive up there into the field."

"I think I saw you in the Park on Saturday," she said.

Uh, oh, he thought.

"Could be," he said. "I was there, along with a million others."

"How'd you enjoy it?"

Enjoy? He was enjoying her soft brown eyes; her brown hair, long and held back by a blue plastic barrette. Her skin was smooth and she had an overall welcoming way, scrubbed and fresh in her white uniform.

"Oh, that was a crazy, fun afternoon," he laughed. He checked his watch. It was eight-fifteen.

"I just dropped off my daughter," she said. "What grade do you teach?"

"Eighth," he said. The space she was leaving was the only one available and he didn't want to seem impatient. "English."

"Oh. I thought maybe science or something."

He shook his head. She didn't move, but he lifted his hand and made a little wave. "Got to get to my class," he said. "You working in a hospital?"

She nodded. "SF General. On a medical ward."

"Oh," he nodded. "Wow!"

"What do you mean, "wow"?"

"Nothing . . . important work, that's all."

"Well, your work, too. What's your name?"

"Josh . . . Josh Lowen." He smiled and looked at his watch again.

"I'm Claire Durand," she said. "I'd better get going."

"Right . . . me, too."

"Maybe we can talk sometime," she said.

"That'd be nice."

Josh's regular solo piano gig at The Cormorant ran from eight-thirty to eleven. He'd had the job for the last year and a half on the third Tuesday of the month, and he was looking forward to the evening, but thoughts of the nurse in the white uniform kept popping into his mind as he drove along the Embarcadero.

I'm Claire Durand.

Maybe, he thought. Maybe. It hadn't occurred to him that he'd been softly whistling a tune all day long, but now he smiled when the recognition dawned on him.

Someone To Watch Over Me.

The smile became a chuckle, then a giggle as he pulled into the parking lot. Okay, he thought. Who knows? Maybe something will happen.

The old wooden building stood on a pier by itself with the bay's green water rising and falling in big sloshing surges on both sides. Sea birds flapping and drying their wings roosted on the roof. During the day The Cormorant was a great place to watch the activities on the bay . . . container ships coming and going, sail boats, harbor seals, and just the reassuring views of Angel Island and the hills of Marin.

The front room just in from the street was long and had an old-fashioned carved mahogany bar along the left hand wall. Locals called the place Coot Heaven, but it wasn't for the little duck-like black birds that float on the water. It was just an expression of pure pride and love for the reliably constant collection of old guys who could usually be found nursing tumblers of Scotch or sipping glasses of Anchor Steam along the historic bar. The Cormorant was their club.

Beyond the bar was a large room with tables for four, all crowded together, and there was always the comforting aroma of onions, potatoes, and fish frying. The broad windows on three sides gave views out over the water that made you feel you were on a ship. The bandstand was in one corner with its small upright piano, and when it was dark outside Josh could sit at the keyboard, look around the room, and see the faces.

Still humming the Gershwin melody, he sat down and began a legato eight bar intro into the song. People were watching him, nodding and smiling. At this hour it was just half an audience. One woman seemed to be singing the words to her date across the table . . . *Someone To Watch Over Me.*

It was a cozy feeling and he felt completely at home there. The crowd was generally appreciative, and playing solo he was pretty much in charge. If he was in the mood he would do requests, but he could also say he didn't know the song, and there were even times when he announced quietly that he only played tunes he loved. No one seemed to mind. He had a large repertoire, and he could play for hours.

Sometimes he would put tunes together that had a theme. Tonight was Tuesday, but he liked Monday songs and did two in a row: lightly swinging *From Monday On* in A flat, and then moving up into *My Monday Date* in B flat.

The Cormorant had different kinds of live music five nights a week, but when he played they put a sign out in front that said "*Josh Lowen, jazz piano.*" Every time he saw that it made him feel good. There were still moments when he marveled that he was paid to play the piano. He was hoping that sometime the management would give him two nights, or even three, a month.

The rest of his musical life was unpredictable, but he had gigs extending out four or five months, playing in several traditional jazz bands, and scattered through his calendar there were weddings, bar mitzvahs, and anniversary parties, too.

The room was filling up and there was more talking, more clatter of dishes. He felt like a fast tune. A bright eight bars put him into the initial two choruses of *I Wish I Were Twins*, stating the melody plainly and taking advantage of the propulsive half-step chord sequence in left hand tenths that gave the song its energy, but then finally moving into freely improvised, shimmering treble runs moving both ways, all supported by his striding left hand with occasional back-beats in the bass to help push things along.

He loved this. There was a delightful freedom in playing solo. The interaction with the audience was closer, and it made him play better. Best was when the crowd was small and well behaved. There were some evenings when his every note and chord sounded almost fine to Josh. At those times he was aware that he was playing beautifully, and yet deep in his soul he knew that when you play jazz, *fine* is something you probably only approach. There were moments when he came close, especially if he kept in mind the way his musical heroes had sounded years ago. That always made the tune richer and more compelling. Still, he knew it always came down to what was inside him.

Heroes? He had quite a few. Jelly Roll Morton, and Earl Hines, and Teddy Wilson, and Fats Waller, and James P. Johnson, and Art Tatum, and Joe Sullivan, and Monk, and Bud Powell. He'd learned something special from each one, and he especially liked quoting them when he was hanging around with younger musicians. He would tell them what Jelly said: "*Jazz music is to be played sweet, soft, plenty rhythm, and breaks . . . clean breaks . . . and beautiful ideas in breaks.*"

He loved describing the way Earl Hines played. "Hines gives you an exhilarating feeling with special emphases, rhythmic boosts, and endless surprises. He's playing with total commitment, inventiveness, and energy; he's always taking chances, always swinging, and probably not quite knowing where things are headed, but he risks it and comes out just fine. If you want to know what joy means, listen to Earl Hines."

And of course he would quote Fats Waller on Art Tatum. "*I only play piano,*" Fats told an audience one night when he saw that Tatum had come into the club. "*But tonight God is in the house.*"

And he reminded everyone how Tatum had maintained that there are no wrong notes—everything depended on the note played next. That was the most important idea of all. It's what improvising was all about.

He had learned, and he knew he'd gotten better and better. Each hero had taught him something special. Josh called it "stuff", and he felt he had put the "stuff" into his own bag, so that he could pull it out whenever it fit the moment. Maybe he would never get to *fine*, but he knew that the more he played the better it sounded. Not a quick improvement over weeks or even months, but by keeping at it and listening to the heroes one got better. Josh was getting closer. He was gaining confidence. His style had matured, but he was still learning and he knew that would continue. Music was always a work in progress.

A week later, on the Wednesday, he saw Claire Durand again at the parking lot. It wasn't as crowded this time and as he pulled in he realized her Volvo was parked two spaces away. She was sitting with the window rolled down, not in the white uniform, but wearing some sort of Granny dress with loops of beads around her neck. The motor was off, and she was reading a book.

He walked over. "Hi, how you doing?"

"Oh, goody," she said. "You broke the ice. I wondered if you'd be here."

"Well, I'm here every day, but Wednesdays my kids have science first thing so I can arrive an hour later than usual."

She opened her door, got out, and pointed to a picnic table at the end of the parking area.

"Sure," he said. "Let's sit over there."

25

On February 15, at five in the afternoon, Josh Lowen stepped out of the elevator on the twentieth floor of the Fairmont Hotel's tower and walked down the corridor to room 2010. He stood a moment, feeling the plush carpet underfoot and taking in the impressive mirrors and gilt furnishings. Then he pressed the buzzer and in a few moments the door opened wide.

"Oh, my God, you're a hippie!" Larry knew very well he was being theatrical, but he was genuinely surprised.

"The ponytail?" Josh said. "Everybody out here wears one."

They embraced, and then stood laughing at each other. Josh had a sudden realization that his friend looked quite a bit older—receding hairline, a little overweight. I remember the boy, he thought. This is a man.

"You look great," Larry said, gesturing at what Josh was wearing. "Very fit."

Josh shrugged. He imagined that in his flannel shirt, jeans, and leather jacket he probably seemed like an overgrown kid to Larry. It was a very clear evening and the corner room had a spectacular view of the lights on the Bay Bridge and way beyond in the East Bay.

"Quite a room," Josh said.

"I have an admission, and an apology," Larry told him. "I've been here a couple of times before on business, and I never let you know. They were quick trips, in and out. I always felt a bit rushed and figured it wouldn't be fair to you."

"Forget it. I'm glad to see you. I've been busy, too. You're here looking at real estate?"

"Yeah, we can talk about that later. How about a drink?"

Larry took a bottle from the desk and held it up.

"Sure."

They sat, sipping the Scotch, in two leather chairs facing out the large window. A tanker had just emerged from under the Bridge and was heading out toward the Golden Gate.

"This is great," Larry said.

"Yeah, the view . . ."

"No, not just that. I mean getting together, you and I, after . . . how many years is it?"

"It was that summer I came home . . . 1953 . . . when I hitchhiked in from Salina, Kansas."

They sat quietly for a few minutes, sipping and enjoying the view, the silence barely broken by the clinking of ice in their glasses and an occasional muffled voice out in the hall.

It was Larry who spoke first. "I want to know what you're doing."

"Oh . . . taking it one step at a time."

Larry eyed him. "Yeah . . . and then?"

"I guess you could say I'm improvising. I don't plan too far ahead."

"But actually . . .?"

"Actually, I'm teaching, and I play music."

He looked over at Larry and waited for a moment before going on. Then he said, "You know, there was a time when I thought about becoming a doctor, maybe because my folks pushed it—subtly, but I got the message. If I hadn't screwed up at Bartlett I probably would have gone to medical school."

Larry looked down at his glass, slowly swirling the ice. "What about that whole thing?" he asked. "Have you put it out of your mind?"

Josh nodded. "In some ways I have, but I'll never really be able to forget what happened and that I was there. Even now I blame myself for being so drunk that I was useless. I still agonize that I wasn't able to change their minds about what they were doing."

"Maybe you really didn't want to go to medical school. Or did you?"

"I did. You remember that summer after freshman year? I was always wearing a pair of white duck trousers. Do you remember that?"

"I don't," Larry said.

"I remember it very clearly, and I wore them all the time because I thought it made me look like a doctor, or at least an interne working in a hospital. It's so weird. Yeah, I wanted to go to medical school."

"But then?"

"Well, it seemed pretty obvious to me that it wasn't going to happen. I didn't know what the hell my future would be, but it sure wasn't medical school. They would never have taken me. Everything was a big scary nightmare."

Larry waited for a moment. "What sort of teaching are you doing?"

"Coming to California was the best thing I could've done. I discovered literature. Anyway, I probably would've been a lousy doctor. I wasn't really interested in the stuff they have to study."

He spoke of the superb professors at San Francisco State. They'd introduced him to Hawthorne, and Melville, and Shakespeare, and Proust, and Joyce, and Whitman, and Homer, and Dante, and Blake. Those were the writers who kept him fired up and exhilarated as they touched on big questions in ways he'd never experienced before.

"That's just for starters," he said. "There is so much wonderful stuff out there, and I found out I was pretty good at it. I could write papers that the professors liked. They said my insights were interesting and helpful. And then finally I discovered I could earn a living—nothing extravagant, but one that was okay for me—by teaching English to kids and getting them to be as excited as I've been about these wonderful books."

"What about the music?"

"That's the other thing. Right after I got here I met a few musicians. One thing led to another and I'm really playing quite a bit. You know the music I love, all the stuff from the early days of jazz. There's still an audience for it even though rock and roll and a lot of electronic garbage have taken over. Kids today don't know about real jazz, but I've ceased to care about that. San Francisco has a whole subculture of people who love the real thing, and there are enough gigs to keep me reasonably busy and happy. Teaching literature is a steady weekday thing. When I play, it's usually on weekends, but it can be nights during the week, too."

"Still single?"

"Yeah . . . although . . ."

"Do you have somebody?"

"No, I live alone, and I've got lots of friends."

"But no one serious?"

"No," Josh said. "Well . . . actually, I met someone just about a month ago. But who knows? It's not really a relationship yet. What about you?"

"I was married for eight years . . . but it ended badly." Larry's voice had dropped. There was anguish in the remark, and to ease the tension Josh was about to move on to a less charged subject, but Larry didn't stop.

"Yvonne was lovely . . . and docile. Always deferred to me. I thought things were fine, but they weren't. She was attractive, tall, slim, had dark hair, and a great figure—a woman other men stare at when you're in a restaurant or at the theatre. We agreed on pretty much everything. You know, how to spend our time, our money, even politics."

"Any kids?"

"No, no kids with Yvonne, but I've got a family in the Philippines."

"You're kidding!"

"I traveled to Manila on business for a couple of years, and on one trip I became ill. Fever, terribly sick, and stuck in a hotel. One of the chambermaids really nursed me back to health. Jalili Galang. She was amazing—a bright, energetic, wonderful human being. So, I got to know her, and then her whole family. Her husband drives a cab. They've got four kids. Anyway, they treated me as one of their family. I could never forget it."

Larry pulled out his wallet, and passed over several photographs, watching as Josh perused them—a two story wooden house on an unpaved tropical street, a mango tree on the left; snapshots of brown Asian faces, the parents behind, the children in front.

"I help to support them. I want the kids to get a good education. I go to their celebrations. We're very close. It's an incredible thing. I know, it's strange to hear, and hard to explain, but they're very important to me."

"That's great," said Josh. "Handsome kids."

"Yeah, they're really special."

"I'm sorry about the marriage."

"It was a mistake. A big one." Larry slipped the pictures back into his wallet. "Things were good the first couple of years. I really loved her, and I think she loved me. Maybe we didn't work hard enough at it. I don't know. Then, one day . . . nearly two years ago . . . I had just completed an important deal. She and I were supposed to go out to a restaurant with some friends that evening. I was feeling like a celebration, and decided to surprise her. I was finished at the office around noon so I came home early and marched into the house carrying a bunch of red roses. She loves roses. I didn't pay any attention to a pickup truck parked across the street. As I opened the front door she was just coming down the stairs in her bra and panties . . . and there was a guy right behind her. He was stark naked.

"They beat it back up the stairs . . . me just standing there. I dropped the flowers on the floor, slammed the door, and went back out to my car. Sat there for a couple of minutes wondering what the hell to do. Nothing was moving in the house. I drove away and cruised around aimlessly for a couple of hours, not really caring where I went. Finally, I got hungry and went into a diner. I had a sandwich and a bottle of beer, and I slept in a motel that night.

"The discussions came later. She cried and went on about how unhappy she'd been. Frankly, it wasn't the best thing for my ego, but I'm lucky to be rid of her. And the financial settlement was not in her favor."

"God, how awful."

"Yeah, marriage wasn't for me."

They left the Fairmont and went to dinner at an Italian restaurant in North Beach. There were moments when Josh saw hints of the boy he'd known, something shy and genuine in the smile that recaptured for him the days when they had played in the empty lot, fooling around with little fires, or clumsily nailing boards together as they attempted a clubhouse.

Larry opened up more and more, allowing traces of a long-ago intimacy to appear as he described complexities and ambiguities in his life.

"My father enticed me into finance," he said. "But it wasn't a total surrender on my part."

After Lehigh, and then two years at Wharton, he'd taken a job at Goldman Sachs, first as an analyst in mergers and acquisitions, and then moving later into actually doing the deals.

"I worked in Europe and in Asia, but on the side I did some real estate deals for myself in the Caribbean and Hawaii, and I'm developing contacts in South Africa.

"What's the real estate deal here?"

"I'm going to build a shopping center. Do you know Danville?"

Josh laughed. "I've played some gigs there. It's out in the boonies."

"There's money to be made in the boonies—a lot of money. People are moving there, and I intend to profit from that."

"I doubt if I'm in a position . . ."

"Not to worry. We can talk about that."

Josh smiled. "I'm impressed—you're a citizen of the world. Projects all over the place."

"It's in the blood," Larry said, an intense look on his face.

"Your father was in that line, too, wasn't he?"

"Not exactly. He did some real estate deals, but arbitrage was his thing. In Europe his family made money exploiting small differences in currency rates between countries, but here arbitrage more often involves fluctuations in stock prices when one company is in the process of merging with or acquiring another. It's betting on whether a proposed merger will go through. He did some of that, but I've done a lot."

"Do you enjoy it?"

"I understand it, I'm comfortable with it, and I can talk easily to the people in that world. I'm in touch with a few of my father's business friends who survived the war and who now live in London, Paris, and Belgium. There are always risks, but I'm alert to them, and I do enjoy the process. I try not to forget that it's all a means to an end—the good life, art, and leisure. I'll know when to stop."

Josh nodded.

"I'd like you to invest with me in this Danville project. It's a local thing, you live here, and it's almost sure to increase enormously in value."

Josh pictured Danville venues where he'd played: a bar, a nearby Elks Club, and an old hotel.

"I'm the general partner," Larry explained. "You'd be a limited partner, like the other investors. I'm asking people to invest no less than $25,000. On this kind of project it's more usual to ask $10,000 as a minimum, but I want a smaller number of investors, so it's going to be 25K. You could put in less, say $10,000, and I'll loan you the other $15,000—just because we're friends. As the profits come in, I'd put some of yours toward paying off the loan from me, and in time you'll own a larger share and will be reaping income from it for years. The IRS requires me to charge you interest, but I've decided I won't do that because of our friendship. They'll never pick it up."

"I wouldn't want to do anything illegal," Josh said.

"No, no. It wouldn't be a problem for you. It's a minor technicality . . . just bureaucracy. The others wouldn't need to know about it either."

"What others?"

"The other investors. If I'm helping you out, that's not their affair. I've done these deals before. To be a winner you always have keep at least a few steps ahead of others."

"Do you ever wonder about the friendship between our two families?" Josh asked.

"Oh, my God—are you kidding? Of course I do. I always liked your parents. I envied you."

"I thought your parents were more interesting. Secretly, I fretted that mine were dull and boring."

"No, they were very natural, very easy. They let you follow your own path."

"Yeah, in a way, they did. My screwing up at Bartlett was a huge crisis, but I came around to seeing that they were still on my side."

"That, in itself, tells you a lot. How often do you see them?"

"Couple of times a year. They're more willing to come out here now than they used to be. There's always some tension, but it's okay. What about your folks?"

"Tense is the word. My mother's in her own double A world. Art and alcohol. She paints, and paints, and paints. And drinks constantly. She's very overweight. Financially, she's okay, but emotionally she's super-fragile."

"What about your Dad?"

"Cool, sarcastic, opinionated. I see him, but it's never wonderful."

"Too bad."

"Yes."

They said nothing for a long minute.

"Anyway," Larry broke the silence. "I've done pretty well, and now I'm on my own, managing my own funds, and developing the other half of my brain."

"I'm all ears," Josh said.

"You've had your changes, and I've had mine. A good part of my work has involved trading. Traders have to make decisions rapidly just to gain an advantage that can be measured in a few pennies in the price of a stock. When you're talking about thousands of shares that can make a huge difference. And I was really caught up in it. Traders are arrogant people. They're impressed by their own importance, and I was right in there with the best. My work came first, my marriage second."

"Are you taking more time off now?"

"Sure, and using it in a better way. Yvonne and I made lots of trips to Europe, but they were short visits and always combined with business. In the back of my mind I nurtured an idea about returning for a longer time, but I didn't think I could afford it. Our divorce changed all that. I left Goldman, and I wanted things to be very different . . . really to start over again. We had a big house in Connecticut, and I hated it—couldn't stand it. We sold it. She did get her part of that, but it doesn't matter—she didn't get much else."

His lips formed a bitter smile. He was looking down at the table, but then he shrugged his shoulders. "See, I don't have to worry about airfares. Up to a point I can indulge myself. I rent an apartment in Italy and I spend a lot of time there."

"Where?"

"Florence. One month there; come back to New York for two—then repeat." Larry looked up. His smile was broad. "I feel fortunate," he said. "I even have a lady friend there."

"Really . . . what's she like?"

"Elegant, sophisticated, and married to a rich guy who's more interested in chasing teen-agers."

"Oh, great."

"No problem. It's okay. Luisa and I get along fine. No demands on either side."

"Terrific."

"Look, I'm not retired. At this point I still need to watch my funds. I can't spend lavishly, and I have no desire for that anyway. I'm comfortable, not super-rich. At Goldman I was in the middle, not at the top."

"What do you do in Italy?"

"I slow down. I don't play the one-upmanship game. I don't try to prove who I am to anyone. And I luxuriate in art."

Josh nodded, and then made some quick circular movements with his right hand. "Come on . . . fill me in. Tell me more."

Larry paused. "You haven't been to Europe, have you?"

"No."

Larry thought for a moment. Then he said, "Okay, here's something that I do. There's a severe looking 13th century building in Florence called the Bargello—looks like a fortress. For a time it was a prison, and now it's a museum, mainly for sculpture. When I'm in Florence I go there a lot. I wander through the rooms, looking at the collection—beautiful, fantastic pieces—things I've seen over and over again. I never seem to get enough of them. Sometimes I can find a chair and I just sit there . . . thinking, marveling. You asked me what I do . . . that's a good example of what I do. Does it seem odd?"

"No, I can see myself doing that."

"I'm becoming more proficient in Italian. And I've been buying paintings—mostly there, in Florence. But of course with the time I've worked in Asia, I've bought pieces in Singapore, Bangkok, and Hong Kong, too. So, money and art, you know—they've come together."

"Meaning?"

"Meaning my mother and father coming together . . . some aspects of them, some of their qualities, in my own life."

"The money enables you . . ."

"Yeah, I have a nice collection now—not huge, but very satisfying to me. I've also sold a few paintings profitably. I can buy in Italy, but when I get a piece home I can decide I'd rather put the money into something else, and often I've been able to do exactly that to my own advantage. Prices in New York are higher than what I pay in Italy."

It was past three when Josh finally got to bed. Initially, he'd felt on edge with his old friend, but things eased and they relaxed, both clearly enjoying themselves over dinner. Now, lying in bed and staring at the ceiling, he was restless, sleep coming intermittently and making of the night a confused procession of wide-awake thoughts breaking up what seemed to be very brief moments of actual dream-filled sleep. People from his past moved across scenes of his life. Zipper, Kenny, Walt and PB were there, arguing about their post-expulsion careers and how getting kicked out of Bartlett hadn't hindered them from making tons of money. Larry's dainty wife was mincing down a carpeted staircase and Josh was trying to get closer to see if he could tell if she was really nude or if she was covered up with some sort of tissue paper. Then he awoke again and felt annoyed at Larry for asking him if he'd gotten over being kicked out of Bartlett. How dare he? How could he pass judgment? His life wasn't so perfect, was it?

And the images flooded his brain—Larry's ex-wife; Larry's lady friend, Luisa; the restaurant's décor; the Chianti; the waiter's face; and thoughts about when and how he and Larry might see each other again.

More than anything, the business arrangement kept him awake. Josh understood the mechanics of the financing, and he had the $10,000 in starter money, but that was about all he had saved. Deciding to put it into an un-built shopping center would be nerve-wracking. Businesses fail. Businesses are subject to things you can't control. Still, it was tremendously attractive to have an investment that might make some real money for him.

He slept again, but it didn't last. The next three hours he lay awake, the restaurant's Italian melodies running through his mind.

26

Josh saw Claire Durand several times in February and March. He found her a down-to-earth woman with a dry sense of humor and a serene, but totally committed dedication to Holly, her eight-year-old daughter. Claire had married Jim Durand in 1958, but he had been killed in a head-on car crash on a rainy night in 1963. Another driver, coming from the opposite direction, had had a fatal heart attack, losing control of his car.

For Claire, with her nursing job at SF General and raising Holly by herself, dating took some arranging. Fortunately, her parents were completely devoted to their only granddaughter, and were upbeat, generous babysitters.

Josh had never met someone with whom he felt so comfortable. He found Claire appealing in a way that far surpassed what he'd experienced with other women. He was thirty-four years old, and had had long relationships with two very different women. At the start, both had been intense and successful. Samantha, two years older than he, was a quiet and intellectual brunette. She'd worked in publishing in New York, but had independent means and had been drawn to San Francisco by the counter-culture scene developing in Haight-Ashbury. The affair had been passionate, but for Josh it gradually fizzled out of boredom.

Samantha had begun to bring most conversations around to what she called "spirituality" and Josh found it painful.

"Groan!" he thought. "It's no different from listening to someone who invokes Jesus in every other paragraph."

Then there was Mitzi—really a girl. Twelve years younger than Josh and a jazz-groupie, she came to lots of his gigs. Mitzi was a nimble and expressive ballroom dancer, but her true preference was to get out on the floor alone and gyrate around without a partner. She attracted lots of attention and Josh found her fun to be with because she was street-smart and quick. She could talk about everything—jazz, certainly, but also politics, film, social injustice, wine, restaurants, and celebrities—so there was never any worry about running out of subjects, but unfortunately she also had a habit of using words inappropriately, and he couldn't hold himself back from correcting her.

One night after a gig they were looking at the menu in a new seafood restaurant on the Wharf.

"Supposably this place has good fish soup," she ventured.

"Yeah, I've heard that," he said. "You mean *supposedly*, not *supposably*."

"Jesus, don't be such a snob," she snapped. "There's plenty of ways of communicating."

"True, true. There *are* plenty of ways."

"Oh, just shut up!"

Eventually it dawned on him that having an enjoyable and meaningful conversation with Mitzi was impossible. She just loved to talk, but he didn't want to hear it any more. They had been together for quite a while, but after a year he went his own way.

On their first date Josh took Claire to a Chinese restaurant. The room was crowded and noisy, but the food was good and they told their stories to each other. Claire had grown up in the Bay Area, acquired a nursing degree at Stanford, fallen in love with Jim Durand, and married at twenty-one.

"That night, when the police came to tell me about Jim, I fainted," she said. "I actually crumpled. They were very kind—grabbed me just as I fell—and put me on the sofa. Holly woke up and started crying. The officers waited with me until Mom and Dad came over."

With emotional and financial support from her parents, Claire had gradually come up from the depths. For the first two years after Jim's death she'd had no interest in dating. Later, she had successively been with three other men, but none had any lasting effect on her. She had her child and she had her work. That seemed quite sufficient to her.

"Life is a journey," she said. "Maybe you know that, too."

"I've been on one for a while."

He started telling her: Brooklyn, Queens, and then Bartlett.

"Oh, God," she said. "How awful for you."

"It was; it is. It never goes away, but it's a pretty big part of my journey."

She asked if he knew anything about the others who'd been kicked out of the school.

"Just occasional bits of hearsay," he said. "They're leading ordinary lives, I guess. I try not to think about them, but even though that's probably for my own good, it's cowardly."

"Why do you say that?"

"Because I was there. I was part of the disaster. I'll never be able to shake the uneasy feeling that maybe I could've done something to stop it."

"It's not cowardly to get on with your life."

"I know that. Of course, the main thing that keeps coming back is that Tom Grillo died. We were responsible . . . he was as much a hero in the war as any other soldier who saw action and got wounded. And his values were good. Who knew at the time? But, later . . . I understood. I saw what kind of guy he really was. We cut short the life of a good man. Who knows what he might have done during the rest of it . . . the part we took away from him."

Claire sat looking down at the table, dabbing her eyes with a tissue and shaking her head.

"Anyway," Josh said. "I'm not sure how to think about it. Those four guys still inhabit my memories, and it isn't as if I don't want them there. They're part of my life even if I get depressed thinking about them. And ashamed, too, but I also know I've been fortunate in my life since then."

He talked about his love of literature and the rewards of teaching, his need to express himself in music, and his little place in the Sunset district.

"I don't look at other people and covet what they've got," he said. "I wouldn't trade."

Claire nodded. "Ah, that's good," she said, her face brightening and her eyes glistening.

A few days later he called and invited her to a movie. "It's *Who's Afraid of Virginia Woolf?*" he said.

"Oh, I definitely want to see it, but my book group meets that night. I'm sorry."

"Maybe next week?" he suggested. "Everybody says it's a brilliant film—depressing, but great."

The following week was agreeable, but the only place showing the film was in San Francisco, so they met right at the theatre after work and saw the six o'clock showing. When it was over they came out on to the sidewalk, finding it difficult to speak, and each seeking the other's hand.

"Oh, my God," Claire said.

The film's relentless emotional intensity and the harsh tearing down of the characters' defenses were cruel and hard to bear.

"What'd you think?" Josh asked.

"It's pretty awful to think about . . . about what life can become for some people. But it was honest, brutally honest."

Josh nodded. "Shall we have some dinner?"

They settled on pizza and found a quiet place nearby where the lighting was subdued, arias from Puccini were playing, and the waitress was believably cheerful and optimistic. Sitting across from each other in a cozy booth they drank their beer and shared a pizza with mushrooms and onions. After a few comments about the movie their mood lightened.

"How often does your book group meet?" Josh asked.

"About every four to six weeks. It depends on everyone's schedule."

"Friends from the hospital?"

"No, only one is a nurse—the others are women I've become friendly with over the last few years."

Claire talked briefly about what they were reading. "But it's been much more than books. These are women who were there for me after Jim died; and I need to continue to see them. We talk about anything and everything, including personal and family issues as they come up. And we trust one another."

"A support system," Josh said.

"Yes, but more than that. I think of them as friends—good friends."

Their next date was to Yank Sing on Broadway for a *dim sum* lunch. Another was an afternoon visit to the de Young Museum. And some days after that they had a stroll on Ocean Beach on a cold and windy Saturday. They walked briskly along the hard packed sand and found a rhythm to their pace. She took his arm. He smiled at her, then turned away and scanned the horizon. A sailboat, heeled over, was beating its way north.

"Do you think things are moving too fast?" Claire asked him.

"Too fast?"

"Between us."

"Oh, no. I don't think so."

He marveled at her candor.

"Do you think I'm too forward?"

He laughed. "Oh, come on."

"You don't want to have this conversation."

"I'm open," he said. "Keep talking."

"Okay," she went on. "That first day . . ."

"In the parking lot."

"You seemed interested," she said.

"I was, but you took the initiative; you started the conversation."

"No, you actually said 'hi' to me first."

"Everybody says 'hi.' And you asked me a bunch of questions—did I teach science or something?"

"Just being friendly," she said.

"Yeah, but you suggested we talk, and then you showed up that other time."

"*Touché.*"

"Yeah, right. And, that time, I was a little disappointed—the Granny dress. I think your white uniform is . . ."

". . . fascinating?" She laughed.

He stopped, turning to look down at her face, and pulled her close. "That, too. But—it's more that I want to capture you, keep you all for myself, embrace you, have you."

She smiled up at him and moved her lips closer. "Well?" she said. "Here we are."

Things moved rapidly from that Saturday. Each responded to humor and to frankness, and that was fortunate. There was no question in their minds that they wanted to be together.

"I can't just move in with you," Josh said. "And you can't just move in with me."

"Are you saying we have to get married?"

"You said that, not me."

"That's not a helpful answer."

They had met in January, and now it was April. They were in Josh's apartment and had just made love. A late afternoon sunbeam made oblique shadows on the rumpled sheets.

"You would marry me?" Josh seemed to be thinking out loud.

"Is that some sort of abstract wonderment, or are you proposing?"

"I'm asking a question."

"Yes, you're definitely asking a question."

"Okay, how about marrying me? I think it's a great idea."

Claire snuggled up to him. "So do I," she said.

But, how? Holly wasn't the problem. She liked Josh, and he was thrilled that this bright, fun-loving, and joyously confident child was drawn to him. He saw in her the nascent qualities that would develop and define the woman she would become—a woman like Claire. That was wonderful. Nor were Claire's parents the problem. Lou and Eve Johnson were warm and easy-going people whose principal motivation seemed to be the happiness of their only daughter.

The question was one of courage.

For Claire, it meant taking a bold next step. She had learned that total commitment contained the seeds of heartbreak and tragedy. No commitment, no risk—at least, not that risk. Yet she found Josh irresistible. She detected no veneer, no pomposity—in fact nothing harsh. He was a gentle man, but along with that she admired his passion for teaching and literature, and his ardor for playing jazz. He was self-assured, but modest, in both of those two activities that were so important to him, and he was unmoved by any hint that others might think his work lacking in prestige or status. Claire found that a very attractive kind of strength, and she didn't want to give it up.

For Josh, hesitation came from a feeling almost of disbelief. For the last few years he'd been comfortable going along as he had, yet all the while knowing that the life he was leading was far from what his parents had envisioned. He also sensed that the Johnsons were probably judging his double career as teacher and musician just as Sid and Mae Lowen did. Most days, the shame of remembering his own part in the death of Tom Grillo existed on a not-too-distant horizon of consciousness, always there as a stain that couldn't be washed off—a sign of inferiority that others would, and probably should, inevitably scorn. Was it even possible that he could be entitled to someone like Claire?

Increasingly, they were seen as a couple. Holly looked forward to going out to dinner with the two of them, and if Claire's parents came along it seemed like any ordinary three-generational family. Mae and Sid Lowen were kept informed by phone and by letters, and on a recent August trip to California they refrained from asking, but it was clear that they liked Claire and that they thought Josh was lucky to have finally found someone worthy of him. When the Lowens met Lou and Eve Johnson, the four talked among themselves as if they wondered what was causing the delay. Even Josh's musician friends had gotten used to seeing Claire. She came along to his gigs often enough to be on joking terms with them, and she knew that they were prodding Josh to go ahead and take the giant step that they all concluded he was just building up sufficient courage to take.

The October wedding was at the Johnson's home in Ross. A garden ceremony was planned, but the weather prediction of only a ten percent chance of rain turned out to be overly optimistic. By mid-morning dark clouds had moved in and the downpour was heavy. Fortunately, the twenty guests, including the Lowens who had flown in from New York two days before, were in high spirits, and with the lights on and the flowers placed at strategic places through the living and dining rooms there was an air of festivity that the weather couldn't quench. The Johnsons were long-lapsed Catholics, but Claire had decided that in honor of Josh's Jewish background they should be married under a *chuppah*. Its blue and white cloth was Sid Lowen's *tallit*, carried on four poles by musician buddies of Josh. Friends from Claire's book group read poems, and a Stanford nursing school classmate who was also a Universalist minister led the brief service. After the official pronouncement, even the traditional glass was crushed under Josh's foot and a few calls of *mazel tov* were heard.

Claire said they should postpone a honeymoon, but Josh insisted on at least a weekend away. Lou and Eve took Holly for four days, and the newlyweds drove up the coast to Mendocino where they rented a small house on an isolated bluff overlooking the Pacific. There was breeze from the north, but the sky was blue, and the sides of the deck facing the water had a thick hedge of Monterrey cypress giving ample privacy and shelter from the wind. It was there that they spent sun-filled hours making love, sleeping, and gazing out at the immense blue ocean.

27

Friday nights Josh was playing in a septet at the Brass Bucket in Santa Rosa. It was a traditional hot band with a front line of three—Dave Sloane, trumpet and leader, Will Barton, trombone, and Ed Howell, clarinet. The rhythm section included guitar, drums, and Rich Mariani, Josh's first musician friend in San Francisco, on string bass. The aim was collective improvisation—call and response, keep the melody in mind, and swing, baby, swing. The repertoire was mostly Armstrong, Morton, Dodds, and early Ellington tunes, but in every set they added a couple of contemporary things, and they had a pretty regular crowd of the faithful who came and danced.

A band is a whole; its parts are personalities. Each band is different, but musicians are expressive people and they don't necessarily always mesh. A good leader expects adherence to the overall goal, but he also respects the guys who are trying their best. To play in an improvising jazz band one goes with the plan, even if its true essence resides in the need for each musician to communicate in his uniquely individual voice. One submerges it only to the degree required to make a good collective sound, because in the end one really wants a conversation.

The evening was going well and Josh was smiling. There was nothing like playing in a band when all the guys were listening to one another and acknowledging in their own improvisation what the others were doing. Sometimes the excitement was so high that you felt like you were flying. Josh often had the feeling that he was not only playing piano—he was playing the entire band. It was an illusion, but a wonderful one—making the entire thing go.

They played *Sugar* as their next-to-last number, and Rich Mariani sang it in a gravelly voice filled with irony. The couples on the floor were dancing cheek-to-cheek and the rhythm was perfect.

There was a quiet ripple of applause, and then it was time for the final tune. Dave announced *Tiger Rag*. "It's a good one to end the evening on," he said. Then he raised his left hand, stomped his foot twice, and they settled into a moderately fast tempo.

A few people were putting on their coats to leave, but five couples were still out on the dance floor. The band moved through the different melodic strains with the trombone doing the traditional tiger's roar, and then they each took a solo chorus on the last strain. Finally, they raised the volume and got into the out chorus. Just as they neared the end Dave put up his left index finger again indicating he wanted an extra chorus, but up a whole step from A flat to B flat. The band was a little flustered by the unplanned ending, but even with some faltering they managed to get it together and ended gracefully. The audience was clapping enthusiastically, and the leader was smiling sheepishly, but Will Barton was angry.

"Christ, man," he said. "That was a helluva way to end."

Dave Sloane flushed, and then turned to challenge Will. "Don't ever criticize me in front of the audience," he said quietly.

Will walked off to one side, set his trombone in its case, put on his coat, and then stepped quickly back to confront the leader. He waved a rolled-up sheaf of band music in Dave's face. "You can take this and shove it up your ass," he barked, throwing it at Dave. The sheets of music fluttered down to the floor as Will turned on his heel and stomped out of the Brass Bucket.

"Looks like we'll need another trombone player next week," Josh said to no one in particular.

Claire was still up and in bed reading when he got home at midnight. She had put a letter on his pillow. Right away he saw the Italian stamp.

November 10, 1967

Dear Josh,

Your invitation was forwarded from New York along with other mail. I just opened it, having returned to Florence after a week in Zurich and Basle. I feel especially bad about missing your wedding. When we talked back in January you said you'd met someone and I am amazed at how rapidly things progressed. Congratulations. I wish you much happiness.

The shopping center in Danville is moving along. Safeway decided to put in one of their stores. They've signed a fifteen-year lease, so they'll be the "anchor" for the whole project. There are only two small spaces left; several stores are competing for them.

I'm active in the art market here, buying things for myself, but I keep an eye out for pieces I know will sell in the States.

I send my best wishes to you and to your lucky bride. Let me know how things are going. I'll keep you informed about Danville.

Ciao!

Larry

"Who's L. Gerst?" Claire asked.
"Larry, my friend. We talked about him coming to the wedding."

"The one who never bothered to let us know?"

"He lives part of the time in Europe, and just got the invitation in mail that was forwarded to him"

They talked for a while before turning off the light. He told her about two boys growing up together, about the friendship their parents had had, about how the Gerst's divorce had affected Larry, and about the particularities of a friendship that he found hard to explain.

"I know we're very different, but we go way back. In fact, he's the only one from those times that I keep up with, although years have gone by."

He told her about his visit to Larry's room at the Fairmont in February. "An evening like that is pretty amazing," he said. "We talked and talked. I think we got to know each other again. And yet, I'm not sure how close we are. I would say I'm more curious about him, than close to him."

"Sounds like it might not be possible to be close to him, but anyway I feel badly he wasn't able to come to our wedding."

"*Bad*," Josh said. "*Feel badly* means there's a problem with the nerves in your fingers."

"What?"

"*Badly* is an adverb. It modifies feel."

Claire bolted upright and looked down at him. "You're criticizing my grammar?"

"Sorry . . . I'm just . . ." He was suddenly hit by a flash of memory from his time with Mitzi: *Don't be such a snob . . . Shut up!*

"You're sorry?"

"Claire, relax."

"Relax? No, let's get it straight. I am not one of your students."

"Okay, okay. I said I'm sorry."

"I am quite serious. We were having a conversation and you effectively ended it by nit-picking."

"I'm sorry, Claire. Really, I'm sorry."

Claire lay down again. "I accept your apology."

They were both silent, but after a few moments she asked, "Do you like him?"

"Larry? Yeah, I do. We go way back. It's friendship, but I guess there's also something in the way."

"And you trust him with this investment?"

"I do."

"Turn off the light."

He reached over and switched it off. "Oh, I forgot," he said. "Our trombone player quit tonight."

"Mmmm."

He lay back, unhappy at knowing that his apology hadn't at all matched the fervor of her anger. How could it? What a jerk he was. He could only hope that things would be better in the morning.

The room was dark, but light from cars passing along the street moved erratically across the ceiling. A little breeze blew in through the open window. Even up here in the hills he could make out the marine scent of San Francisco Bay.

No more comments about grammar, he told himself.

28

Quarterly reports from the Danville investment came regularly and the gradual increase in its value was evident even to Josh. He'd been under the impression that it would take a couple of years before his debt to Larry would be paid, but now it looked as if that would happen sooner. The shopping center was fully rented, more families were moving into the area, and several articles in the *Chronicle* had noted a concurrent rise in East Bay property values.

Every time a report came in the mail he would glance briefly at the figures and then put it into a loose-leaf folder. It was also an occasion for Claire to want to talk about his friendship with Larry.

"When am I going to meet him?"

"You make it sound like he's some sort of mystery man," Josh chuckled. "I'm sure he'll be out here one of these days."

"He was an important person for you, a big part of your life before we met."

"Well, sure, and you have friends from your past that I don't know, but that's okay, isn't it?"

"Absolutely. Well, he sounds interesting—and complicated."

"That he is." Josh described Larry's connection with his adopted family in the Philippines. "The last time I saw him he was clearly very devoted to them. I was surprised that he got involved that way, but I thought it was great."

"It's pretty unusual. I don't know anyone who's doing anything like that."

They were both moving around in the kitchen getting things ready for their dinner, and Holly was setting the table.

"What are you talking about?" she asked.

"Just about a friend of Josh's."

"Why is he interesting and complicated?"

"Oh," said Josh. "When you grow up, and then you see one of your old friends from when you were little, and he's lived a different sort of life—maybe he's moved to another country—then that's pretty interesting—or maybe he works at something that seems strange to you."

"Where does he live?"

Josh opened up the story. He talked about his boyhood, about the friendship between the Lowens and Gersts, about the things he and Larry enjoyed as kids. "We were pals," he said. "Now he lives some of the time in Italy, some of the time in New York. And he has a family in the Philippines."

Claire put plates of meat loaf, gravy, peas, and mashed potatoes on the table. "Okay," she said. "Let's sit down."

They ate quietly.

Moving into Claire's place had been the almost obvious solution after the wedding. With her parents' help she had bought the small home in Mill Valley a year after her husband was killed. She and Josh had talked frankly and often about Jim Durand because it was a thing that couldn't be avoided, but it required caution and sensitivity in the handling. There were self-evident possibilities for hurt and jealousy, and they knew that ghosts from the past hovered, but they also felt strongly that if they could maintain honesty and candor their love and commitment to be with each other would enable things to work.

Josh's teaching job being in Marin, he wasn't unhappy that his former daily commute from the city was over. Besides, his cramped apartment in the Sunset would have been impossible. These days he had to pinch himself when he realized he now had a family. Although Holly had frequently talked to Claire about Jim Durand, wanting to know all sorts of things about a man she barely remembered, that didn't interfere with her quickly and easily forming a strong bond with Josh. He was "Josh" and "mommy's husband", and he played the piano and taught her little tunes, and told her stories about when he was a boy and when he came to California by himself. Months later she was still calling him "Josh", but when she spoke of him to her friends she was saying "my Dad."

Josh was astounded that this remarkable thing had happened to him. A bachelor life extending indefinitely into the future had been his vision for himself, and although he'd equated that solitary life with freedom, now it embarrassed him to see how below the bravura there had been emptiness, loneliness, and even a lack of purpose—all of it overlaid with a strange quality of guilt about how self-immersed he had been. If he'd had concerns that nostalgia for his single years might mean a degree of sadness or even loss, it soon dawned on him how needless that was. Life with Claire and Holly was full of warmth and comfort, and he felt so blessed.

29

October 20, 1968

Dear Josh,

I'll be in the Bay Area for three days in January. I hope to see you and meet Claire and Holly. I'd like to take you to The Blue Fox.

Danville is doing quite well. If it continues, you'll soon be receiving quarterly checks. It's an excellent spot. It's also been a very good time to develop that property. It will be a marvelous investment for you.

Do you ever get to Europe? You should—especially Italy.

Warm regards,

Larry

Josh liked the idea, but Claire demurred. "We'll invite him to dinner here. He's not just a business associate; he's your friend. Maybe The Blue Fox is his style, but he can eat there anytime. We'll have him here. You and I don't need The Blue Fox."

"Well, Larry does have style, but I'm all right with him coming here," Josh replied. "I've never even been to The Blue Fox."

"I have," said Claire. "Forget it."

It was another one of those moments when Josh looked at her with pleasure and astonishment. The stunning woman in the parking lot who had taken the first step, who had been straightforward about seeking him out, was no pushover. Her loveliness was coupled with strength and resolve that he increasingly found magnificent, and she managed it without being intimidating. He marveled at his happiness.

"All right, I'll let him know."

Their guest arrived on a cold, drizzling Saturday in late January. Claire, glancing out their living room window, watched as the rental car pulled into the driveway.

"He's here," she called to Josh.

They were both at the front door to welcome Larry. He was carrying a gift box and some flowers, and when Josh saw that it was a bouquet of red roses he said, "Oh!"

"What's wrong?" Claire said.

"Nothing," he whispered. "I'll tell you later."

"This is so special," Larry said, handing Claire both the bouquet and the box.

"Thank you," she smiled. "Such lovely roses, and chocolate, too."

Larry embraced Josh, took off his trench coat, and emerged very spiffy in a blue blazer with gold buttons, a blue and white striped button down shirt, a paisley ascot, gray flannel trousers, and highly polished brown loafers.

"I've always regretted missing your wedding," he said, approaching Claire. He bowed and kissed her hand. "There . . . I feel much better now."

Holly came out from her room and was introduced. She tended to be shy with newcomers, but she was curious to see what an old friend of Josh's would be like.

"And this is for you," Larry said, pulling a small package from his jacket pocket. Holly pulled off the paper wrapping and held up a small, embroidered purse. "Something from Florence," he told her. "You can keep your money in it, or anything else you like."

They sat around nibbling cheese and sipping Merlot. To Josh, Larry appeared much more at ease than on his last visit to San Francisco. Memories of an embittered friend recounting the uncomfortable and sordid end of his marriage seemed nearly inconsistent with the dapper, urbane man who had come to dinner. Larry was talkative, yet not dominating in the conversation, and Josh observed him almost as if he were a new species.

"You have to tell us about Italy," Claire said. "I was in Florence once during college."

"Junior year abroad?"

"Only a semester, but it was wonderful. Of course, two years ago there was that big flood."

"Ah, terrible destruction. So many paintings ruined. There are little plaques all around town showing how high the water came. It's hard to believe."

"Sometime I'd love to go back," Claire said. "By the time I left I knew quite a bit of Italian."

Larry described how he divided his time between New York and Florence. "Most of my business I can do by phone. I'm in touch with things no matter where I am, but I know my soul is in Italy."

He had a long-term lease on a two-bedroom apartment just a short walk from the Arno, and he said he never worried about locking it up and returning to New York for several months. He was buying sculpture and paintings all the time, sending most of it to his place in Manhattan, but thinning out that collection by selling pieces he didn't want to keep. Five or six different dealers in New York, Philadelphia, and Boston were almost always willing to take things on consignment, and apparently they had no difficulty finding local American buyers. "It's not a big market," Larry said. "But there are Americans who love European art and who know that it's a good investment. The great days of the American robber barons amassing huge collections of stuff from Italy, and even from France, Germany, and England, are over. That was the nineteenth century, but it's still possible to discover fine pieces. My situation is ideal, maybe even unique. I know there are Americans eager to buy and willing to pay good prices. By living a third of each year in Italy, I find out lots of things and I'm not shy about exploiting the advantage it gives me."

Most assuredly, he was also enjoying it.

"And your lady friend?" Josh asked. "How's that going?"

"Luisa?" Larry smiled. "Couldn't be better. We understand each other very well."

"And the family in the Philippines?"

"Wonderful," Larry said. He pulled out his wallet. The photos were new, the children a little older. "I see them usually twice a year. They're doing fine. The kids are great."

He told them a little more about each child, about the work the parents were doing, and about the satisfaction of knowing he was making a difference in their lives.

"Since I don't have a real family of my own it's pretty important to me."

"I'm sure," Claire said.

They sat in silence for an uncomfortable moment.

"Do you buy art in Asia, too?" Claire asked.

"I do, but I'm mostly interested in Italian art."

"How do you actually go about it?"

"Could be hereditary," Josh ventured. "Larry's mother is an artist."

"Oh," Larry said. "I'm sorry—you don't know. Mom died just six months ago." He told about Betty Gerst's slow decline from cirrhosis to liver cancer. "It was pretty awful. But, you're right, Josh. You and I used to watch her paint down in her basement studio in our house. I was always intrigued by it and some of her passion for art rubbed off." He talked about the interest developing further in college and then on many trips, business and otherwise, to Europe.

"I love having it around me," he said. "It's more than a hobby, more than an infatuation. Of course, collecting is another story. Art is art, but it's also . . ."

". . . an investment?" Claire asked.

"True, very true . . . it's a complicated business."

There was something about the way Larry said it that made Josh want to change the subject, but watching his old friend he detected no nervousness there. Larry merely made a smooth transition to a suggestion that Josh ought to come to Europe. "It would be good for you," he said. "And you've never been, right?"

"Never."

"I wouldn't try to see too much; just pick one country. Find out what the great spots are and focus on them. Take your time. Figure you'll go back on other trips."

"We will," Claire said. "This may not be the ideal time, but we will. I'll see to that."

"I'd recommend Italy, of course. Come . . . I can show you lots of wonderful things."

"Sounds great," Josh said. "We'll pick a time, and we'll come. Definitely."

"I'd like to go," said Holly. "We can all go."

"I think dinner is ready," Claire said. "Let's sit down."

After Larry left and Holly had gone to sleep, they were putting things away in the kitchen.

"I was struck by the change in him," Josh said. "He's got a lot of varied business interests, but I think this art thing has really grabbed him. He's not just a dilettante. His mother's love of art seeped in."

"There's something very sad about him," Claire said. "Something missing."

"I know. He's had his problems."

"Go on, tell me."

"He had a bad marriage."

"When he was just coming to the front door you said you would tell me something later. What was it?"

"It was that bunch of red roses."

Josh told her Larry's story . . . the anticipation of celebrating a successful business deal, the unremarked pickup truck across the street, the awful, lurid moment as Larry entered his home, and the dropped bouquet of red roses he'd chosen for his Yvonne.

"Oh, my God," Claire said.

"Yeah, horrible, but I think he's recovered."

"I wouldn't bet on it. He's carrying around a lot of pain."

Josh nodded.

"When you were growing up did you feel competitive with him?" Claire asked.

"What are you getting at?"

"You and he are very different."

"No doubt."

"I wonder what you even have in common."

"Growing up together. Our parents were friends—although that ended when the Gersts split."

She was drying a large bowl and stooped to put it in its cabinet. Then she stood up.

"I don't like him," she announced.

"Okay," he said.

"Will that bother you?"

"Probably not," Josh said with a little laugh. "Anyway, we're here, and he's there. Pretty far away, right? I mean—Florence, New York, the Philippines. And you're entitled to your opinion."

"I don't want to hurt your feelings."

"I'm a big boy."

"But you're tied to him in some way."

"I'm tied to the Danville shopping center because it's making us some money, right?"

"I've asked you this before: do you trust him?"

"Probably."

"Probably? You have some doubts?"

"I think he's shrewd enough to make things work the way he wants them to work."

"I think underneath his suave manner, he's a pretty tough cookie. Anyway, I hope your trust isn't misplaced."

"I don't imagine we'll be seeing Larry Gerst very often."

"Still, there's something in you that feels a loyalty to him."

"Look . . . I like Larry. I admire him for his expertise in whatever it is he does. Loyalty—what do you mean by loyalty?"

"It's just a feeling I have."

"To know about loyalty it would have to be tested, wouldn't it?"

"Probably. But I hope it doesn't come to that."

They lay side by side. The room was completely dark.

"Do you ever think about that Be-In?" she asked.

"Be-In?"

"You know—last year. Golden Gate Park. It's where we met."

"You saw me there, but we didn't meet . . ."

"I know, until later. But I think about it in relation to us. We were both there, but do you think you were a part of it? I know I was just an observer. But I'm asking you . . . do you consider yourself a part of that?"

"Why, because I'm a musician; because I have a ponytail; because I've smoked weed a few times?"

"No, I guess you're not. I just think, here we are, lucky to have found each other."

He rolled over and hugged her. "I love you."

She lay still, but then said quietly, "He's lonely, isn't he? Your friend."

"Maybe, but he's leading an interesting life."

"He reminds me a little of Jim," Claire said.

Josh waited. He always waited when she mentioned Jim Durand.

"Not as good looking," she said. "But he has a similar no-nonsense, straight-ahead determination. Many men exude it."

Josh said nothing. His eyes were closed, but he wanted her to go on. What was she leading up to?

Finally, she said, "You and he are totally different."

"Who?"

"You and Jim."

Now he hoped she wouldn't go on, and she didn't. In a few minutes he heard her steady breathing and knew she was asleep.

30

The school day at Los Arboles ended at 3:10, but Claire's work schedule at SF General made it impossible for her to get back to Mill Valley in time to pick up her daughter. Eve and Lou Johnson had always been happy to assume that responsibility, but now, since Josh worked at the school, it was natural for him to do it. It didn't take him long to realize that spending those few hours every day with Holly was building something valuable. Gradually, the girl was accepting him, and he was beginning to think of her as his child.

I'm a thirty-five year old guy with no child-rearing experience, he told himself, marveling at the fantasy that he might even be good at it. I didn't go through the early stages of feeding her with a bottle or changing diapers, but I think I'll be okay with this.

Holly talked easily and often seemed enthusiastic about listening to what Josh's teaching day had been like.

"I think I could be a good teacher," she said on one drive home. "I think the kids would listen to me."

"I'm sure they would. I certainly like listening to you."

"Did you always want to be a teacher?"

"Not always. Sometimes you meet a person who influences you, someone whom you admire. Then you start thinking—Gee, maybe I could do that. And then one thing leads to another, and before you know it you're older and you're following a path that you'd never imagined."

"Did you meet someone?"

"Sure, when I was in college I met some really good teachers."

"And you met my mom, too."

"I did." He looked over at her. "Are you glad about that?"

Holly turned shy at that moment, shrinking into a smaller space in the car, but nodding and saying very quietly, "Yes."

"I'm glad, too."

After school a few days later, Josh was waiting for Holly in his classroom before their drive home. He heard footsteps coming down the hall and Holly came in with another girl and a parent.

"This is Renata," Holly said. "She's going to ride a horse. Can I go with her?"

"I'm Tina Davis," the mother said. "I'm glad to have Holly come along. Renata's just going to have a lesson in the ring at Gormley's stable and Holly can sit with me."

The woman looked wholesome and responsible.

"Okay," he said. "I know Gormley's. I can pick her up there. How long is Renata's lesson?"

"An hour, but afterwards she likes to stay a few minutes to give the horses sugar cubes. Holly might like doing that, too."

"All right. I'll be there at five."

He walked them out to the parking lot and watched Tina Davis's black Mercedes drive off.

Had he made a mistake? It was certainly something that parents do every day, yet he was uneasy. It had seemed completely natural and safe, but for the first time he knew the small, heavy feeling that comes with the burden of parental responsibility.

No, it's all right, he told himself. I'll handle it.

When he arrived at Gormley's the girls and Tina Davis were waiting by the ring. Holly was smiling, but her hands were dirty and there was a big greenish-brown smudge on her white blouse.

"A small mishap," Tina said. "Renata's horse has a sweet tooth and Holly didn't step back quickly enough."

"You look like you had fun," Josh said.

"Oh, yes," Holly replied. "When I was holding out the sugar he pushed his head into me. I fell, but I didn't hurt myself."

"You're sure?"

"I'm fine. Could I take riding lessons?"

"Really? You think you'd like to do that?"

"Well . . . I'm not sure."

"Let's see what mommy says," he said.

They got off the freeway at Blithedale, drove through downtown Mill Valley, then up Throckmorton into the Heights. It was a warm day and he was happy that the little girl beside him had had her small adventure. The Volvo was parked in the driveway, and when they went in Claire, with arched eyebrows, stared at Holly's blouse.

"What happened?"

Holly and Josh took turns telling the afternoon's story.

"But you didn't hurt yourself?"

"No," Holly giggled. "The horse didn't mean to push me over. But can I take riding lessons?"

Claire flashed an accusing eye at Josh, and it was suddenly clear to him that she wasn't ready to relinquish her exclusive authority over Holly's activities. The quick look was full of meaning, and she immediately went back to Holly.

"Go take a shower and get into something clean," she said. Then, without giving Josh a glance, she went into the kitchen.

"You're mad," he said, following her. "But Holly's okay. Tina Davis was with her the whole time."

Claire spun around to face him with moist eyes, but said nothing, and then turned away again. He went up, touched her shoulders, and felt her relax.

"Don't worry," she said. "I'm not blaming you."

"No, I know that."

She moved away, leaned against the counter, and wiped a tear from her cheek. "Just a nervous mother," she said. "During these years it's all been on me, and it's hard to trust her with anyone else."

"I did worry a bit as I watched Tina's car drive away."

"No, I think it was okay. This is kind of a big step for me," she said. "And for you, too. I'm not mad at you. Just . . . shaken up, I guess. Anyway, Tina Davis's husband is a venture capitalist and I don't think we need to encourage Holly to take up an expensive hobby. I certainly grew up without horses."

Josh nodded. "Me, too," he said. "But Holly had a nice afternoon and I felt good about that."

"I know you did."

He understood. After Jim died, Holly was all Claire had, and Holly adored her. There was heavy responsibility, but there was also total love in both directions. She certainly wanted Holly to feel close to Josh, too, but she hadn't counted on the sense of loss that came along with sharing the child's affection with another.

PART FIVE

1977
Jazz

31

After Will Barton's hasty and inelegant defection from the Brass Bucket septet, the surviving six lamented the absence of a trombone. The band sounded top heavy and impoverished without the bottom voicing, and although a few substitute players helped out for a while, none of them connected with the music the guys liked to play. One night, after six or eight months of feeling tonally denuded, Rich Mariani invited Moe Pruitt to one of the band's infrequent rehearsals because he'd heard him play at another session and had a feeling they should give him a chance.

Rehearsals were usually in Berkeley at Dave Sloane's house in a room just off his garden that looked out over the bay. Moe, only twenty-three, had already gigged around in Northern California with groups that played various types of music, but he was hoping to find a jazz band that would be busy enough to keep him playing frequently.

That rehearsal at Dave's was a night to be remembered, and everyone regretted that no one had thought to record it. Moe Pruitt had total command of his instrument, great versatility, and an impeccable sense of time. He could play with a velvety tone like Tommy Dorsey's, but he also had humor and a real feeling for the blues, with a growl that made you think of the great Vic Dickenson. The balance among the band's different instruments was now close to perfect. The guys were listening to one another, and what came out was hot, authentic jazz with a refreshing clarity, admirable lightness, and a never-faltering infectious swing. Moe's trombone was more than equal to the clarinet and trumpet phrasings. His musical ideas were appropriate, helpful to the overall sound, and always tasteful. It was serendipity to the nth degree, and Josh found the band's new freshness thrilling.

"Moe's a terrific addition to the band," he told Claire. "It's been a long time since I've enjoyed playing with other musicians this much." The band had been offered a steady Wednesday night gig at a Sausalito restaurant and people from San Francisco and even the Peninsula were making reservations for dinner two weeks in advance so that they could hear the band and dance until the midnight closing.

She smiled. "You're a lucky man."

"In lots of ways."

He wondered if she might interpret that response as a willingness to go back twenty-six years to his misadventure at college and how he'd dealt with it. At times she carefully circumvented around that, but Claire wasn't really shy about bringing it up. Neither of them considered Josh's expulsion from Bartlett taboo. They'd talked about it often enough, and fortunately these days he was rarely plagued by the sudden unexpected surges of intense shame he'd felt before. Nevertheless, it existed as a knot of pain in his past, and Claire wasn't one to avoid difficulties.

"Lots of ways?" she ventured. "Do you want to talk about them?"

"Well, you for one—you brought me luck."

"No, you've done that yourself."

"Meaning . . ."

"Meaning that you've had your issues, but you've faced them. You haven't been passive, and you've found your own way."

He chewed his lip. "I've tried," he said.

"You've more than tried. You were involved in a horrible tragedy. You got drunk, and although you didn't kill someone, you went along with a group that did a stupid and shameful thing that led to Tom Grillo's death."

She stopped, letting her words have their effect. He sat silently, shaking his head from side to side.

"Having to face your parents afterwards was an enormous calamity for you. Am I right?"

Josh nodded, but he added, "They got over it . . . eventually."

"What?"

"It was hard, at first, but later . . ."

"Sorry, I don't think you know what I'm saying. I know your parents, Josh. We've been married almost ten years, we've seen them lots of times on holidays and birthdays, and I've got a pretty good understanding of their values. If you don't think Bartlett was a grotesque horror in their lives, as it was in yours, then you're more naïve than I've imagined. The entire debacle went against everything they tried to teach you as you were growing up—the stupidity and arrogance of the fraternity crowd, the whole jock culture, even just being drunk. The shame of it; the anger they must've felt."

Josh watched her face. Claire's skin showed color easily, and now it was flushed, with little beads of sweat forming on her upper lip.

He said nothing for a long moment, and then finally took a deep breath. "Yeah, it was more awful than anyone can appreciate."

"Of course, but the point is that lots of people would've been ruined by your experience." She said it softly, almost caressingly. "I can't begin to imagine how I would have handled it. No one can know in advance, but the truth is that you went through a calamity, and it devastated you, but somehow you absorbed what it meant and it actually strengthened you—I'm absolutely sure of that."

A smile flickered across Josh's face.

"What's funny?" Claire asked.

"No—something just occurred to me. What you said kind of goes with what I know about music."

"What is that?"

"When you play jazz, there is some sort of plan. Sometimes we call it a road map. But lots of times we never know what comes next. And we try different things. No matter what note we play, we want to be able to fit it into the overall thing. It all depends on the note we play next. That's what improvising is. So, I guess I've improvised in my life, too. Anyway, all that horror is behind me now."

"Not really," she said, shaking her head. "It's as much a part of you as growing up in Queens, as being a musician, a teacher."

He shrugged.

"There's something else," she said. "What books do you have your students reading?"

He stretched his arms and scratched his head. "Right now we're reading *Huckleberry Finn*. Next it'll be Anne Frank's *The Diary of a Young Girl*, and then toward the end of the term Hemingway's *The Old Man and the Sea*."

"And you picked those?"

"Yes."

"They're all stories that have to do with facing the hard things in life."

"Sure."

"They're all about you, too. It's an unconscious thing. You don't even know why you're choosing those books, but it comes from deep down inside you."

"Oh, I don't know. I'm an eighth grade English teacher. Those books are no different from what teachers in other schools choose for kids of that age."

"Maybe so, but I think it fits you. You can call it playing the next note, but however you see it, I know it's actually a wonderful thing."

Holly was now eighteen. She had done extremely well in school, and had gotten into both Stanford and U.C. Berkeley, but her heart was set on Pomona College and she was thrilled when she received its acceptance letter.

Josh and Claire drove her down and got her settled in her dormitory. For a time, standing and watching the clustered groups of parents saying last minute goodbyes to their children, Josh was surprised by the acuteness of his own feelings. This was something beyond his experience—a rite of passage he'd skipped. That long ago, solitary arrival at Bartlett had lacked the jubilant ambience he was seeing here, and he was happy that Holly would possess and remember it long after her graduation. That was a wonderful thing, and it stood in stark contrast to a strange state of mind he was feeling. Part of it was disappointment that the spirited cheers of welcome and nostalgic songs of alma mater rendered by Pomona's glee club held no meaning for him, but even more it was a painful discomfort that made him squirm as it brought back Bartlett College's own songs. Those had once given him a sense of participation and belonging, but all of that had been shattered by his stupidity and weakness. Catching glimpses of the blue, white and orange Pomona streamers and hearing the melodies, he decided he was experiencing the mixture of isolation, detachment, and bewilderment that an anthropologist felt when observing the rites of a lost exotic tribe. He could look on, but he was excluded.

The whole thing excited Claire. The pleasant, manicured lawns and handsome buildings with the majestic backdrop of the San Gabriel Mountains, the bright sun, and the general exuberance of the day had great appeal for her. "It wasn't that long ago that I was starting out this way," she told Josh. "Different campus, but the feeling is the same." Her smile was broad, and her fair skin just a little flushed with happiness.

Holly's roommate was a girl from Texas—talkative, friendly, and apparently addicted to chewing gum—and when Josh mentioned that he and Claire would come back the next morning to say goodbye, Holly said, "No, you don't have to—I'll be fine. It's a long drive back for you. We'll talk on the phone, and anyway I'll be home for Thanksgiving."

They agreed, although Josh saw that Claire was rather surprised, and even a little hurt.

"I guess it's best this way," she said as the car pulled away and Holly stood waving at them from the sidewalk. "One has to let go."

The next day's trip north was easy enough, but Josh drove the whole way. Claire had awakened with a headache and except for sporadic intervals of knitting she spoke little and dozed.

The phone calls began a week later, and it became apparent that the beginning of Holly's freshman year at Pomona College was going to be harder than she'd anticipated. She called home almost daily during the months of September and October, and the conversations were punctuated by sobs and complaints about not having made any close friends.

"But you've just gotten there," Claire reminded her. "It takes time."

The Texas roommate had decided to move into another room with two other girls, so Holly was now by herself. Academically, she was doing beautifully. She'd already received laudatory comments on two papers in English and one in philosophy, and when prodded she admitted that she'd gone to several museums in Los Angeles with two or three classmates.

"So, you do have some friends," Claire pointed out.

"Yes, but it's not the same."

Claire remembered her own first year at Stanford and wasn't worried. She would be available to Holly by phone anytime; she would listen; she would be rational, patient, and optimistic. Despite the long and sometimes awkward pauses during the phone calls, she knew Holly's strength and had confidence that adjustment would come and that her daughter would end up loving Pomona.

Josh heard only the northern end of the conversations, but he couldn't keep from smiling as he regarded his wife's uncanny facility for saying precisely the right thing. Reassuring, but realistic; calming, but pragmatic. When Claire would get off the phone she'd look at Josh, raise her lovely eyebrows, shrug a bit, and go back to whatever she'd been doing before the phone rang.

"You're perfect," he told her. "You're letting go, but she knows she can count on you."

There were definite advantages to the "empty nest syndrome." The telephone made it possible for Claire to monitor Holly's process of adjustment, and feeling connected that way assuaged her concerns.

The stresses of freshman year seemed to melt away with each week that passed, and Holly actually began talking about how much she liked the school, her classes, and her growing group of "friends."

Josh and Claire now had the Mill Valley house to themselves and they quickly took advantage of unanticipated freedoms. They began eating out more, often picking a restaurant on the spur of the moment. Thai lemon grass soup, Mexican food, sushi, pizza and beer, Indian cooking, even an Ethiopian restaurant—they would never run out of new places to try. Their group of friends, acquired over the years, gave them just the right amount of social life, but they enjoyed being with each other more than anything.

Claire continued to work at SF General, but only three days a week. The cost of living in Mill Valley was high, and they needed their two incomes if they were to make ends meet. Josh couldn't avoid some evening gigs, and Claire was sometimes tempted to earn more by working nights, but neither of them wanted that.

She was very loyal to her book group and adamant about attending the sessions. "I always try to get them to have the meetings on nights when you're playing somewhere," she told him. "I don't like when it takes time away from you, but I can't give it up. During those years when I was alone it was one of the main sources of strength for me. Those women helped me to grow up to the point where I no longer felt I needed to lean on someone. I could face problems as they came up. When I realized I could solve some things on my own it was a great day for me . . . a source of pride."

It was during one of those shared times at home that Josh, rummaging through a carton out in the garage, finally rediscovered some notebooks and papers that had disappeared years before when he moved from his San Francisco apartment into the house in Mill Valley.

He carried the box into the living room where Claire was reading.

"Look," he said, setting it on a side table. "Treasures." He held items up for her to see—a loose leaf binder in which he'd collected old, long forgotten jazz tunes; a folder of letters from his parents; a packet of other letters held by dried out rubber bands; a well-worn AAA map of the western half of the United States.

Claire nodded and went back to her book.

Looking through the music binder, he came upon the infrequently played verse to *Ain't Misbehavin'*, the complete words and music for *Purple Rose of Cairo*, the verse and chorus of *Blue River*, the melody and chords to *Duff Campbell's Revenge.*

"I was sure these were all lost," he said.

He opened letters—some from his parents, a few from Larry—and then began going through the other papers.

For ten minutes he said nothing.

Then he said very quietly, "Oh."

Claire looked up.

He had unfolded a white sheet and held it out. "My expulsion from Bartlett."

He handed it to her and she read it. "I think you can throw it away," she said. "You don't need to keep that."

"Yeah."

He took the paper from her and, as she watched, ostentatiously tore it into tiny bits.

"Of course, my destroying that doesn't undo what happened."

She watched his face, thumb in her book, and waited for him to go on.

"Back then I talked about it with my folks," he said. "Very hard doing that, but by sticking to the bare facts as I remembered them I could tell the story without getting into a panic or starting to bawl. You're the only one I've really opened up to about it . . . talked about how it affected me."

Claire murmured approval.

"The question was always whether I could've done anything to stop it. Drunk or not, couldn't I have prevented it? Sure, it changed my life, but that's not the point. I love my life. By some lucky chance I met you. No, the point is, in a crazy way, what happened in Tom Grillo's room that night made me see who I really am. I can see the phony parts, and the true ones."

"What do you mean?"

He waited for a few moments, trying to figure out how to put it.

"I had no business being there that night. Even joining the frat was just cowardice. I needed something outside of me for support. That's cowardice, isn't it? Not being able to stand up on my own. It was shameful. I know that. I knew it then, too, but I never had the guts to face it . . . that takes time."

"Of course it does."

"I was involved in Tom Grillo's death. A part of me says I could've stopped it, prevented it. And it destroyed me. I felt unworthy, dirty, stupid, ashamed. Deep down I knew that some of my old self-confidence was pure bullshit—the admired wrestler, the excellent student accepted by the jock fraternity. All that stuff puffed me up. It was a pose. When I say the experience changed my life I'm talking about grasping who I really am."

She put her book down and folded her hands. "Who are you?"

"I think all that achievement stuff was phony. It wasn't me, wasn't my core."

"I think you're exactly right."

"I have no interest in being a leader. I want to be in the background. I could never be the guy playing trumpet, standing out there in the front, chatting up the audience, leading the band, attracting attention, responsible for a whole group thing. Quiet is better. Fading into the surroundings."

He paused again.

"That's a new kind of self-confidence, you know. I'm certain of it. No matter how it may strike you, or others, I don't feel I'm shying away from anything important. I just know who I am, what I need, what suits the real Josh Lowen. I need that—and I hope you understand it."

Claire was smiling. "I do," she said quietly, giving him quick little interrupted looks.

They were both quiet for a while; then she went on. "Can I tell you something, too—about me?"

Josh had a quick flash of memory—of a moment years ago when she'd remarked that he and Jim Durand were "totally different"—and it brought back keenly everything he'd understood about that dormant, but abiding and essentially unknowable matter. He would forever have to move carefully through the thicket of Claire's feelings for Jim, and now a small cloud of unease came over him.

"Sure."

"You look a little worried," she said. "Do you know what I'm going to say?"

"Something about Jim?"

"You're perceptive," she replied. "Maybe even clairvoyant."

"Well, I am looking at you."

"What?"

"*Claire? Voyant*?"

"Oh, my. *Touché*!"

"Well?"

"No, I mean it, but I was only going to say that for me, in 1958, although Jim was the right husband, I'm not sure how long it would've lasted."

"How do you know that?"

"It's a feeling, that's all. Just as you've gained perspective about a hugely important moment in your life, I've done the same. Sometimes my marriage to Jim seems like a dream to me. There are times when I can barely remember those days. I do know that I wanted Jim's certainty, his self-assurance, and self-confidence . . . his self-regard. I needed that. It buoyed me up. I was less of a person then—a child, really. His death changed all that. Suddenly I was alone with total responsibility for Holly. That's what nudged me into adulthood."

Josh nodded and waited for her to go on.

"Do you doubt that?" she asked.

"Not at all, and I think you and Holly have a closer relationship as a result of that. I think it was hard for you to share her with me."

"A little, at first," she said looking away from him, her gaze intent, but focused on something only she could see.

She turned again and faced him. "But not now. I love seeing how she looks up to you."

"Sometimes I can't quite believe it, but I love it, too."

"Josh, Holly was four years old when Jim died. You're her father."

He looked down at the floor, not able to speak for a moment. Then he said, "And I feel it, too. Before—maybe not so much now—I felt that she came first for you, and that I came second. It bothered me because I knew it couldn't have been that way while Jim was alive. I thought a first love had to be a deeper, more intense love, and so I always asked myself where that put me. I know it's not healthy always to be comparing myself with others, but I used to wonder a lot about Jim."

Claire's meditative expression disappeared, and now she was smiling. She put her book aside, got up, and, standing before him, put her hands on his shoulders.

"Josh, I loved Jim, but I was a kid then. I had gone from being a child in my father's house, to being little more than a child bride. My feelings are totally different now. My understanding of love, my definition of love, is far richer and far better than what it was. You say you've been lucky, and I don't disagree. I've been not only lucky, but also blessed. It's very clear to me that ultimately I was looking for someone more nuanced, someone more complicated, more empathetic. And you're all of those things."

32

A few jazz bands were being invited to play on cruises to Mexico and the Caribbean, and the subject frequently came up.

"I don't know about a cruise," Dave Sloane said one evening. "But there is a possibility of our playing in Wales."

The guys were taking a break during a rehearsal and drinking bottles of Anchor porter. Several years before, Dave had played with a British band and had recently gotten word that a tavern in Cardiff now had music every weekend and was looking for an American jazz band.

"Any interest?"

Everyone had questions and opinions. Most of it revolved around when, how, and how much.

"I'm willing to write to the manager of the place and find out what the deal is, but only if we have at least a core group that's up for it."

They chewed it over for a while, and at length decided Dave should find out more and get back to them.

When Josh mentioned it to Claire that night she was initially enthusiastic. "Wonderful," she said. "I've never been to Wales. I'm sure we'd love it." Then she shrugged her shoulders. "But we need more details, don't we?"

In two weeks she had them. The band would play at the Cardiff tavern on two weekends; there was no guarantee that any other gigs in the area would be possible; the musicians would be put up individually in local houses; they would have to pay their own way to the UK and back; and the actual bread for the gigs was no better than what they were paid in the Bay Area.

"I guess we're not going to Wales," Josh told her. "But, I'd still like to go to Europe sometime."

He continued to find work as a solo pianist satisfying, and his job at the Cormorant had recently been increased to two nights a week. The band had also recorded three albums, but it wasn't only his musical life that was going well. More than ever, Josh was happy in his work at the school. His students adored him.

When he came home from school late one afternoon, Claire was just taking groceries out of the station wagon.

He grabbed the bags, and leaned over to plant a kiss on her cheek. "Guess what?" he said.

She gave him a curious look and cocked her head to one side.

"Best teacher," he said. "Your husband . . . me."

Such an award had been talked about for several years, but members of the board had been timid about going ahead with it. Some had questions about its usefulness to the school, but mainly there were worries about the possibility that singling out teachers could promote resentment and unhealthy competition. The idea was repeatedly shelved, and it came as a surprise to everyone—students, faculty, and staff—when the principal made the announcement.

"We had a full school assembly at two o'clock," Josh said. "A performance by the combined chorus groups, and when it was over Jack Vincent came out on the stage and said it was a pleasure for him to tell everyone something that he hoped would be an annual thing."

Three teachers had been selected as best teachers and Josh was the first named.

"Oh, that's wonderful," said Claire. "But, I thought . . ."

"I know, they've debated it forever, but apparently the board now thinks it'll be good for teacher morale."

The procedure included confidential balloting by students, consideration by the nine member Los Arboles board, and finally by a committee of seven of the more senior teachers.

"They assuaged their concern about resentment, favoritism and competition by deciding to spread the honor among three," Josh said. "That way there's hope for everyone—eventually. Right?"

Claire was smiling, and now she burst out laughing. "My God," she said. "You're too good; already worried about everyone else."

"Well . . ."

"You deserve it. Just enjoy it."

"Okay, I'm enjoying."

"I mean it," she said. "You're a wonderful teacher. They're so lucky to have you."

PART SIX

1985
Italy

33

On a cold, clear March night Larry Gerst stood on the Ponte Santa Trinità, held for a moment by sparkles of reflected light from street lamps along the Arno that glistened on the broad, rolling flow. A crescent sliver of moon hung over the dome of the Church of San Frediano, and the air's chill made him wish that he'd worn his down jacket instead of the light raincoat. He pulled his collar up and adjusted the muffler higher on his neck before going on with his after-dinner walk home to the apartment on the other side of the river.

His days in Florence were regular. Breakfast of *cappuccino* and a *cornetto alla marmellata* at the bar on Piazza Santo Spirito; then a visit to a museum, a church, or an art gallery; a *panino di prosciutto* and a glass of *vino rosso* for lunch; and the rest of the afternoon taking a long walk, reading newspapers, and perusing books on Renaissance and Medieval art. He usually ate dinner at one of the many good restaurants that flourish in the city, but a couple of nights each week he ate at home. He was not without a goal. Italy had become a passion, and his quest was art.

That was a complicated thing. After all, unlike his mother, he didn't make art. People who painted or sculpted had an inner need, and their hunger was fed by the act of creating.

His ardor was different; he wanted to own the art, but insistent questions often bothered him.

What did it mean to be a spectator, and not an actor? What was the cause of his unrelenting hunger? Was it purely sensual? Was it a status symbol? The pondering was endless, and there were times when he resolved to put it permanently out of his mind. Really, there were so many more important things in the world than concerning oneself with abstractions. Art enriched his life. Living with bare walls, or, worse, with trite, bland commercial art was not an option. He wanted the stimulation of good art that enlarged his perspective historically, intellectually, and aesthetically. For all his cogitation, that, finally, would have to be sufficient.

Two weeks before, an interview with a sixty year-old real estate tycoon in New York had been printed in the *International Herald Tribune*. The man was well known as a collector in modish Manhattan circles, and the names of prominent contemporary artists were scattered through the article. "I work with an art consultant," the tycoon divulged proudly. "I always want to know what the trends are and who's buying what, and I absolutely rely on her advice. Of course, I only buy what I love, but being knowledgeable about the market is critical. When I buy a painting I not only want it, but I want a good return."

The words had remained, uninvited, but chafing. Larry was clear about his own quest for art, and he was certain there was no possible equivalence. The guy's concept was contemptible. If there were ever to be a chance meeting between the two, it would be a silent encounter. They had nothing in common.

It was 1985. Ronald Reagan was in his second term; the US government had approved a new blood test for AIDS; citizens in Lebanon were being killed with car bombs; and terrorists were hijacking airplanes in Europe and Africa.

Most of these things carried no more than mild background interest for Larry. He had his phone and his FAX machine, and they kept him in touch with his business pursuits. It was no longer difficult for him to be away from New York for extended periods of time, and he was feeling moderately self-congratulatory about it. In fact, more and more, and for the first time in many years, he had sufficient leisure to be able to reflect on everything that had happened—not that being introspective was totally new to him. His life had been too full of activity and events, family and otherwise, for him to have been unaware that thoughts about his past were always churning and tumbling through his mind. But the time and energy he had spent building up his assets hadn't, until after his divorce, allowed for the kind of real freedom he now felt. He was quite satisfied with how he had managed to arrange things. These days he had control over the pace of his activities. No more rushing frantically—physically and emotionally. That was finished.

When he pondered his personal life he realized that "undemanding" was an apt word. His twice-yearly visits to the Galang family in Manila were enjoyable and satisfying for him, but Luisa Orlando was even more important. After eighteen years, she was still his *amante*. It was an easy relationship—not at all burdensome—open and comfortable for both. How ironically perfect, he often thought, that this long affair with a married woman still gave the two of them pleasure and the added comfort of a trusted friendship. Both had suffered flawed marriages and the consequent predictable burden of a sense of personal failure, but their own unorthodox accord had brought back a healthy equilibrium. If the early passion in their liaison had matured, it hadn't gone away, and nothing of jealousy or recrimination had ever come between them. They genuinely looked forward to their times together.

Luisa continued living in the villa near Fiesole with her husband. That was a matter of sensible practicality. In return for the respectability she conferred on a philandering husband, Enrico Orlando gave her complete freedom. Luisa was a romantic, but she had no qualms about looking out for her own interests, and leaving Enrico was out of the question. He traveled constantly, was always finding new ways to enlarge his fortune, and had a chronic inability to curb his appetite for younger and younger women. It was a game for him—game, in the sense of hunting. The chase could be competitive at times, but business was also a game and he was very good at that. He had proven to himself that the risks with women were notably slighter than with investments, and his philosophy boiled down to "why not give it a try? There's so little to lose."

Enrico's game worked well for Larry, too. Luisa—lithe and dark-haired—wore exquisite clothes and an intoxicating scent. Her family had married her off at nineteen to Orlando. Their three children—two girls and a boy—were all now on their own. For Enrico, Luisa was an important symbol of his credibility in Florentine society. They hadn't been lovers for many years and he was perfectly willing to turn a blind eye to whatever Luisa might be doing in her private life. In fact, he assiduously avoided asking questions, and in return she did the same. Both got what they wanted from the marriage, and neither had any intention of endangering the delicate balance. Their conversations were civil and matter of fact, but romance was excluded by mutual agreement. He had his freedom, and she had her beautiful home, servants, and her own definition of freedom. There was plenty of money to sustain her need to get away from time to time. Sometimes it was to Paris or London. And often, with considerable regularity over the years, it was to Larry Gerst's apartments in both Florence and New York.

Larry paused again and took in what was before him, especially the architectural aspect of well-known buildings lighted up for the evening—crenellated Palazzo Spini; the Roman column beyond it in Piazza Santa Trinità; the sculptures representing the seasons at each of the bridge's four corners; and the long view upstream to the Ponte Vecchio and the Torre d'Arnolfo rising behind. By now they were all good old friends for him, and he smiled to find himself moving his lips, pronouncing the names, perhaps a silly way of certifying his familiarity, but a thing that seemed almost necessary to feeling that he was actually present. The city of Florence was splendid. In fact, it was beyond words—always changing, yet the same, and, no matter how many times he had taken this walk, he never tired of it. It only made him marvel at what he thought might be the most compelling characteristic of the city—a pleasing spatial arrangement of architectural forms. He wondered if it might have almost a therapeutic effect on one's brain. Maybe it was analogous to what music did by connecting with some basic neural circuits as patterns that soothed and satisfied a built-in requirement for equanimity and balance . . . or even happiness.

34

It was raining the next morning as he made his way to the Accademia. A small line of people under umbrellas waited to get in, but Larry showed his priority card and was promptly admitted. He walked quickly through the first rooms, barely glancing at David and the other Michelangelo wonders. His destination was the upper floor where a group of early Italian paintings showed the evolution of expressive change from the late medieval era into the early Renaissance. He had made many visits to these particular rooms and was beginning to think that this transitional period in Italian art might be his favorite.

A self-education in Medieval and Renaissance painting took time, and his had been methodical and painstaking. Both of his apartments, in Manhattan and in Florence, were filled with shelves of books devoted to the subject, and he subscribed to catalogs from the big auction houses.

His own small, but very good collection of seventeen paintings, acquired one by one over the years from various sources—some from dealers in New York and in Italy, and some from auctions—dated from the mid-1200s into the early 1500s. What he looked for were sensitive faces, simplicity, and genuine human feeling. Anything merely decorative turned him away, and he had little patience for the late

Renaissance with its Mannerist excesses and what he liked to call its "decline" into the Baroque. He felt excitement in the quest; pride in his accomplishment; but more than anything an immense pleasure in the paintings themselves.

A single guard drowsed in a chair with part of a newspaper on his lap and the rest scattered on the floor at his feet. Larry was alone, and he exulted in the luxurious feeling it gave him.

The Accademia's collection wasn't large, but it was spectacular. These were religious paintings, and not generally loved by contemporary viewers, but Larry went his own way. What others liked or didn't like wasn't important. For him the old gold backgrounds were charming, and he was especially held if he detected individuality in faces. Some artists of the period painted only bland, standardized portraits, but in the best pieces he felt he was looking at real people. One needed to spend enough time standing quietly before a painting, and then it paid off. All sorts of human qualities might be seen: delicacy, toughness, distinction, cunning, and even deception and dishonesty in some of the faces. Patient absorption in the work made it all worthwhile.

Despite the dim light in the rooms, the colors used by artists seven hundred years ago could still beguile and captivate. Some of the artists he knew from work hanging in other museums, but there were also unfamiliar names, and he passed along slowly, savoring the feeling he was getting from each painting, and then jotting down impressions in a small notebook. Later, back at his apartment, he would read about the particular artists.

Today he was happy to learn the origin of the Italian word for a painting: *quadro*. Earlier pieces from the late medieval period, for example religious triptychs with gold backgrounds, often had, as part of the frame, little spires and spandrels extending above the painted figures. Later artists in the earliest days of the Renaissance deemed such ornamentation old-fashioned, and by eliminating it they squared off the work, making the painting a quadrilateral. Hence, *quadro*.

Once again, he was rather pleased to find that he was able to discern the notable features of the International Gothic style that characterized Italian painting from about 1370-1450: elegance of form; flowing lines; decorative richness; and the rediscovery of naturalistic detail. It was easy to understand why some art historians also called it "the beautiful style." Clearly, these paintings were just a short step away from the changes associated with the Renaissance.

By one o'clock he was hungry. Hidden behind the stalls at the edge of the San Lorenzo market was a small restaurant where he had enjoyed simple Tuscan cooking and he set off down Via Ricasoli. The rain had turned to the finest drizzle, and as he walked along the Duomo and Giotto's bell tower came into view. On Via de' Pucci he turned right and in five minutes he was seated on a bench with his back to the wall in the lively atmosphere of Osteria da Sergio Gozzi where he ordered a kind of potato gnocchi that went by the name of *topini*. It was delicious, but as he recalled that *topo* means mouse, he suddenly laughed out loud with the realization that he was eating "little white mice." It was the kind of small thing that made him love being in Italy. He cherished New York, but he also needed this . . . getting familiar with the city of Florence, feeling more and more comfortable after his many visits, and being able to unwind mentally and emotionally.

"Why do you laugh?" Someone sitting alone at the next bench was speaking to him. He saw a querulous, interested expression in a deeply tanned, intelligent face with gray eyebrows arching over surprised, wide-open eyes. The skull was bald and shiny, and framed by a curling and surprisingly luxuriant fringe of white hair. The man held a knife in one hand, a fork in the other, and both were raised above his table in a gesture that said, "So, fill me in. I like a good joke, too."

Larry leaned over. "*Topini*," he said. "I'm American, but I'm interested in words. *Topini* . . ."

"Ah, *sì, certo*," the man replied. "Where are you from?"

"New York."

And the conversation continued. Larry knew a number of Florentine art dealers and over the years they had come to recognize him as a serious collector. From a few he'd bought paintings, while with others he had only chatted and absorbed their opinions about seemingly random fluctuations in the art market.

However, meeting Piero Gherardi at Osteria da Sergio Gozzi was the chance beginning of an acquaintance that grew into what, before long, Larry sensed as almost a friendship. The initial tableside conversation ended with a walk together along narrow streets in the direction of the river to Piero Gherardi's small gallery. He had owned it for almost twenty years and had clients in the States as well as in England, France, Germany, and Italy itself. In the window there was a single gold-ground painting of the Madonna and Child by a follower of Giotto. Inside, there were marble sculptures, other paintings of the Baroque period, a wood box with lions' feet and intricate cornices along the edges of its cover, several tapestries on the walls, and a few pieces of antique Tuscan furniture.

Larry showed Gherardi some small photographs of paintings he already owned, and was pleased when the dealer indicated his approval.

"Ah, *sì. Ha un occhio per l'arte*! You have a good eye," he said. "*Bellissimi! Sì, sì, bellissimi*!"

Gherardi showed off his inventory, named a few prices, and told Larry he should come back because he was getting new items all the time. Perhaps they could have lunch together next week.

Larry asked him the price of the Madonna in the window, but Gherardi shook his head. "*Impossibile*," he said. An export certificate for that piece was out of the question.

"It can't leave Italy—but the Uffizi has some interest in it. *Beh, vediamo*. We'll see."

35

Saturday, August 2, 1985

Hi, Larry –

Can you remember telling me I should visit Europe? Here I come . . . finally. Our band has a tour in October. We start in Amsterdam, go on to Dusseldorf, Florence, Torino, and finally Zurich. The Florence gig will be at 9 pm, both Friday and Saturday nights, October 4 and 5, at a place called Chiasso Swing. I'm sure you'll be able to find it.

By the way, Claire will be with me, and we actually have a couple of extra days in Florence. So, I'm looking forward to seeing you at our gigs, and otherwise if you're free. I hope October will be one of the months you'll be there.

Holly graduated from Pomona College, spent two years in Honduras in the Peace Corps, and is now in medical school at UCLA. She hopes to become an Ob-Gyn.

Let me know if our plans are going to coincide.

Best,

Josh

36

Larry folded the letter and stood quietly for a few moments at his living room window looking out over Piazza Santo Spirito. He would invite Josh and Claire up when they came to Florence so that they could actually experience something of his current life. The third floor walk-up apartment was small, but perfect for him, and he knew he would feel pride in showing it to them. Down below, the square's outdoor market was bustling. Stalls had been set up and people were moving about buying vegetables, eggs, kitchen implements, clothing, old books, and even hardware. At the far end of the piazza stood the plain stucco façade of the church designed by Brunelleschi. It was one of Larry's favorites, and he'd spent many hours there, studying the paintings and sculpture, and enjoying the serene ambience of the classic architecture.

The Oltrarno had become his neighborhood and he knew its streets and alleys as well as he knew midtown Manhattan. He was a regular in several restaurants and hardly a day went by when he didn't run into someone he knew—a neighbor, a merchant, a waiter, an artisan, or one of the art and antique dealers who populated the maze of alleys on the south side of the Arno.

Josh's letter took him back to his last visit to California. So much had happened since seeing Josh and Claire in their home. He marveled that they were still in touch, or, at least, that Josh was able to reach him. The letter had been forwarded from New York with the usual packet of mail that Larry's secretary sent on to Florence each week, and it was the only personal item. He glanced at the business reports, credit card statements, and letters from his bank, and found nothing there to worry him. Things were going well and he was making money without a lot of effort on his part. His goal of spending more time in Florence was already a reality. As long as he was able to maintain contact with New York, his schedule was as flexible as he wanted it to be. At the moment, he had no definite plans, not even a return flight reservation. He would go back to New York when he felt the urge, and he thought that this time he might remain in Florence for three or even four months.

How would he explain this kind of life to his old friend? Of course, he didn't have to explain it to anyone, but he wondered what Josh and his wife thought about him. They had taken such different roads, he and Josh. And from what he could recall of that evening more than fifteen years before, there was something about Claire that made him feel she was judging him. She was a very attractive woman, and Josh had seemed comfortable and happy, although a little in awe of his own good fortune finding himself married to someone like that. Poor Josh. He had a childlike innocence. And wasn't that ironic, especially after being involved in the death of the student, a war veteran? Wouldn't that make someone grow-up fast? Perhaps by now he had. Still, playing in a jazz band—wasn't that something kids do?

Piero Gherardi had called him to ask if they could meet for lunch. He had something that Larry might find interesting. At two in the afternoon they met at Osteria da Sergio Gozzi.

"They have *sgombro* today," Piero said. "You call it mackerel, and I recommend it. They do it *alla brace* over a wood fire. Squeeze a little *limone*. Some roasted potatoes, some spinach. Very healthy. Easy to digest."

"What is it you called me about?"

"Ah, I'm so hungry," Piero said. "First, we eat, then we'll talk."

Larry wondered why they couldn't do both, but he went along with Piero's recommendation and they made small talk about Florence and the weather until the waiter brought their plates. Eating broiled fish on the bone requires care and attention and what little conversation they were having now broke off until they'd finished.

The waiter cleared the table and both men sipped white wine. "I have a picture you might like," Piero said. He had a mischievous smile on his lips.

Larry raised his eyebrows. "What is it?"

"A little *complicato*, but it's a very nice painting. An *Annunciazione*. At any rate, you must have a look."

"Where is it?"

"In my place. We'll go there now."

Larry divided people who visited his New York apartment into two groups: the majority who paid no attention to the art, and a minority who did. He thought a few in the first group might be timid about saying anything, but most were simply oblivious and probably didn't notice art or its absence in doctors' offices, airports, galleries, or even museums. He didn't understand that group at all, but he tried not to judge them. After all, he had no interest in physics, or in professional football. Live and let live. It was their loss.

The people who noticed his art could also be divided. It wasn't quite as distinct a separation, but in his mind he thought of it as people who were either mystified by his taste or who shared it. To be sure, owning paintings from the Middle Ages or the Renaissance was an uncommon passion today. Contemporary tastes ran to various types of abstract art, to Expressionism, and even back to Impressionism, but religious paintings were an oddity in a New York apartment. Some people, both Jews and non-Jews, couldn't fathom Larry Gerst hanging explicitly Christian art on his walls. That was especially true if they knew about the Nazi deportation and murder of his father's family, but when they expressed surprise, Larry usually smiled and said only, "It's art, just art. I haven't converted." In buying his paintings, religious in theme though they clearly were, he had scrupulously avoided what he felt to be Catholicism's obsessive fascination with martyrdom. He owned no crucifixions, or bloody depictions of saints. What he looked for were pieces that showed people he could relate to—lovely faces in the women, sensitivity and intelligence in the men, interesting landscapes as background, and small depictions of animals and plants. And among Medieval and Renaissance subjects, the visit of the Archangel Gabriel to the Virgin Mary almost always moved him. The moment when Mary is told that she has been chosen by God to bear a son who will redeem mankind has probably been painted by every artist of these periods. Yet despite the common subject, each rendering is different.

"I'll leave you alone with the painting for a few minutes," Piero Gherardi said. "I must go upstairs to make a telephone call. When I return we'll talk and I'll tell you more about it."

The vivid scene, painted on a wood panel and larger than what Larry had imagined, measured about three feet in width and somewhat over two in height. As in many Annunciations, the angel hovered inches above the ground at the left, while the Virgin sat with her open book in an architectural structure on the right which attempted to show a knowledge of perspective, but which achieved it only partially. On the other hand, the two figures were startlingly alive. The moment for Mary showed her feeling much more than the usual drowsy surprise. She was certainly still a girl, but there was something in her face and in the attitude of her body that indicated active participation rather than the anemic passivity that Larry had seen portrayed in dozens of depictions of the subject. The colors were vibrant, although spotted sections of the surface meant that a careful cleaning might be appropriate.

Larry owned two Annunciations. Both were smaller than this one, and simpler. Neither was by a known artist, but the curator at the

Metropolitan in New York had assured him that they dated from the late 14th century and were clearly Tuscan, probably Florentine, in origin.

This painting, if it was genuine, was certainly going to be more expensive than what Larry had usually paid. By now, after considerable self-education and experience with dealers at home and abroad, he had learned to respect his first impressions. If he felt immediately drawn to a painting, and if the interest lasted after seeing it a few times, it was usually something he wanted to buy. He felt that the Annunciation before him could very well be one of those.

It pleased him to know that the subject was particularly honored here in Florence. From the mid-1200s until almost Napoleonic times, Florentines considered the New Year to begin on March 25 with the Feast of the Annunciation, exactly nine months before the birth of Jesus. Moreover, Mary herself was extraordinarily important to the city. Florence's Duomo, Santa Maria del Fiore, is dedicated to the Mother of Christ, and when Florentines pass between the figures of the angel and Mary as they come into the church they can perceive themselves as entering and now occupying the space in which the Word becomes Flesh. In this way they themselves are becoming a continuation in time of the Incarnation of Christ. It creates a theological parallelism between the Virgin Mary and the Church, which, like Mary, is "mother." Thus, as citizens of Florence become "children of the Church", they are also becoming Mary's children and receiving her protection.

Larry's doubts and skepticism about Catholicism's hierarchy didn't prevent him from finding the theology interesting. Its complex philosophical constructions were far-reaching and provocative, and he couldn't help being struck by how well the Church had managed to spread its message of impossible miracles to the uneducated masses in Europe after the decline of Rome. Some of its success in buoying up Catholic belief systems among the illiterate had surely been partly through the telling of stories through pictures. It was an early, and apparently effective, form of visual education.

Theology aside, the longer he looked at this Annunciation the more excited he became thinking that it might be a possibility for his collection, but he had a growing suspicion about meeting the price. This painting is beyond me, he told himself. It's probably unattainable. I can desire it, but I will be disappointed.

Piero was coming down the curving iron staircase from his office above the gallery.

"*Allora*," he said. "How does it strike you?"

"It's a lovely painting . . . really lovely."

"Yes, of course. Do you see the way the young girl is different? How she understands what she is being told?"

"I've never seen anything like that in other Annunciations."

"Yes, it's what makes this so special," Piero said. "Come upstairs. I'll show you something."

Gherardi's small office was organized for efficiency. There were two filing cabinets, and along one wall there was a long table holding an IBM computer, trays of business correspondence, and a number of open books. There were two chairs at the table, and on the wall above it were shelves filled with art books and catalogs. A handsome painted wood sculpture of the grieving Madonna stood in one corner—early 15th century, Larry imagined—and there were also two fussy late 18th century paintings of swooning female figures, one in an outdoor setting, the other in an ornate room with chandeliers and lute players in the shadows.

"No, those are not your style," Gherardi told him. "I don't love them either, but someone will buy them, you can be sure."

Larry laughed. "You're right," he said. "I took an immediate dislike to both."

Piero pointed to one of the open books. "Look," he said.

It was a monograph with a faded green cover that bore the title *Ugo di Paolo Menchini*. Larry opened it to see the date of publication. "1925 . . . sixty years ago," he said. "I've never heard of him."

"I'm not surprised," Gherardi answered. "He's not well appreciated by the general public, but he was an important painter. Art historians know him—a Florentine artist of the second rank whose paintings hang in the gallery on the upper floor of the Accademia."

"Oh, I've been there several times. Now that you mention it, I do remember his name."

Piero Gherardi took the book from Larry and opened it to the pages showing the paintings. "Look," he said. "Look at his work."

The old monograph had only black and white photographs, but there were a number of close-ups showing an exquisite rendering of faces. "These are Renaissance faces," Gherardi said. "Ugo di Paolo Menchini was brought up in the International Gothic style, but he was ahead of his colleagues. These are people you and I know, real people."

"I remember some of these from the Accademia—and you think . . .?"

"Yes, I'm certain this Annunciation is one of his works. I've already shown it to the two most reputable art historians for early Italian art, Professor Latini of Perugia, and Professor Mastrangelo of this city. Both are eminent scholars who receive nothing for attributions. They are interested only in perhaps writing an academic essay about the work. But they're in agreement that it's by Ugo di Paolo and done around 1420. To decide where it fits into the development of Italian art, just try to recall three paintings that I'm sure you know."

Gherardi held up one finger at a time as he counted them off.

"Simone Martini's Annunciation, painted in Siena in 1333. It's in the Uffizi. You've seen it?"

"Of course."

"Gentile da Fabriano's Adoration of the Magi painted in 1423 in Florence. You know that one, too."

"Yes, I love it. I've spent a lot of time enjoying its color and the stupendous panoply of characters, including the little rascal at the bottom of the painting who is stealing a gold spur from a nobleman's ankle."

"And the third is Masaccio's Adam and Eve being evicted from Eden. He painted it around 1424. You've been to the Cappella Brancacci, of course."

"Many times."

"This painting is a marvel, and it was done at about the same time that Masaccio was working. He and Ugo di Paolo were contemporaries. Did they meet? Did they have a conversation? Did they know each other's work? It's impossible to say."

"But it's intriguing."

"Consider—Simone Martini's Annunciation is wonderful, but it's really completely in the Gothic period. There's no comparison between Simone's Virgin, and Ugo di Paolo's Virgin. One is stiff; one is a real person. *D'accordo*?"

"Absolutely."

"Gentile da Fabriano's painting is at the tail end of the International Gothic period. It's almost Renaissance, but not quite. Do you see?"

"I do, and, of course, Masaccio's Adam and Eve is a totally new concept. It's firmly in the Renaissance. Is that what you're saying?"

"*Sì*, and Ugo di Paolo is a kind of forgotten figure, but he knew what was coming. You can see it in the face of this young woman. She is not just an empty vessel. She is a complex human being, with a mind of her own, with an ability to make decisions. She is not just a passive receptacle. You see that?"

Larry nodded. He watched the other's face. Was Piero Gherardi just selling him something—or did the painting genuinely excite him?

"I've known the owner for a long time," Gherardi said. "Ercole Miglio is eighty-six years old; he's the patriarch of a family in Arezzo. Although he's lived in a certain high style, his cash is running out and he wants to sell the painting before he dies so that he can distribute the money to nieces and nephews in his family."

"What does he want for it?"

"He asks 500 million lire."

Somewhere between two and three hundred thousand dollars. Larry shrugged. "Out of my reach," he regretted.

"Ah, I understand, and that is surely up to you," Gherardi said. "But I have an idea." He cocked his head to one side and raised his eyebrows.

"Tell me."

"*Beh*, Ercole Miglio is in a hurry. He doesn't want to spend his time investigating the painting's real value. At the same time, he's shrewd."

"You think he'll take less?"

"No, that's not what I mean. I told you that the whole thing is *complicato*. I'm afraid he is *un po' disonesto*."

"Dishonest."

"*Sì*. He has fabricated a story to inflate the painting's worth to more than what he knows it to be."

"I don't follow you."

"The painting has been in the family *cent'anni*—at least one hundred years. No one has ever talked about it in any special way. About a year ago, Ercole called me to say that a visiting French gallery owner had seen the work and thought it might be by Iacopo da Monteloro. One of Iacopo's paintings on wood hangs in the Church of Santa Felicita, and a fresco of his is in the cloister of the Church of San Moisè in Empoli."

"I don't know anything about him."

"A Tuscan painter of perhaps the fourth rank."

"But still valuable?"

"Not to what Ercole imagines," Gherardi said, shaking his head. "But his story is not true. When I asked him for the name of the French dealer, he changed the subject. Ercole's not a good liar. And he doesn't take the lie far enough."

"So, he's promoting his painting and trying to make the most of it?"

"I don't blame him for that. After all, we are Italians. But he is not an art expert. He would go into shock if he found out by how much he's underestimating the real value. He's fabricated a story, but he's way off. Clever, *certo, ma innocente. Capisci*? A work of Ugo di Paolo Menchini should bring at least four times Ercole Miglio's asking price. With the lira around 1900 to the dollar, I'm thinking one million U.S."

"Wow!"

Piero Gherardi's brow was furrowed, but then his face broke into a broad grin.

"So what's your idea?" Larry asked.

"A painting like this may not be for your collection, but it is still an opportunity. A group could be formed; each member would invest something in the painting. Not to keep it, but to sell it to a big buyer, someone who can pay *prezzi grandi*. There could be a satisfying return for the investors."

"Buy it as a group from Ercole Miglio? That is, pay him a price he'll agree to, and then sell it to someone who can really afford it?"

"*Sì*, you understand. What do you think?"

"Well, you called it *complicato*. Tell me the details of the process. How would it go?"

Piero Gherardi was willing to bargain with Miglio, and eventually to advise him to accept a price of 300 to 400 million lire. A small group of investors would be formed to buy it from him. The next step would be selling the painting—aiming for one million U.S. dollars. Gherardi would charge the investors 47 million lire to guide Miglio in the desired direction.

"You understand what I'm saying?" he asked. "I would receive 47 million for persuading the old man that 300 to 400 million lire is a proper asking price."

Larry nodded.

"*Sì*, it takes a lot of work," Gherardi added. "And I can arrange other possible investors—but, of course, I would also be paid for that service."

37

It was a heady proposition with its allure of fresh and intriguing adventure, but also with musings on sheer, potential profitability. Yet as much as Larry was drawn to Piero Gherardi's idea, for the rest of the week he didn't feel at all well. His months in Florence had always been the most relaxing parts of his year, but now, for the first time, he was having trouble sleeping. Hot, muggy weather had descended on the city and there was little comfort in his apartment. Even with a fan running all night his skin was bathed in sweat, mosquitoes tormented him, and constant sneezing and coughing from an allergy were wearing him down.

Still, despite such physical nuisances, his main preoccupation came directly from the meeting with Gherardi. Yes, the dealer could get a group of investors together, but what about the next step—selling the painting? Who would spend that kind of money?

It was in Larry's nature to think ahead. His mind had always worked that way—puzzling over any deal, and never assuming that things finding their own way would necessarily lead to the desired result. If he'd learned anything from his successes in business it boiled down to the need for a diligent consideration of all possible outcomes and for paying scrupulous attention to detail.

And one paid a price for that lesson.

It was called anxiety.

He didn't have long to wait.

"*Ciao*, Larry."

Piero Gherardi was on the phone. It was just a week after their last meeting.

"You're still interested in *L'Annunciazione*." It was a statement, not a question.

"Of course."

"Can you come to a meeting Tuesday morning? I've arranged a small group of people."

"About the painting?"

"They are possible investors."

"That was quick."

"Good. You will come?"

"Sure, where do I go?"

"Palazzo Guglielmini. You know it?"

"Facing on the river? With the statues on the roof?"

"*Sì, esattamente*. Go to the entrance and ask for Signor Buscemi's apartment. Come at 11:30. We'll talk, and then perhaps have something to eat together."

On Tuesday morning Larry got up early and hurried over to the Accademia where once again he headed for the quiet rooms on the upper floor, this time just to pay attention to the small group of paintings by Ugo di Paolo Menchini. As Gherardi had indicated, they were right there, and the dealer was certainly correct. Ercole Miglio's Annunciation had to be by Ugo di Paolo. The enigmatic expressions in the faces, the arrangement of architectural forms, and subtle use of color—everything became clearer to him the longer he looked.

What a wonderful thing! He was feeling better already—this could be an enterprise to remember. Moving along slowly, making notes in his little book—subjects, dates, and even tiny diagrams of each of Ugo di Paolo's works—he took his time, and finally sat down on the backless wood bench in the center of the room to contemplate the works from a slightly greater distance. He certainly regretted that Miglio's painting was too expensive for him, but that was overbalanced by the surge of anticipation he felt about the complexities of the whole project and the promise of a nice profit. There were lots of questions to ponder, but also lots of possibilities.

He checked his watch. Thirty minutes remained before he had to be at Palazzo Guglielmini and he wanted some fresh air and a coffee. He walked down the street to a bar where he stood with other customers and enjoyed the feeling of being a part of the Italian morning. It was pleasing to know enough of the language to be able to order his coffee and to grasp the gist of the several conversations going on around him—not full comprehension by any means, but sufficient to feel that he almost fit in.

His way to Palazzo Guglielmini took him down the street of Gherardi's gallery. There were other galleries and antique stores along the way, and he walked slowly, stopping before windows. One place had copies of well-known sculptures—replicas in bronze or marble of Niobe, of Aphrodite, of Mercury, and of Michelangelo's Pieta. Another had a full-size bronze duplication of Lorenzo Ghiberti's gilded bronze plaque depicting David's slaying of Goliath. A third shop had several unimpressive eighteenth century portraits of wealthy men and women.

Piero Gherardi's window outdid them all. The gold-ground painting of the Madonna with Child was no longer there; the Uffizi Gallery had purchased it. Now, resting on a plinth covered by wine-colored velvet stood a white marble bust of St. John the Baptist. Larry immediately saw its similarities to pieces he had seen somewhere in Florence, but he couldn't place it. Clearly, it was an exceptional sculptural work, probably of museum quality. It must date from before the start of the fifteenth century, he thought, and that gave him encouragement and reassurance about Gherardi's reliability. In fact, the window proved it. There was nothing shabby there—just high quality, simplicity, and superb taste.

Palazzo Guglielmini extended its symmetrical late baroque structure on the north bank of the Arno. It was built around a central courtyard, and the distinguishing feature of its façade was the balustrade along the roof's edge with interspersed statues of mythic figures and alternating large terracotta vases. Larry had never been inside, but during his early inquiries to find a place that would suit his needs he'd heard that one wing of the Guglielmini had been turned over to a real estate firm for division into luxury apartments. The palazzo being right on the river didn't appeal to him. Cars were always going by on the Lungarno and he decided that something quieter and less imposing would be more comfortable. Now, never having looked into it as a real possibility, he was curious to enter and observe.

From the courtyard it wasn't clear where he was supposed to go, but a uniformed guard stepped out of a doorway and asked him what he wanted.

"Signor Buscemi?" he asked.

The guard took him into a small office and picked up a phone.

"Your name?"

"Gerst. Larry Gerst."

The guard spoke a few words into the phone, nodded, and hung up.

"*Prego*," he said. "Come with me. The lift is down there."

They were in a long mirrored corridor. The frescoed ceiling showed a stormy ocean with Neptune driving through the waves in a chariot drawn by muscular winged horses.

The guard pressed the button and extended his arm to hold the door. "First floor, then turn to the left," he said. "You'll see. It's the only apartment."

The elevator was new and quick, and Larry stepped out cautiously. He saw the door. A small brass plate on the wall bore the word *Buscemi*. Right away, from emphatic bits of Italian conversation that filtered out into the hall, he knew that the others had preceded him. He heard words, and even a few complete sentences, but it was mainly the impassioned engagement of the speakers that struck him. It would be rude to delay going in, but he waited another moment, listening, and finally he rang the bell.

The talk ceased abruptly.

It was Piero Gherardi who opened the door.

"*Bene*, Larry . . . *avanti, avanti*."

Three other men in business suits had risen from chairs—looking and appraising. It was a spacious room with a high ceiling and expensive furnishings. On an easel in one corner he caught a glimpse of Ugo di Paolo's Annunciation.

The introductions were quick and friendly.

Their host, Santo Buscemi, tall, white-haired and distinguished, was the real-estate lawyer who had presided over the division of Palazzo Guglielmini into luxury flats, and this apartment, his own, was clearly at least one of the best. He spoke English slowly, but well, had a warm smile, and a quiet manner, and Larry liked him immediately.

Piero Gherardi said a few words about Larry, telling of his interest in art, his love of Florence, and his "excellent" Italian.

"No, no," Larry said. "Certainly not excellent, but I try."

Piero went on to Orfeo Malizia, a big man with a disproportionately small head. He was introduced as an engineer and appeared to be in his fifties. Somewhat over six feet in height, he had unusually broad shoulders and large reddened hands that hinted of manual labor. At the same time, he gave an impression of being shy, a listener more than a talker. When Larry shook his hand Malizia didn't face him, but seemed to utter his "*piacere*" to the middle distance. He was smiling, but not connecting.

The third man, Arturo Zampini, lived in Argentina, and was an old friend of Piero Gherardi. He was also an art dealer, and he made frequent buying trips to Florence.

Larry listened and nodded, but he felt intrusive and out of place. How would this go? Fortunately, the others seemed equally uncomfortable.

"Let's have a drink," said Santo Buscemi. "Some red wine? I have saved a very nice Chianti Classico Riserva. A good friend of mine makes a few hundred bottles, and this was an excellent year."

He poured and they raised their glasses. Larry disliked being a specimen under a microscope and needed to break the unease. "Well, I'm very happy to be here," he said, looking around at the others. "In Florence, of course, and here, too, meeting all of you."

A serving woman came in with a tray of shaved slices of pecorino on pieces of flat bread.

"What do you like especially about Florence?" Santo Buscemi asked.

"To walk, to look, to feel the history," Larry said. "The other day I climbed up to San Miniato and took in the wonderful view of the city, and then I went into the Church and sat down to rest. I looked around and I thought maybe this was what heaven must be like. You know . . . the serenity."

The others smiled and nodded.

"Of course, I thought about the charming story of Minius, an Armenian serving in the Roman army, and about his martyrdom, and then about his carrying his own severed head up the hill to where the faithful later built the church in his memory. I don't especially love the story, but I did linger for an hour in one of the back pews, just absorbing the marvelous green and white marble interior and the wonderful painted wood ceiling that seems like the inside of an overturned ship's hull. Two monks arrived at five-thirty for a service in the crypt. I stayed to hear their chanting, and then I left to walk back down the hill."

Everyone relaxed now, and the conversation became more general, but after a few minutes on the history of Florence and its art they all fell uncomfortably into another lull. Larry looked around, hoping for something more substantive.

"You are a collector?" Arturo Zampini broke the silence.

"On a small scale," Larry said.

"Yes, of course. And that one?" Zampini pointed to the easel across the room. "What is your opinion?"

Larry swallowed, but his mouth was suddenly dry and he coughed.

"Oh, quite high," he finally managed. "I'm very interested to hear what you all think about it." He made what he wanted to be a polite inclusive gesture toward the others.

Piero Gherardi nodded. "Yes, let's look at it. That's why we're here." They followed him to the opposite corner and stood before the painting. Larry remained quiet, listening to the others. Santo Buscemi and Arturo Zampini were already commenting to one another in quiet, but rapid Italian. He heard mention of Ercole Miglio, and of Ugo di Paolo Menchini, and caught the word *ladro*, which he knew meant "thief", and then there were several back-and-forth remarks about prices in lire. Orfeo Malizia was silent. He hadn't said a word, and Larry couldn't restrain himself from sneaking quick looks at his face. There were unsettling hints of boredom or maybe even annoyance there. Why was Malizia here if not interested in the painting?

Once again, Larry was struck by the painting's vividness, especially by the unusual degree of active engagement in both the angel and the young girl. This was a Virgin unlike any he had seen, a person of real interest, someone to know. He liked her very much.

"What a lovely painting," he couldn't help saying to Arturo Zampini.

All the others nodded.

Piero Gherardi turned and began walking back to their chairs. "*Allora*," he said. "Is this an opportunity? All of you have expressed an interest. Are you willing to buy it from Miglio? He wants 500 million lire."

"You'll tell him less," Santo Buscemi said.

"*Sì, assolutamente*. I think perhaps 300 million, and then we could go up some. Maybe to 400 million. What about that?"

Buscemi and Zampini nodded, but Orfeo Malizia had a sour look on his face. "It's no good if there's no buyer," he said.

"*Certo*," Gherardi reassured him. "And that will be a responsibility for all of us." He looked around at the others, who nodded in agreement.

"I'm not in the art business," Malizia said. "But I don't like the uncertainty. I mean, to get stuck with the painting . . ."

"Stuck?" said Arturo Zampini. "I wouldn't put it that way. It may take a little time . . ."

"How much time?"

Piero Gherardi shrugged. "Look, this is about each of you putting in maybe 80 million lire, but coming away with, say, 320 million. The risk is in time spent waiting, but eventually we'll have a buyer."

Santo Buscemi turned to face Malizia. "It's a sure thing, Orfeo. Really. You should come in; you won't be sorry. It's a clean deal."

"Clean," Larry thought. Odd word . . . *clean*. But it slipped from his mind because he was wondering how they would actually find a wealthy buyer. Gherardi and Zampini were in the business, of course, so probably they already had some ideas. Would it be an Italian? A German? An American?

"*Va bene*," Orfeo Malizia said.

The others nodded their approval, and looked at Larry.

"I'm in, too," he responded. "It's an attractive opportunity."

Piero Gherardi spoke for a few minutes about details. They were each to give him 40 million lire within a week. He would confer with Ercole Miglio and pay him 200 million lire. The rest, depending on the final agreed price, they would pay within 30 days. Gherardi would continue to keep the painting in his gallery on Via del Moro.

"The piece is in excellent condition," he said. "No restoration is needed, just a little cleaning . . . and I'll find a better frame. Meanwhile, we should all be thinking about potential buyers."

38

Larry's phone rang that evening. It was Luisa.

"I'm going down to Chianti the day after tomorrow," she said. "Will you be free? We can be together."

"What's doing in Chianti?"

"I've had some shoes made in Panzano and I want to pick them up. Besides wouldn't you like to see me?"

"How can I resist an offer like that?"

"I'll pick you up . . . Porta Romana at ten."

"I'll be there. You're free for the whole day?"

"And the evening, too."

"Marvelous."

Thursday morning he walked the length of Via Romana. It was already hot and muggy at 9:30, but maybe out in the countryside it would be cooler. Everything along the street was familiar to him: the pharmacy with its lighted green cross sign; the barber shop where he had his hair cut; the several deconsecrated small churches built as early as 1050 A.D.; the Pirelli tire store; the stone plaques marking former residences of Giosue Carducci, the national poet of modern Italy, and Jessie White Mario, a nurse to Garibaldi's soldiers; the meat market;

the bakery. At the far end of the street Porta Romana, an enormous stone arch, came into view and it always made him think of the story he'd heard many times from local people. In the summer of 1944 the Germans blew up the bridges over the Arno to slow the Allied advance. Only a few days later, American troops were entering the city through the somber, massive portal in the ancient walls, and Florence was soon liberated. Once more, Larry realized that it was this vivid consciousness of being in the presence of history that made living here so special. Despite the heat he smiled and looked ahead—to being with Luisa, to the drive, to some breeze, to lunch in Panzano, and to the evening.

He waited in the shadow of the arch, and at two minutes after ten the Alfa Romeo pulled up to the curb.

"You drive," said Luisa, cool and fresh in a light blue cotton sundress and white sandals. She got out of the car, they embraced, and he kissed her lips. She smelled wonderful.

Years before, when they had first met, they'd been very circumspect about their trysts and had moved with great care. For a city with an international reputation for culture and an unsurpassed place in history, Florence was a surprisingly small town, and both had felt the need for caution. People knew Luisa; people knew her husband. But Enrico Orlando counted on his wife for only two things: complete freedom in his own personal life, and an unwavering commitment to remain with him as wife and mother to his children. Whatever her life was apart from those two demands was her business. In his own way, he was a liberated man, and he understood that liberation worked both ways.

Larry knew the road—Via Senese to Galuzzo, then east to the Via Chiantigiana, and finally south through Greve to Panzano.

Driving here wasn't that different from driving in the States. Maybe one needed to be a bit cheekier, but the main thing was to relax. Getting from point A to point B was always going to take longer in

Italy. Distances were stated in kilometers, but you had to think miles. On any given road the traffic was going to be worse than in the States.

Of course, there were headaches, like drivers right behind you who couldn't tolerate even one or two car lengths of empty space. But he wasn't going to let that spoil the day.

"Tell me about shoes," he said. "We're going all the way to Panzano to pick up shoes?"

"Don't make fun of me," she laughed. "Carlo Fagiani's a real artist."

"I wouldn't dare make fun of you."

"I love his shoes. They're stylish, interesting, comfortable, and they last. And the colors are always great—subtle, different—and I can order my own combinations. You should look, too. His men's shoes are very handsome."

Before long they were in Chianti. The air was a bit cooler, but the fine haze blanketing the rolling terrain of vineyards and olive groves gave things a mystical, otherworldly quality. With each turn in the curving road the vista changed. Wooded stretches with glimpses of a stream gave way to distant views of a grand villa silhouetted on a hilltop. There were fenced fields with patches of red poppies; then alleys of cypress trees leading up to stone farmhouses. The grapes hung lush and dark blue, and Luisa said that the harvest would be earlier than usual this year.

Picking up the shoes was quick and easy. While Luisa tried hers on to make sure of a perfect fit, Larry looked through the stock of men's styles. All were well done and as handsome as she'd described, but he wasn't convinced that he wanted to splurge on hand-made shoes. He looked through the rack of leather jackets and belts, and was also quite happy to leave them for others.

"You didn't find anything?" Luisa asked. She looked disappointed.

"Not my style," he said. "Let's go have lunch."

They drove to a small restaurant and sat on an outdoor terrace overlooking the valley. It was very quiet and peaceful. Only the intermittent hum of bees and the chirp of small birds somewhere not far off broke the silence. They ordered a bottle of Badia a Coltibuono

Sangiovese—dark ruby color, intense nose with a bouquet of cherry, cinnamon and cloves, and a well-balanced, warm and persistent taste—and took sips with a first course of *panzanella*, a Tuscan salad with pieces of stale bread soaked with olive oil and vinegar, chopped tomatoes, lettuce, cucumber and anchovies.

"I met some people recently," Larry said. "I wonder if you know them, or if you've heard of them."

"Who are they? Where did you meet them?"

"They're people interested in a painting. I met them through Piero Gherardi."

"Gherardi, the antiquario? On Via del Moro?"

"Yes, do you know him?"

"Not personally, but he has a good reputation. He's honest. What is the painting?"

"It's a long story, but basically he has put a group of investors together—to buy the painting, and then to sell it—and I'm one of them."

He described the Annunciation by Ugo di Paolo Menchini. "We stand to make a nice profit."

She cocked her head to one side. "Maybe," she said. "But you must be careful. It's a tricky business."

"What should I be watching for?"

"Ah, you know, there are so many regulations. But who are the others?"

"A lawyer named Santo Buscemi . . ."

"Yes, I don't know him personally, but people say he has powerful political connections. Who else?"

"Another dealer, a friend of Gherardi's . . . Arturo Zampini. Lives in Argentina."

"I don't know the name."

"And a businessman named Orfeo Malizia."

"Ah, he has a reputation, too. Very clever. Also very connected."

"He seemed rather hard when I met him. Doesn't smile much."

"Well, I don't know, but I hope you have success."

"I've been in plenty of investment arrangements, but never in an art deal quite like this. It makes me a little anxious, but I suppose it could lead to other similar projects. It would keep me more connected in Florence."

"Then it has my approval." She leaned over and kissed him.

The waiter brought their second course, *tagliata di manzo con rucola*—strips of rare steak on a bed of arugula.

"What a wonderful meal," Luisa said

"It's especially wonderful with you. Thank you for needing to come to Panzano to pick up your shoes."

"I know, I know. Shoes are a fetish for some people, but that's a sexual thing, isn't it? For me they're just an ordinary obsession."

"I'm glad you have an obsession. It makes you especially attractive—and lovable."

They were sipping the last part of the Sangiovese. Larry pointed to a small shaded garden with wicker chairs and sofas off to one side of the terrace. "I think we'd better sit over there for a while before I attempt to drive back," Larry said.

They finished the meal with a pear tart and coffee, and then went over to sit on one of the sofas that had a spectacular view out over the countryside.

"You are a strange man, Larry Gerst."

"More strange than other people?"

"Everyone is strange," Luisa said. "But you used the word "lovable" just now. That's extraordinary for you."

"Come on, you know my history. Once bitten, twice shy."

"I know just as much about that as you—but I'm glad you said I'm lovable."

He picked up her hand and kissed it.

A little breeze stirred and they sat quietly. In the valley below, the pattern of vineyards extended west and south to a line of hills forming the far horizon. Siena was somewhere over there.

The haze had lifted. Only a few puffy white clouds softened the fiercely blue sky. The world seemed filled with light.

39

On Friday, three days after the meeting at Palazzo Guglielmini, Larry returned to Gherardi's gallery to deliver his part of the initial investment, but also to have another look at the painting. He'd called his broker at Merrill-Lynch to move some cash into his Italian checking account.

"My share," he said, handing Gherardi a check for 40 million lire.

"*Grazie.* Buscemi and Zampini have paid. I just have to collect Malizia's share and then I'll drive down to Arezzo and confer with Miglio."

They stood before the painting once more, chatting amiably about the qualities they both found appealing. Piero seemed pleased at Larry's genuine interest in the way stylistic features enabled one to move toward an accurate attribution. "Exactly," the dealer said. "That's what art history is. Or perhaps that's connoisseurship—blending science, or at least meticulous observation, with aesthetic appreciation. And passion, too."

"Oh, I like that. A good definition."

"Someday I will write an essay," Piero laughed.

"Tell me about the others," Larry ventured. "I take it Santo Buscemi is a real art lover . . . Arturo, too. What about Orfeo? He seems different."

"He's a businessman, and very successful, too. I don't think he'll cause any trouble."

"What kind of trouble?"

"No, I mean he will be quiet, but he'll go along with the group. He's very loyal."

"Why do you put it that way?"

"Ah, he's from the South—Briatico, a little seaside town on the coast of Calabria. Loyalty is everything. Down there it means much more than written contracts. *Calabresi* take it very seriously. Orfeo comes from a large family. They were poor, but hardworking. He helped them all up from the lower classes. Imagine, he began in the garbage business. Don't they call it sanitation engineering? Yes, and he still runs it down there."

"What does that mean?"

"Anything having to do with that business goes through Orfeo. He makes all the decisions. And he does it very well. He's helped the people of Calabria, and he's highly esteemed. But he has many other business interests including here in Tuscany."

"Why would he be interested in investing in a painting?"

"Why would anyone? Profit—he's quick to take advantage of a possible profit."

"What about Santo, and Arturo?"

"Santo's family is Sicilian, but they moved to Firenze in the 1930's. His father, a soldier, was a casualty of Mussolini's insane invasion of Ethiopia. His mother remarried, but she and her second husband were killed during an Allied bombardment of this city. That was a great tragedy, but Santo is very intelligent and he became a lawyer, a real-estate person. He knows important people in government. He's not flashy, but he gets things done behind the scenes, and he's a very cultivated gentleman . . . passionate about literature, opera, painting, and sculpture. We didn't see much of his collection yesterday. Most of it is in his villa near Settignano where he spends about half his time."

"And Arturo?"

"Arturo and I lived in the same *quartiere* here in Firenze when we were children. We went to school together. He studied history and politics at the university, and then went into our diplomatic service. He's lived in Japan, in France, in Canada, and now in Argentina."

"You told me he's an art dealer."

"Yes, it's a kind of side business for him."

"What's his role in the diplomatic service? What does he do?"

"Ah, well, I don't talk with him about that."

40

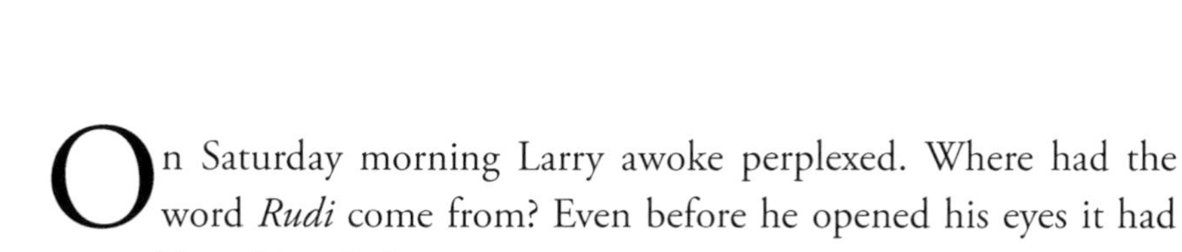

On Saturday morning Larry awoke perplexed. Where had the word *Rudi* come from? Even before he opened his eyes it had popped into his mind.

Rudi?

He swung his legs down and sat calculating on the edge of the bed. The lira was trading at 1900 to the dollar. Buy the painting from Miglio for 400 million lire. That came to about $210,000. Divide that among five investors—say, $42,000 each.

What about Gherardi's prediction of a sale price four times what they'd pay Miglio? Could he trust Gherardi? It could be a sweet deal. He'd make a profit of about $126,000. Nice. Clever. Or could he lose the whole thing?

Rudi?

That name . . .

Rudi? *Rudi*? Where'd it come from?

From below in the street came the sounds of an accordion. The same grizzled old man would be sitting on his wood box in the sun, leaning against the building, his black cowboy hat set low on his forehead, and playing his weekend concert for the neighborhood. *Volare; Funiculì, Funiculà; O Sole Mio.* Looking down at the sidewalk Larry could just make out the man's leg and the tin cup standing before him. Always the same music, non-stop, repeated over and over.

He showered, dressed, and left the building. The musician swayed lazily as he squeezed and extended the battered accordion. His eyes were closed, but when Larry's coin dropped into the tin cup, he blinked and, with a tiny nod, smiled in acknowledgement.

In the bar at the corner, cool jazz was playing on the radio. *Take Five*, wasn't it? Brubeck and Paul Desmond? Larry had a quick thought of Josh's upcoming visit to Florence. He needed to check the calendar.

Tiberio, the owner, was wiping the counter as Larry mounted one of the stools.

"*Buon giorno*, Signor Lorenzo. *Cosa desidera*?" Tiberio, an imposing, plethoric, genial extrovert, took pleasure in engaging his habitual American customer in Italian, even granting him the esteemed name of the city's arguably most famous son, *Il Magnifico*, Lorenzo dei Medici.

"*Ciao,* Tiberio. *Buon giorno.*"

Larry asked for his usual *cappuccino* and *cornetto alla marmellata.* These were soothing moments of relaxation—abstracted, daydreaming observations of Tiberio's quick, practiced coffee-making maneuvers, and his careful expert placement of the pastry with its tiny paper napkin on the white plate. There was something very satisfying about watching someone do a job well—any job—especially if the doer seemed to find pleasure in the work.

Almost immediately, other customers began coming in, and Tiberio turned his attention to them.

A new song was on the radio . . . *God Bless The Child* . . . Billie Holiday.

Yes the strong gets more
While the weak ones fade
Empty pockets don't ever make the grade

Larry sipped the hot cappuccino and wondered if Josh liked Billie Holiday. They'd never talked about that.

How would it be having Josh and Claire in Florence? What would they be interested in? Claire had been in Florence as a student. She probably loved the art, but he had his doubts about his old friend. Josh had his music, and he had his teaching, and he had his wife. Not that Josh was smug or self-satisfied. Larry just didn't see him as being tuned in to Europe and its history and art. Josh had had his big trauma, and surely he cherished his domestic security and comforts. Perhaps his translocation to the west coast of America had been his grand adventure. Why would Italy hold appeal for him? Florence was an acquired taste. It wasn't for everybody.

And then, in a flash . . . *Rudi*!

Rudi Nathanson!

Someone his father had known in Europe. But . . . who was he? Why did the name pop up out of the blue?

There was no one to ask. Abe Gerst had had a stroke in 1979, and had lived only two more months.

What else was there?

There had been that nasty argument. What was it his father had said back then? 1947 or 1948? Around the time of the divorce—anyway, late 1940's. Nearly forty years ago.

Slowly, it began to come back.

Geneva! And an art collection!

How well had Abe Gerst known Nathanson? Were they contemporaries, or was Rudi Nathanson in an earlier generation?

How would one track it down? Was it even possible? Just a name. A name, and a city.

PART SEVEN

1985
Mill Valley

41

Claire's packing list caught Josh's eye one Sunday morning. He was on his way down to breakfast and that quick glance at a scrap of paper started him thinking. His wife's organized approach to items she wanted to take to Europe made him smile. Three bras, six underpants, six blouses, black slacks, red skirt, and on and on. Some things were crossed out because they were already in her suitcase, but he could see from the writing that others were added at different times because another pen or pencil had been used. They had two weeks to go before the band left, but Claire planned ahead. Josh wondered about a list for himself, but it seemed present more as a vague notion that he ought to give it some thought. More important were large facts lying ahead: traveling with others; the enormity of Europe; language; food; and, infiltrating everything, a nebulous fog of conflicted musings on the entire trip.

Everyone talked about Europe; everyone seemed to like it. What if he didn't? If you think about something for a long time, build it up into a grand dream . . . does it make disappointment more likely?

Claire was clearly looking forward to the trip. The almost daily additions to her packing list, some of them carefully underlined, showed determined and steady attention to the adventure. This wasn't going to be just a casual interlude for her. She was always upbeat and happy whenever she spoke of her college time in Italy, and Josh liked seeing her eagerness to revisit those places.

"Oh, there are so many things I want to see again, and to show you," she said. "The churches, the museums; Michelangelo's sculpture; Botticelli's paintings; the Fra Angelicos in San Marco; Masaccio's frescos in the Brancacci chapel."

"I've been looking at the guide book," Josh said. "So far, it's a confused blur, but I'll enjoy following you around."

"I hope we'll have enough time to see it all, and that we can be by ourselves."

"Oh, I'm sure we can. The other guys will go off on their own."

"What about Larry?"

"I'm sure he's got his schedule, too. We'll see him, of course, but I don't think he wants to hover."

"Good."

Contemplating Larry, and also the guys in the band, occasionally ushered in thoughts about marriage—what made a good one, or a bad one. Not infrequently, Josh would meditate about what he and Claire shared, and it always ended with an acute consciousness that he was lucky—very lucky.

Three of the band members were bachelors. Two were divorced and remarried. Josh's old friend, Rich Mariani had been widowed, but was happily remarried.

Moe Pruitt, wonderful trombonist and perennial bachelor, was misogynistic and exploitive with women. He talked endlessly about the current lady in his life, but it always ended with her rejection of him. Good looking and affable, he also had a kind of intensity that could be frightening. There was something scary in the way he looked at people, and it didn't help his case that he persisted in telling demeaning jokes about women. Josh would shake his head and move away, but he saw that Moe would never grow up. Something was missing. Empathy? Common sense? How could such a superb musician be such a jerk?

The other three spouses were coming on the trip. Claire knew them all, and was friendly with Rich's wife, Frannie. The other two wives were bright women, but Claire knew them only from the band's Bay Area gigs where they sat listening to the music and made cautious, and sometimes-uncomfortable conversation about non-controversial topics. No easy socializing had ever developed. Somehow the musical part of Josh's life remained separate. He'd never made that an absolute requirement, and neither had Claire, but there it was—a compartment. Divided . . . music and life. Life was Claire, Holly, home in Mill Valley, and teaching literature at Los Arboles. Music was his soul, his passion, and his oxygen. Life and music—should a person uncouple one from the other?

It was different with Rich Mariani. Completely *simpatico*, Rich was very much there in both. Besides being the first musician Josh had met on arriving in San Francisco back in 1952, Rich had become a close friend. He and Josh were soul mates, able to talk endlessly about music, but also very easily about other things. Rich's first wife had died after years of battling the many hellish manifestations of systemic lupus. That was a devastating time for Rich, and Josh had spent hours with his friend, just sitting together, and being quiet and available. Years later, at a rehearsal where the guys were talking about new tunes the band ought to consider, the guitar player suggested *When I Lost You*.

"It's a good melody written as a waltz," he said. "We could start it in 3/4 time and then move into 4/4."

"No," Rich said quietly. "Definitely no."

The other musicians looked a little startled, but Josh knew immediately. Irving Berlin had written *When I Lost You* in 1912 out of grief at the death from typhoid of the young woman who had been his wife for just five months. It was a slow and sensitive song, and Rich felt the connection in a deeply personal way.

Eventually, and indirectly through a friend of Claire's, Rich had met Frannie, an effervescent blonde who looked after him and also managed to write poetry that got published in *The New Yorker*. They were a perfect couple, and Frannie was coming along on the trip.

Rich, growing up in a working class family in San Francisco, had completed only two semesters of community college after graduating from high school. He'd learned to play the string bass practically on his own, and that became his modus operandi. A true autodidact, he had immersed himself in literature, and history, and even in ornithology.

"When I heard Charlie Parker's recording of *Ornithology* I had to look up the word," Rich explained. "I didn't know ornithology from optometry." Then he discovered the Audubon Society, began going on their hikes, and bought binoculars. It didn't take long before he was leading some of the hikes.

Rich could hold forth on the sublime textures of Count Basie's rhythm section, on Samuel Johnson's philosophical insights about human happiness, and about the trans-world migrations of Red Knots, Short- and Long-billed Dowitchers, and Semipalmated Sandpipers. He had taught himself Spanish; had voraciously devoured biographies of the Founding Fathers, on whom he often lavished praise for their skepticism about organized religion; and had never failed to manifest cynicism about current politicians in either party.

"Are you excited?" Claire asked Josh one evening. "Are you looking forward to this?"

"I'm trying to."

"You've always been envious of other bands that go on cruises and tours. Now you're not so sure?"

"Don't hate me for saying this, but I have my doubts about everybody getting along. It's going to be pretty close quarters, don't you think?"

"We're all adults," Claire said. "Except maybe Moe, but even he probably wants to go off hunting by himself, don't you think?"

"I don't want to hear any more of his stories." Josh muttered. "Do you think he could learn how to edit the narratives of his romantic exploits? Except that *romantic* isn't the right word. Maybe *desperate*, or even *hopeless*."

"Forget it. Just be happy he's the right trombone guy for the band. We'll have fun. Everything will be fine."

PART EIGHT

1985
Geneva

42

Larry's search took only three days. The American Express office had telephone directories and there were several possibilities listed in Geneva. Four calls proved futile, but one to an Alain Nathanson was promising.

"Mr. Nathanson is away at present. I am his secretary. Who may I say is calling?"

"My name is Gerst—Larry Gerst. I'm looking for the family of Rudi Nathanson."

"What is this in regard to, Mr. Gerst?"

"I'm looking . . . You see, my father's family . . . they were friends of the Nathanson family. Before the war . . . in Berlin."

"Yes?"

"If you can . . . that is, if you will . . . please let me know if this is the same Nathanson family."

"Mr. Nathanson will be here tomorrow. If you call again, at about this time . . ."

"Thank you. I shall do that."

Indeed, it was the same family.

Alain Nathanson's quiet voice was guarded. "I may've heard the name—Gerst, you say—from my father," he said. "But I must tell you that I know nothing of their friendship."

"That's all right," Larry replied. "I know just as little. I realize it's quite odd for me to call you like this so unexpectedly."

"Where are you?"

"In Florence. I'm here for part of every year."

"You're American?"

"I am."

"Please tell me why you're calling."

Larry paused for a deep breath.

"I'm calling about a piece of art, a painting."

"A painting . . ."

"Years ago, when my father mentioned your family's name he told me that your father had a wonderful art collection."

"Is that so?"

"Is it still in existence?"

"Is what in existence?"

"The art collection."

Nathanson was silent for a moment. "Look . . . I don't know you, Mr. Gerst, and I generally don't discuss personal things over the phone this way."

"I understand completely, Sir, so let me be brief. As I said, I live in Florence at present, and I'm one of a group of five investors. We've purchased an exquisite early fifteenth century Italian painting and we're looking to sell it. Would you have any interest in that sort of thing?"

Nathanson chuckled. "I'm amused at how you put it," he said. "But, I don't know. Tell me more about the painting."

"It's an Annunciation. Two art historians have attributed it to Ugo di Paolo Menchini."

"Ah, really. That would be quite remarkable."

"You know the name?"

"Of course. Anything by him is very rare."

Larry waited.

"I've seen his paintings at the Accademia, of course," Nathanson said. "Perhaps you have, too."

"Yes, I have seen them."

"I've never heard of one coming on the market."

"This one is. Are you buying paintings?"

"I maintain our collection. It's intact—and continues to grow some."

"I can send you a photo . . ."

"Before you do that," Nathanson broke in. "Tell me more about what you think the connection is between your father and mine."

"Mine came to America from Berlin in 1927," Larry replied. "Being Jewish . . . well, I'm sure you know."

"Of course."

"My mother was an artist and I heard discussions about art almost daily from the time I was a little boy."

"But how did your father know my father?"

"He never told me. All I remember is the name *Rudi Nathanson* and that my father said that he had a very good collection. It was during an awkward argument with my mother about what constitutes good art. He mentioned your father as someone who had good taste. I should add that my father had strong opinions about a lot of things."

"Yes? What sort of work did he do?"

"In Germany the Gerst family worked in finance—currency arbitrage. That sort of thing."

There was another long moment when neither spoke.

"Look," Nathanson said. "I have an appointment just now. How about calling me back the day after tomorrow?"

"Are you interested in the painting?"

"Interested . . . no. Curious . . . perhaps."

"The photograph is really excellent . . ."

"Fine, but I don't buy paintings offered in a telephone call. I need to know a lot more."

"Couldn't we start with the photograph?"

"I don't think so . . . that doesn't mean we can't have another conversation about this. As I said, I don't know you, but I shall think about it. If you call me the day after tomorrow I'll be here."

"Okay, sure, I'll do that."

It was disappointing, but Larry realized he should have expected hesitation, and even suspicion, from Nathanson. If the roles had been reversed he wouldn't have been any more eager to bite. What a strange and tenuous thing it was—calling someone you don't know and offering for sale a work of art that's not only very particular, but also exceedingly rare and quite valuable.

Thou shalt not covet—but sophisticated collectors certainly coveted paintings like the Ugo di Paolo Annunciation, and Larry was passionate enough about owning pieces of art to know how it felt. For someone like Nathanson, he hoped, it might be irresistible. Meanwhile, he could only wait, and during the next two days he eased the tension by walking his favorite routes.

Of course, he told himself, Gherardi and the others are all supposed to be looking, too, so I don't have to be the one to find the buyer. But I want to, and if I succeed I'll feel like a winner.

He climbed up to Bellosguardo for its panoramic view of Florence. Leaning against the low stonewall along the narrow road, he gazed out at the domes and towers, the churches and palazzi spread far and wide below. Every building, everything he saw, had its history, and he lost himself in time and in the mosaic of colors—red roofs; ochre, sienna, and umber walls; the green hills toward Fiesole; and the bright blue sky.

The next day he walked downstream along the Arno and then crossed over to the long green park called the Cascine, where for a while he watched trotting horses being worked by drivers in sulkies.

That was already a considerable hike, but he wanted to see one more thing. Heading back past the railway station, he made his way to Via della Colonna to view once again the unusual painting of the Crucifixion by Pietro Perugino. Larry had seen it many times, but now, quite tired from his long tramp, he sat quietly, facing the monumental fresco. Completed in 1496, it filled an entire wall. No one else was in the room, and he stayed for a long time, allowing its serenity to replenish his energy and savoring each part and each detail of the great painting.

Unlike the terrible drama of most portrayals of the Crucifixion, Perugino's has a remarkable softness, a meditative effect produced by the tranquil pastoral landscape that serves as a luminous background for the people in the foreground. Despite the grim subject, those six individuals appear strangely quiet and detached. Again and again, Larry's eye was drawn to the hills, streams, rocks, and trees. The scene was restorative and very welcome to him.

43

The second phone call was more encouraging.

"Do you know a lot about your family?" Nathanson asked.

"You mean about the war?"

"Yes, Father was rather silent about the whole thing."

"Sounds familiar," Larry told him. "And, like you, I'm equally ignorant about how well they knew each other, although I know my father held Rudi Nathanson in high regard. He admired him."

"Really . . . that's interesting. Quite interesting."

"Can I assume that during the last couple of days your interest, or shall I say your curiosity about this painting might have increased?"

Nathanson laughed. "Well, possibly."

"I hope that's the case," said Larry. "Because I'm obliged to say that the other investors in our group are also looking for a buyer."

"Who are these investors?"

"Piero Gherardi. He has a gallery in Florence. Arturo Zampini. He's also a dealer, but lives in Argentina. Santo Buscemi, a lawyer in Florence. And a businessman named Orfeo Malizia."

"The names aren't familiar."

"I'd really like to send you the photo, but then if the painting appeals to you, I would recommend acting on it soon."

"How soon?"

"I can't say, but it's a remarkable piece and there will certainly be other bidders. I'm sure you understand that."

"Yes, I suppose so. What about coming up here to Geneva? Would you consider that?"

"I think I should just send the photo."

"You could do that," Nathanson said. "But, you know—this may strike you as odd—I would feel easier if we could meet first. The trains are quick and efficient. Bring the photo with you, and any information you have. Would you mind doing that? We probably have some things in common, wouldn't you say?"

"You mean about our fathers."

"Yes, that . . . and the background of Germany, the war, and what happened."

Larry thought for a moment. A train-ride up through the mountains suddenly sounded appealing, and he wanted to be a winner. "All right," he said. "I'm willing. How about this Friday?"

"That's fine."

"Good, I'll come then."

"Excellent."

Friday. September 13. Good luck, or bad luck? Larry shook his head. This was not the time for superstitious nonsense. Selling the painting was the serious matter at hand and there was no point in wasting energy straying from the goal. Nathanson was no fool, but rather an obviously bright, careful, and motivated man. And those qualities were entirely appropriate for this exceptional painting.

Every plastic chair in the Florence rail station's crowded waiting room was taken, and Larry stood looking around at other travelers and guessing their histories. A lot of faces showed fatigue and anxiety and it made him happy to feel that by comparison he was quite relaxed and confident. Bringing Nathanson in as the buyer would require some earnest convincing on his part, but the day was sunny and he was optimistic about his chances. He checked the big black board for new information clicking into place on arriving and departing trains. Now it was his train's number—Geneva, track 7, leaving in ten minutes. He looked at his ticket—car number 10, seat 32.

The train moved through the outer parts of Florence and Larry sat quietly, glancing out at a receding dusty landscape of apartment buildings with tiny terraces, drying laundry, and walls defaced by spray-painted graffiti. He closed his eyes.

He was spending more time on this deal than he'd anticipated. Wasn't his time in Florence meant to be for himself—for himself as a person? Was he completely unable to keep himself from turning all activity into yet another variety of business?

No, that wasn't the point at all. This would be a pleasant diversion, and inordinate self-criticism was uncalled for and stupid. Why should he even hesitate to interrupt his Florentine routines? He had no obligations except to himself. Besides, Nathanson intrigued him. The post-Berlin futures forced on both their fathers had developed differently. And now weren't their sons—he, and Alain—in some kind of mysterious, historical and generational connection?

It was three o'clock when he arrived in his room at the Tiffany Hotel, and he called Nathanson right away.

"Yes, come over, and plan to stay for dinner. How about in an hour? Would that suit you?"

"Perfectly."

Nathanson gave him directions for the taxi. "It's just fifteen minutes by cab."

Larry washed up, put on a clean shirt and tie, picked up the manila envelope with the photograph and went down to the lobby.

Nathanson's villa stood at the crest of a hill above the city and its lake. The hazy mass of Mount Blanc was still visible forty or so miles to the southeast. The taxi ride from the hotel had given Larry time to think about how to present the proposal to Nathanson. He felt rather proud of the way he had introduced the probability of competition in the sale. The idea had just popped unplanned into his mind, but it was definitely clever. After all, the point was to sell the painting.

A wrought iron gate stood open between two tall stone pillars, and the short curving drive led directly to the house. The day was cool and autumn leaves fluttered down from the trees. A maid wearing a black and white uniform opened the door. Behind her, the tall bearded man in a maroon turtleneck and gray flannel trousers was Alain Nathanson.

"I'm glad you agreed to come," he said. He had a high forehead, kind but penetrating eyes, and a friendly smile, all of which suggested deep thought and little patience for fools.

"As you predicted, the train was comfortable and efficient." Larry handed him the envelope. "Here's the photograph."

"Oh, good."

Nathanson walked ahead and led the way through a long hall hung with modern paintings.

"This is only a part of our collection . . . some that Father collected, but also a few that I've added." Nathanson pointed and named artists: Klimt, Max Ernst, George Grosz, a landscape by Cezanne, and an interior scene of an old man sitting on a bed, It was by an artist Larry didn't know, Jozef Israëls.

"Very sad, that one," Nathanson said. "Mid-nineteenth century. He was a Dutch Jew. Often painted that melancholy feeling."

Larry nodded. "Maybe prophetic—about the future?"

"Or maybe how Europe's Jewish past had shaped his world view."

"Wonderful paintings!"

They went into a large sitting room with sofas and antique tables. At the far end stood a grand piano with its lid raised.

"Who plays?" Larry asked.

"No one, actually. It came with the house."

"Really, that's unusual."

"My parents bought the property from the estate of a couple who had died. There were no children, and the heiress was a niece who lived in London at the time. She was anxious to sell and the piano came along with the whole package. Do you play?"

Larry shook his head. "No," he said. "I have a friend who does—a jazz musician. As a matter of fact, his band is coming to play in Florence in a few weeks."

Nathanson put the envelope on a table and pointed to an easy chair.

"Sit down, please," he said. "I've made Bloody Marys." He gestured toward a sideboard. Larry saw the pitcher of tomato juice and glasses with ice.

"I'd love one."

Nathanson began to talk about spending two years at Harvard where he had become enthusiastic about certain aspects of American culture. "It opened things up for me," he said. "I am a Swiss, and I can't put aside my need for order which goes along with that, but I am a great admirer of your country."

He handed the Bloody Mary to Larry. "And I'm an admirer of your drinks as well," he said. "Cheers!"

They clinked glasses.

"What did you study at Harvard?"

"I got an MBA there, then came back and took over from Father."

"What sort of . . ?"

"It's quite varied—property, some manufacturing. Chocolate, actually. And finance."

"Is your father living?"

"No, he died several years ago—and my mother a year before that. I have two sons working with me, but my wife and I were divorced a while back."

Larry nodded. "Your father was able to bring his art from Germany?"

"He was rather fortunate in having some important friends who facilitated things," Nathanson said. "Certainly it was a terrible time, and I'm sure you're well aware of that, but it is also true that Father helped other people. He was able to buy items that they wanted to sell. Supply and demand, you know. So he took advantage of that opportunity to acquire some new paintings. People were selling their art and whatever else they could get rid of in order to gather enough money to emigrate."

Larry listened. "Yes," he said. "It was a horrible time."

"And a very touchy subject," Nathanson said. "I'm acutely conscious of our family's good fortune, but I know my father did what he could to smooth things for others."

"I'm sure he did."

"You and I were children then, and I don't know how it affected you, but personally I have times when I feel . . . when I feel awful about that period. The Jews my father bought paintings from were fleeing for their lives. He was paying them, but they were at a disadvantage. Still, he may have made it possible for them to survive."

"Of course."

"You told me your father went to America in 1927. Why did he leave Germany then? Did he realize what was coming? What happened to his family?" Nathanson asked.

"Yes, he left six years before Hitler was made chancellor, but even then Nazism was getting stronger. My father was aware of that, but he was also attracted by America's newness and the possibility it promised for breaking away from the rigidity of German society. He did well in New York, and married my mother, an American Jew, but his parents and sister were all murdered in Auschwitz."

"Oh, God," Nathanson shook his head. "Terrible, terrible . . . and you grew up in New York?"

"I did."

"How do you happen to be involved in this business of art? Was your father a collector?"

"Not at all, but my mother was quite a good artist and I probably caught the virus from her. I certainly don't paint, but I have a passion for art. I love having it around me."

"So, you do collect?"

"I do . . . in a small way."

"Interesting," Nathanson said, smiling. "And how are you able to live part of the year in Italy?"

Larry gave a quick outline of his business career. "And now I'm in a new time in life," he said. "I must be attentive to my affairs, but I'm able to nurture this other part of my soul . . . maybe it's selfish, but I'm content with my arrangement."

"Good for you," Alain Nathanson said.

"It's hard to believe that I've made this connection with you," Larry said. "Sitting in this room is amazing. There's a lot of talk about the children of Holocaust survivors, and I keep imagining what my father would think or say if he were here with me. If he'd stayed in Berlin his fate would have been that of his parents and sister, but by going to America he survived, and so I am the child of a survivor."

"True," Nathanson said. "You and I share that. What was he like—your father?"

"Strong. Stubborn. Impossible at times."

"That sounds familiar, too. We do have a lot in common."

They sipped the Bloody Marys and Larry's eye took in the tasteful details of the room. It reminded him of his favorite spot for studying in the library at college—a room with floor to ceiling bookcases and very comfortable easy chairs that, if one were not sufficiently motivated to study, easily induced somnolence.

"Your father was from Berlin originally?" Larry asked.

"That's right."

"I assumed that was the case, but it's so strange. Here I am today, and it's entirely the result of the name *Rudi Nathanson* coming into my mind close to forty years after I heard my father say it. As I mentioned, he and my mother were arguing about art and he used your father's name just to show her that he knew someone who had what he considered to be good taste and who had managed to acquire a collection."

"If his family was in finance in Berlin that might have been the connection. My own father continued to work in finance after he was allowed to come to Switzerland."

"Do you want to look at the print?"

Nathanson nodded, reached for the envelope, and pulled out the photograph. Larry watched his face, pleased as he saw the immediate smile and the other's eyebrows raised in an expression of pleasant surprise and appreciation.

"Lovely," Nathanson said. "Of course, a photo isn't the same as seeing the work itself."

"You'd need to come to Florence."

"I know."

Nathanson said nothing for a few minutes, just continued looking at the photo, holding it out and then bringing it closer to see details.

"When I see it I'll know for sure," he said. "But I can almost tell you right now what my decision will be. You know, there are paintings . . . and then there are paintings. And I will admit that when you mentioned Ugo di Paolo Menchini it fairly took my breath away. What a tremendous thing! Few people have even heard of him, but I know his work from my many visits in Italy. There's something about those early paintings that almost makes it possible for a person to re-enter a time hundreds of years ago. Do you know what I mean? It has to do with the nearly unspeakable, enormous differences between that period and what constitutes this frantic and complicated modern life. Maybe I'm stupidly romantic, but owning such a painting certainly appeals to me. I'm well aware of the importance of Ugo di Paolo's work. He's a pivotal point between two stages in the development of Italian art. So, we will most likely need only to talk about price."

Larry had a pang of anxiety realizing that he'd just completed only the first step toward his goal. Price, of course, was what really mattered.

"Yes," he said. "The group wants one million U.S dollars."

"No, I won't pay that."

"Do you doubt that it's by Ugo di Paolo?"

"On the contrary—this is an excellent photograph, by the way. I'm reasonably confident the painting is what you claim it to be, but the price is too high. What about other prospective buyers?"

"I'm certain there will be some. We are a group of five and we're anxious to sell. In fact, I've sensed a certain impatience in the others."

"About what?"

"About getting our investment back. About taking our profit. About avoiding the tensions of waiting."

"Quick and easy, eh?"

"That's right."

"Your group has possible buyers in Italy? In Germany?"

"Yes, in both. The others certainly know more people . . . more prospective buyers than I do. It's pretty remarkable that I thought of you."

"I very much appreciate that. Indeed, I do. Naturally, I must see the painting itself, but it's extremely likely that I will want it."

"I'm happy to hear that."

"How will you let the others know?"

"I'll just telephone them. I can do that now if you like. What's your offer?"

"A million dollars is out of the question."

"Give me some reasonable figure."

"I don't want to get into a situation of competitive bidding."

"How so?"

"I want to have assurance in advance."

"I don't follow you."

"If I give you a figure, I want to feel reasonably certain it will be accepted."

"If it's a high enough bid you're very likely to get it."

"If there are to be other bids, I'd feel better about everything if I knew that you were on my side."

"I'm already on your side. I would like you to have the Ugo di Paolo."

Alain Nathanson hesitated. “And I like Americans,” he said, smiling. “Your naiveté is charming, but you aren’t accustomed to bargaining in a market.”

“Do you want to give me a figure?”

“My figure for your group will be one thing, but now I would like to be very frank with you. Perhaps I’m the one being naïve because I feel I must reiterate what I said just now about your being on my side.”

“I assure you that I’ll use whatever influence I have to make certain that you get the painting.”

“Good—and I’m very grateful you came to Geneva on your own. You’re rather like a ghost from the past. Not my past, but my family’s past.”

“Well, yes. I think our generation has been very lucky.”

“Of course.”

Alain Nathanson searched Larry’s face for a moment. “Look,” he said. “If I see the painting and love it, I will pay $800,000. Cash. That will make the Italians happy. But I’ll pay you something extra . . . call it a finder’s fee.”

“If I ensure that you get the painting?”

“Do you think you can?”

“I’ll do my best.”

“I would pay you an extra $100,000.”

“Oh?” Larry’s eyes widened.

“You’re puzzled? Or you doubt what I’m saying?”

“No . . . go on.”

“I’m entirely serious. Naturally, I could change my mind about the painting when I see it, but your photograph tells me otherwise.”

Larry frowned.

“You’re uneasy about what I’m saying,” Nathanson suggested.

“I wouldn’t put it quite that way,” Larry said.

“You’re thinking about the others in your group?”

“Yes, I am. We’re a group with one focus, and I don’t know them well.”

"I understand that, but this would be entirely between the two of us."

Larry watched Nathanson's face. This was the Harvard Business School graduate, the dealmaker, and he had to smile at that. They definitely had more things in common than just a family connection that went back fifty years.

"You're amused."

"Not exactly amused," Larry said. "It's the juxtaposition . . . you, on the one hand, and my group of fellow investors, on the other. So peculiar . . . a feeling of knowing you better than I know them. It's got something to do with their being Italian . . . with the barrier of language and culture. None of them know America the way you do. And of course our two families."

"That's all very true," Nathanson said. "So, what about it? This needn't be awkward. I'm appreciative of your role in this and willing to take that extra step."

"I understand, but it makes things more complex."

"Only for you and me."

It was all very clear to Larry, but images of faces—Gherardi, Malizia, Zampini, Buscemi—passed through his mind. There were aspects that were imponderable.

"I could pay your supplement with a check, or with cash. Do you have an Italian bank account?"

"Yes."

"I can place deposits there."

Larry didn't say anything, merely nodding slowly a few times. He wasn't accepting immediately. It was much better for Nathanson to see that he was thinking and considering. Were there other implications? Was he missing anything? Take your time. Appear careful . . . prudent.

The calculation itself was quick—it was a remarkable bonus.

"Look," he said. "Wouldn't a sudden large deposit to my account raise eyebrows in the wrong places?"

"That is possible. I think a combination of cash and a smaller deposit would be best."

"You're quite generous."

Nathanson's face showed no emotion. It was clear that he had made his case and had no intention of saying more until he had an agreement or a refusal.

Several moments went by in uncomfortable silence.

"I hope I don't disappoint you," Larry said finally.

"You're accepting my offer?"

"I believe I am."

"Ah, good."

44

In the taxi taking him back to the hotel Larry had twinges of embarrassment about their talk. He didn't really know Nathanson, but he liked him, and it did seem better for the painting to be in a collection where it was certain to be protected and well appreciated. Nonetheless, he was uneasy about suddenly becoming so intimately involved with a stranger. Was it going to be worth all the trouble? Never one to minimize the attractions of a good deal, he was elated about the near certainty of a large profit, and he also knew that his qualms about the finder's fee wouldn't last long. He would use it to buy more art for himself. A nice plus . . . a very nice plus. No need to feel uncomfortable about it. It was the way lots of business got done—maybe even more so in Europe. There was no point in being falsely moralistic about it. He had no way of knowing if any of the other investors would come up with a real buyer, so his role in this might be just the piece that would make the whole thing work. Accepting an offer of an extra $100,000 made him more than an equal among the members of Gherardi's group of five, but he had put himself out and ought to be compensated. Anyway, no one else would know, and, actually, all things considered, his extra bonus wasn't that much. He had made a special effort to find

Nathanson, so that made him literally the finder of the buyer. He'd played his part well.

He called Gherardi from his room.

"You're calling from Geneva?"

"I have a buyer," he said. "Do you know the name Nathanson?"

"No."

"I'm not surprised. He has a good collection, but he's managed to avoid publicity."

"That's to be admired. What's his offer?"

"He wants to come down to Florence to see it."

"Of course. When?"

"Sometime in the next week or ten days. He'll let me know."

"He didn't make an offer?"

"He'll do that when he sees the painting, but I think he's a real possibility."

"I see."

"Have there been any other offers?"

"Two—one from Argentina. $850,000, but it's going to be very difficult to ship it out of Italy."

"Why is that?"

"It will require a special permit. We'll have to pay someone."

"You mean bribe someone?"

"I don't want to put it that way."

"What about letting it go to Geneva with this Nathanson? Won't that be an issue?"

"Not necessarily. It would be easier than to South America."

"You said there was another offer."

"It's from Belgium, and only for $600,000, but it's problematic."

"How so?"

"A dealer in Brussels has a client there and is buying for him. Arturo Zampini knows the dealer, and it turns out I know him, too, but indirectly."

"What's the problem?"

"The problem is that I don't trust that dealer. He will shake hands, but then always has an excuse for paying less than what was agreed."

"Oh, that's not promising."

"No, I won't get involved with him, but we still have time. Anyway, I'm glad you called. I hope your Mr. Nathanson is serious."

"I'm quite certain that he is."

"Listen, Larry, the others—Arturo, Santo, and Orfeo—were asking about you."

"What about me?"

"They wanted to know how I know you, how we met, what you do. It's nothing, but they are curious people. They want to know about a person if money is at stake."

"That makes me feel uncomfortable. It's a pretty straightforward investment. Am I correct?"

"It's a question of trust. Italians depend on trust."

"Everyone depends on trust. What did you tell them?"

"I told them how we met. I reassured them."

"Thanks, glad to hear it."

"Don't worry yourself."

"I won't. See you in a few days."

"*Va bene. Buon viaggio. Ciao, ciao.*"

He wished sleep would come, but his mind raced, ruminating for a few moments on one thing, and then abruptly veering to another. So many disconnected thoughts, all moving inexplicably with an obscure logic. What about the issue of the painting leaving Italy? How much of an impediment was that? And why was Alain Nathanson so eager to acquire this particular painting? Such a quick decision to buy the Ugo di Paolo. Was he privy to something that the rest of them didn't understand? Was he endowed with an unusual fund of courage? Or was he just very wealthy? Doubtless, the work was a splendid piece. And the collection in the Nathanson family villa on the mountain was clearly first rate. But was there some hidden motivation? Nathanson had said Ugo di Paolo was "*a pivotal point between two stages in the development of Italian art.*" That seemed a valid enough reason, but there was something elusive about it, perhaps the hint of a partial truth best left unstated.

No, he told himself. Don't dwell on that. The main issue is doing the deal. Finish it. Take the profit. Then put it all behind. Go on to something else.

How convoluted and shady this art world was. Ercole Miglio concocted a story to make potential buyers salivate. Piero Gherardi stated things quite directly, but had no aversion to slyly bamboozling Miglio with a cute plan for purchase and payment. And what about Orfeo Malizia and the other investors? Anyone meeting them for the first time could see that they were nicely dressed and probably dependable, but who knew? Who could figure what Malizia's semi-belligerent attitude might be about?

And now, here was Nathanson, a potential buyer, entering into a cordial relationship with a guy he'd just met, in order to make a deal under the table that would insure his acquisition of a picture.

And I'm in it, too, Larry knew. Culpable, just like the others. I'm not blind to the unsavory side of the art market, and I share in it as much as anyone else. I'm drawn to the culture and beauty, and to transcendence, but at the same time I accept the shame of what amounts to a marriage with greed, money, and deception. Layers of dishonesty—Miglio, Gherardi, maybe the other investors, Alain Nathanson, and myself.

Okay—enough. This will get me nowhere.

PART NINE

1985
Florence

45

Four days later Larry and Alain Nathanson met Gherardi at the gallery on Via del Moro.

"I thought it easier for just the three of us to be here," Gherardi said. "If we can come to an agreement I'll let the others know. I'm sure that will be acceptable."

He led them to the back of the gallery where the painting, covered by a large green cloth, stood on an easel.

"Larry tells me you're familiar with this artist's work," Gherardi said. "That's a very good beginning. There aren't many collectors who are so knowledgeable."

He carefully removed the cloth and the men stood quietly, taking in the lovely scene of the angel and the young girl. Larry saw immediately that the painting's surface had already been cleaned. That was fast, he thought.

No one spoke for several minutes. Larry felt a sense of imminent loss, knowing that someone else would own this painting. He would never be able to live with it, and would never have the complete freedom to see it again and again in his own home on sunny mornings, or at night before going to bed. It would never be possible for him to have, at a random moment, the remarkable pleasure of catching a glimpse of it out of the corner of his eye as he passed from one room to another, knowing confidently that it was his to possess until the day he died.

"I'm very grateful to be able to see this," Alain Nathanson said in a low murmur.

Piero Gherardi looked at his visitor and waited. He watched the other's face, trying to decide whether to speak or to preserve the silence a little longer.

Larry's eyes roved around the room, recognizing objects he'd seen before, and thinking ahead to what his role should be in the negotiation.

Nathanson nodded and turned to face Gherardi. "I know that you're asking one million U.S.," he said. "I can't pay that. On the other hand, I like it very much, and I'm prepared to pay $700,000. I believe that would be a very fair price."

Gherardi frowned, and shook his head. "You know, we have others who are interested," he said. "I don't want to mislead you, but some have offered more, and since we knew from Larry that you'd be coming from Geneva we agreed to hold off making commitments."

Nathanson threw a quick look at Larry, and then at Gherardi. "Your other investors," he began. "Do you all need to vote on the decision? Or can you and Larry here come to a final agreement with me?"

"Just tell me a more realistic figure," Gherardi said. "Then Larry and I will go into the other room and discuss."

"What about the problem of exporting it out of Italy?" Nathanson asked. "It's a very good, very old painting."

"Ah, yes," Gherardi said. "But this is a private sale. A painting that has been in someone's family for years and he's decided to sell it. A quiet sale, do you see?"

"But I'm not buying it from that family. I'm buying it from you." Nathanson scrutinized Gherardi's face and awaited a reply.

Gherardi, who was standing quite close to the other two, took a step back.

"It's a private sale," he said. "A very quiet, private sale."

Nathanson turned to look again at the painting for a few moments. Then he faced them and said, "My top price is $800,000."

Gherardi nodded to Larry. "You and I will go in there," he said, pointing to a side door.

Paintings covered with brown paper stood stacked against the walls of the tiny room and dusty tapestries hung above them.

Gherardi kept his voice to a whisper. "Will he go any higher?"

"I don't think so," said Larry.

"It's not what we were hoping."

"Yes . . . but it's what we have."

"I can see you're a practical man," Gherardi said. He searched Larry's face with a look of appraisal that combined fatigue, irony, and, finally, acceptance.

"*Bene*," he said.

"We'll agree?" Larry asked.

"*Sì, d'accordo*."

Final arrangements were easier, and Larry was pleased, but somehow not surprised, that the buyer had thought of everything.

"Cash is always better, isn't it?" Nathanson said.

Piero nodded. "Of course."

Larry knew very well that it was in Piero's interest to shield the sale of the painting from the authorities. Everything had to be done secretly, and so far that was already a fact in this deal. He and the other investors were not going to talk about the sale and Nathanson clearly knew how to do business in the Italian art scene. Everyone was aware that avoiding taxes was as Italian as soccer or spaghetti. Larry smiled and congratulated himself on being in the know about local transactions. He'd been here long enough to lose his naiveté. Receiving a big bundle of cash would be a new experience, but he felt confident that he'd be able to hide it.

"I don't like to put things off," Nathanson said. "I often make decisions quickly—in this case, that I want the painting—and then I move."

Larry looked at Piero Gherardi. "The others?" he asked. "We need to tell them."

"Don't worry," Piero said. "I'll talk to them. It'll be all right."

"By the way," Alain Nathanson said. "I'll take the painting with me. I shall rent a car here and drive back to Geneva."

Gherardi nodded. "I think that will be fine," he said. "You shouldn't have any trouble. I'll wrap it up and give you documents which indicate a low value, say one thousand dollars, and a certificate that it was painted by an Italian art student in 1912."

"I like that," Nathanson said. "Very good, indeed . . . and I have the cash right here."

After Alain Nathanson left, Piero turned to Larry. "You did well, my friend, very well."

"Thanks, I'm happy you agree."

"I think you and I could have a little arrangement."

"What sort?"

"You travel to New York and other places. Sometimes that can be very helpful to me. Here I am in Florence, but my customers are from anywhere. If you find a buyer for something I have, a buyer outside of Italy, you and I could come to an agreement."

"I would be an agent?"

"Why not? Call it an agent."

"I couldn't guarantee anything."

"But if you're successful in finding someone for me we could call it a commission."

"I see."

"Say a certain percentage of the sale price."

"Such as?"

"*Beh*, perhaps three or four percent?"

"Oh," Larry shook his head. "I was imagining something more, but I wouldn't mind."

"Then why don't we say six percent?"

"Sure, that seems fair. I'm willing."

"Good. It will be beneficial for both of us."

46

The evening of October 4 was cool and clear. Although he'd never been to *Chiasso Swing* Larry had an idea where it was and looked forward to a pleasant twenty-minute walk to the north side of the city. He felt good about his part in selling the painting. The Ugo di Paolo was in Geneva, and he had a wad of U.S. dollars stashed in his Santo Spirito apartment. Moreover, his Italian bank account had a very comfortable balance. Alain Nathanson had certainly confirmed the Swiss reputation for efficiency and reliability.

Crossing the river on the Ponte alla Carraia, Larry headed in the direction of Gherardi's gallery, but then turned left down another street. To his surprise, people were going into the Church of Ognissanti. That was unusual at such a late hour, and he didn't know it to be a special day. Beyond the main entrance another door was open that led to the room of Domenico Ghirlandaio's *Cenacolo*, and he decided to go in.

Josh's band was starting at 9 p.m., but Larry didn't feel he needed to arrive precisely on time. Just now he would pay his respects once again to this five hundred year old painting that he loved more than any of Florence's several portrayals of The Last Supper. It was almost always a quiet room, and now, as he'd done many times before, he sat down in one of the Savonarola chairs facing the fresco, open to finding new pleasures in the scene.

It was incredibly lovely—a work of art that got him wondering if the right word was *study* or *enjoy*. No matter—both were apt. There was the overall impression—calming—but, there were also many individual parts that made him pause and observe more carefully, going back to specific things to make certain that he could keep them in his memory: the tonsured Peter with furrowed brow, sitting on Jesus' right, looking almost angry, and holding a knife that seemed much too large and menacing for simple table fare; and Judas, the only disciple without a halo, his back to the viewer, clutching his bag of coins.

There was a pleasing symmetry to the painting that, while not obsessive, was clearly carefully planned. Ghirlandaio had painted a tall narrow window high on the upper left through which light appeared to illuminate the supper scene below. A peacock perched in an opposite window on the upper right. The thirteen men at table were divided into three groups. The central one consisted of Jesus, Judas, and the sleeping John. To the right there was a group of five disciples, and it was balanced on the left by the other five. Everything had been considered, and the overall effect was both fascinating and very satisfying.

Larry had often been the only person in the room, but if other tourists or even large groups of students came in, he stayed, held by the scene, and immersed in a world of pastel color and passion. Ghirlandaio had painted his *Cenacolo* in 1480, and it portrayed the moment just after Jesus has told the others that one of them will betray him. In the faces of the disciples one saw such varied states of human feeling and such shades of emotion—innocence, wonder, worry, weary concern, even pragmatic toughness, caution, questioning, eager readiness, suspicion, matter-of-fact realism, sleepiness, introspection, and resignation. Birds flew through the air beyond the arches above the table. The food and flasks of wine and oil on the long table were real. And the spatial perspective was so marvelous one couldn't believe that it was all painted on a single flat wall.

Finally, one came back to the center—to Judas—and the sense of a story that would go on into a dark future.

A few other visitors wandered in, but they left after only a cursory passage through the room. That always surprised Larry. There was no accounting for the astounding variation in people's interests.

Then he stood, left the building, and continued his walk up Borgo Ognissanti. How lucky I am, he thought. The chill night air carried the not unpleasant organic smell of the Arno, and he wondered at its complexity, inhaling deeply several times. A mixture of things—mud and silt that the river brings down from the mountains of the Casentino; spray in the air as the water rushes through the city; and fresh, vaguely spiced aromas of moldering vegetation. It was all good.

His way led into Via Il Prato with its hair salons, furniture stores, and *trattorie*—jarring structures of the here and now—and he tried not to let them crowd out from his mind the remaining lingering pastel images of Ghirlandaio's transparent flasks of wine, of birds delicately flying, and of Judas and the others, everything vivid and present against the background of light air and classic architectural form. What beauty! And here I am, he thought. This is where I am meant to be.

An alley branched off to the left, and half way down he saw the neon lights: *Chiasso Swing*. Even out on the sidewalk he could hear the band playing *Just One of Those Things* at a medium tempo and it sounded awfully good. A few couples stood at the door waiting for a table, and peering over shoulders he could see that the place was packed. Some people were avidly listening, but for more the music was clearly just background for conversation. Audiences who don't appreciate what they're hearing, he thought, and low pay for the band to boot. How do jazz musicians keep resentment under control?

The hostess at the door smiled at him. "I have a seat close to the band," she said. Larry nodded, and she began guiding him toward a small table. A rotating light fixture in the ceiling flashed red and blue on two couples jitterbugging on the small polished floor in front of the raised bandstand. Right away he spotted Josh sitting at the piano, swaying with the rhythm, his face tilted down, intent on the keys.

In a far corner of the room an altercation was taking place. Two men gripped an inebriated young man who was yelling something incomprehensible, but definitely in English. Another man, tall and broad shouldered, stood in the shadows behind them and seemed to be directing the process of expelling the struggling drunk. It had been only a quick glimpse, but something about the tall man seemed familiar to Larry. Wasn't that Orfeo Malizia?

The whole thing was over in a flash. The customer was pitched out on to the sidewalk. The bouncers, grim-faced, retreated into the shadows. The tall man was gone.

The trombonist was beginning a mellow solo, and then Larry saw four women sitting in the opposite corner. He recognized Claire.

"I'll sit with those ladies," he told the hostess, and turned to make his way through the crowd.

Claire was half-standing and giving a tentative little wave. A memory of his visit to the house in Mill Valley came back to Larry. It had been their only occasion together.

"Was it really seventeen years ago?" he asked her.

She was smiling shyly, but it was welcoming and he took it as a sign that it was all right to embrace her. Then he held her back at arm's length. "Is my math correct?"

"I think so," she laughed. "It's great to see you, Larry."

The women smiled and nodded as Claire introduced them. He heard her words, but the music was loud and compelling, and he turned to look over at the band. Josh was into his solo now, and he wanted to hear his old friend play.

The tune ended with an ensemble chorus and a final resounding drummer's cymbal crash that faded as people stood up clapping enthusiastically.

"They're wonderful," he said.

Josh, getting up from the piano, gave a big wave, and came over.

"Hey, man," he said, hugging Larry. "Thanks for coming."

"Oh, my God, I wouldn't miss it. You guys sound fabulous."

"Yeah, it's going well. We had no idea how Europe would respond, but they seem to like it."

He looked over his shoulder. The trumpet player was announcing the next tune. "I have to go back," he said. "Couple more tunes and we'll be through with this set."

Josh hustled to his place, played an eight bar piano intro, and the band swung into Fat's Waller's *Keepin' Out of Mischief Now*. It was very light, with Josh's opening providing a Basie touch that set the perfect groove for the whole piece. They played two ensemble choruses, and then Rich Mariani leaned into the microphone to sing

> *Keepin' out of mischief now,*
> *Really am in love, and how!*

Larry kept scanning the room for the tall broad-shouldered man, but he was nowhere to be seen. Orfeo Malizia? What an odd possibility.

The dancers loved the easy tempo, seeming to barely touch the floor, skimming and turning rhythmically, spinning adroitly, all finesse and nimble expressive grace.

The band played another ensemble chorus; then a series of fine solos: piano, trumpet, clarinet, trombone; and two choruses out.

"Wow," Larry said, turning to the four women. "Aren't you glad you came to Italy?"

Everyone laughed.

"I keep thinking about Lorenzo il Magnifico," Claire said. "What would he make of this scene tonight? I mean, it's humanism, isn't it?"

More chuckles.

"What a great idea," Larry said. "The Medicis certainly nurtured the high culture of their day. In my book the music these guys are playing fits the bill. If Lorenzo came back he might need a few hours of preparatory listening, but I think he'd be open to it."

"In college my time here was very short," Claire replied. "But it made a big impression. Little things keep coming back to me."

"I want to show you what I love about Florence," Larry offered. "People sometimes ask me why, out of all the cities in Europe, I keep returning here, but I can explain it better by taking you around."

The other women turned to face the band. They would let Claire get reacquainted with her friend.

The gig ended at midnight, and Larry walked Josh and Claire back to their hotel. He was surprised they had picked the Alberti. He knew the place.

Josh talked about the band and how pleased he was with how the evening had gone.

"We're basically a traditional band," Josh said. "But we're not stuck in a rut. We want to combine elements that work for us. We love the collective improvisation of the old timers in New Orleans, with each of us listening to the others and making it a musical conversation. We want the audience to hear that, to get in on the conversation. But beyond that, we've all absorbed enough modern jazz to be able to incorporate some of its elements into our solos. We're lucky because we don't seem to have a problem combining things that way. And, you could probably tell, we play a broad range of tunes. Our only rule is to swing."

"I keep thinking about you playing piano back in high school," Larry said. "Didn't we used to argue about bebop?"

"I remember," Josh said. "Neither of us knew what we were talking about."

Claire was amused, but she was focused on the churches and piazzas they were passing. Larry mentioned a few names and offered historical bits of information, but it was a relaxed stroll, mostly along the river, until they turned up a narrow alley and arrived at the hotel.

The Alberti Hotel was grim and run-down, but somehow it merited a three star rating. Larry knew from experience that it was clean enough, but what had promised two years back to be a passionate one-night affair there with a very seductive young woman he'd met on an airplane had ended as a tedious and awkward time discussing her life's problems. The wasted evening still brought back feelings of embarrassment and futility, and he cringed at the thought that this was a place where he'd been disloyal to Luisa. He decided not to ask Claire and Josh how they had selected the place. Obviously, he told himself, if you play jazz for a living there are compromises you have to make.

47

They met for sightseeing the next morning.

"We should start with Julius Caesar," Larry said as he led them past the great buildings of Florence's center to the Piazza della Repubblica. "Two thousand years ago this was the forum of the original Roman city. Over the centuries it became a place of squalor. Part of it served for several hundred years as the Jewish ghetto, but that was torn down in Napoleonic times. The Kingdom of Italy was unified in 1861, and for a brief period Florence was its capital. Then this entire area of dilapidated buildings was rebuilt so that the present Piazza could stand as a proud and majestic symbol for the future. What do you think of it?"

"Must be an improvement over what it was," Claire said. "But I don't love it. Maybe that's what the 19th century was all about—over-confident and pompous?"

"Agreed," Larry said.

He led them through the narrow alleys behind the Duomo and came to a stop where they found themselves at a street that appeared to make a large rounded curve.

"What do you think of this?" he asked them.

"The curve seems odd," Josh said. "As if it doesn't belong here. All the other streets are straight."

"We'll follow it for a while."

The curve continued; then ended. They turned a corner, went another block, and the curve reappeared.

"This was the Roman amphitheater," Larry explained. "It was outside the city's original wall, and it was huge and glorious. Over the centuries the curve has managed to survive all the building, tearing down, and rebuilding of neighborhoods."

They had pizza for lunch and then stepped out into Piazza Santa Croce.

Josh pointed to the prominent blue Jewish star high up on the church's marble façade.

"That's a little unusual, isn't it?" he asked.

"Definitely," Larry replied. "And Santa Croce is the largest Franciscan church in the world. It dates from the 13th Century, but the façade is much newer."

He led them up the broad front steps of the building to a gray stone block set into the pavement just before the church's great door.

Niccolò Matas di Ancona
Giudicato degno dal parlamento nazionale
Di riposare fra gli altri grandi
In ossequio – al desideri
L'undici di Marzo MDCCCLXXII
Da Lui manifestati morendo
Qui nel MDCCCLXXXVI Fu Deposito
Perche La Facciata di Questo Tempio
Fosse Monumento all artifice

Claire looked at the words. "Someone is buried here?"

Larry crouched down and translated. "Niccolò Matas of Ancona was deemed worthy by the National Parliament to repose here among the other great men out of respect for wishes he expressed as he lay dying on March 11, 1872. In 1886 his body was placed here so that the façade of this temple might be a monument to its creator."

He looked up at Claire and Josh. "Matas was the Jewish architect who planned the façade. Somehow he was able to include the prominent Star of David in his design. Despite his desire to be buried inside with the famous Florentines, it was ruled impossible because he was a Jew. Consequently, his body is not within the church, but under the porch."

"All these thousands of tourists come here," Josh said quietly. "I'll bet only a handful know about this tombstone."

"Larry, it's really special to have you as our guide," Claire said. "Living here the way you do must be wonderful."

Larry accepted her appreciation modestly. "I manage to keep busy, even here," he said.

Josh watched his old friend's face, searching the features of the mature man, and he felt a pang of nostalgia when he detected a palimpsest of the boyish smile, but behind the maturity there was sadness and pain. He remembered scenes of Larry's awkward unburdenings—the hurtful story of the Gersts' divorce, and the protective hardening of Larry's soul that followed; the recurring talk of money, power, and success; and, then, the lurid stairway scene that destroyed Larry's own marriage. If Claire's intuition told her that Larry's retreat to Italy was a wonderful way to live, God bless her. She was usually right, and Josh wanted her to be right, but he couldn't shake the thought that his friend was still encumbered with bitterness and defeat.

Inside the church they looked up at the huge cycle of frescos extending one hundred feet above the main altar. "They were painted by Agnolo Gaddi in the late 14th century," Larry explained. "His father, Taddeo Gaddi, was the most important pupil of Giotto, the great Florentine master. These frescos tell the story of what's called *The Legend of the True Cross*, and that's appropriate for this church, Santa Croce, which means Holy Cross."

Larry outlined the legend: the cross of the crucifixion was made of wood that originally came from the tree of the knowledge of good and evil in the Garden of Eden; the tree was cut down and used to build a bridge that the Queen of Sheba crossed on her way to meet King Solomon around 900 B.C.E.; the Queen told Solomon that a piece of the wood from that bridge would someday cause a replacement of God's covenant with the Jews; Solomon, frightened and upset by the prediction, hid the piece of wood; it was later used to make the cross of the crucifixion; and the Empress Helena, Constantine's mother, went to the Holy Land in 326 A.D. and discovered this piece of wood, the True Cross.

"In the Middle Ages most of the population was illiterate," Larry said. "And the church used these fresco cycles to educate the faithful. I don't think art historians would approve, but I always think of this one as a medieval comic strip."

They walked along the side aisles of the vast interior, pausing at chapels where famous Italians were buried—Leonardo Bruni, Lorenzo Ghiberti, Leon Battista Alberti, Michelangelo Buonarroti, Gioacchino Rossini, Galileo Galilei. "Santa Croce is far more than a church," Larry said. "It's also about civic pride. It's where the great sons of Florence are remembered."

They stopped before Niccolò Machiavelli's tomb. "Power, money, and art all come together here," Larry said.

His words bothered Josh, and he watched Claire's face to see her reaction. She was happy, and interested and curious about everything. Larry was her tour guide and she was taking it all in, loving the wedding of art and history, and feeling lucky to be back in Florence. But Larry hadn't changed. A smart-ass remark from long ago came back to Josh.

Money isn't everything, but being poor is stupid.

Okay, maybe there was some truth to it, but he didn't have to like it. If the relationship between art, money and power was a fact of the real world, it was only a small part of the story. Focusing on it was annoying. It seemed a desecration. Yes, artists had to live, and Josh knew all about the support for the arts by the great Florentine patrons and banking families—the Medici, the Bardi, the Peruzzi, the Pitti— but he didn't want to keep hearing about it. And what was it William Blake had written?

To the Eyes of a Miser a Guinea is more beautiful than the Sun & a bag worn with the use of Money has more beautiful proportions than a Vine filled with Grapes.

Grapes, grapes, beautiful purple grapes. Did Larry see the miracle of grapes? Or was everything just another financial deal for him?

And what if it were? Why should Josh care? Was he jealous? Was it just sour grapes for him? Comparing himself to Larry was stupid and hateful. He'd had an inkling that this reunion after so many years might be awkward, and now it was bothering him more than ever. He didn't like the thought that being with Larry meant he had to feel self doubt. After all, what did he really want? Money? Travel? Larry's life? Wealth, but always alone? A search for happiness in a foreign country?

But especially—to be alone?

Sure, a little extra money coming in would make life easier. It didn't take a genius to figure out that playing jazz was an impossible way to live. How cool it would be to get paid more for the gigs he played.

Still, it would be impossible for him to spend his life in an equation where music was seen as just another commercial transaction.

They dined early at Cammillo so that Josh could be at the piano by nine. The next day was going to be devoted to more sight-seeing with Larry, and the following morning the musicians were taking the train to Torino for the next part of their tour.

Larry knew all the waiters at Cammillo and obviously enjoyed being warmly received as a recognized and valued customer, especially on an evening like this when he brought guests who could see how comfortable he was making all the arrangements. He ordered a plate of *fiori di zucca fritti* to share, and then they had *spaghetti alla bottarga* accompanied by a crisp, light Orvieto.

They arrived at *Chiasso Swing* with ten minutes to spare. Once again, the band was in fine spirits, and the musicians were playing in an even looser, more relaxed style than the night before. The crowd seemed quieter, but more attentive and appreciative, and the evening was unbroken by rowdy disturbance. Midway through the final set, Josh took the microphone and told the audience about the history of the next tune.

"This is a ballad we love playing. You don't often hear *Georgia Cabin* these days, but it was recorded in 1941 by the great soprano saxophonist, Sidney Bechet, and his New Orleans Feetwarmers. If you like to dance, this one is for you."

The clarinet opened in the low chalumeau register with the trombone harmonizing on quiet legato whole notes. People began heading for the dance floor.

Suddenly, Larry felt a hand on his shoulder. He turned and his eyes ran up an arm to the face of Orfeo Malizia.

"Hello, my friend, and welcome."

Larry stumbled slightly as he rose to take the hand. "Signor Malizia! What a surprise. I didn't expect to see you at this place."

"Why not? It's my place, and I have always loved jazz. I'm happy to have you as a guest."

"These are my friends," Larry said, making introductions. "Mrs. Lowen is the pianist's wife. He is my oldest friend."

Malizia smiled and took her hand, making a short bow. "I am enjoying your husband's music very much," he said. "I wish it could be for a longer engagement."

He explained how the club tried to please all musical tastes. "Usually we have rock music," he said, almost as an apology. "That's what the young people want. But, you can see that there are still those who like the older kind. I know I prefer it."

Larry was still standing. He gestured to Malizia to sit with them, but that seemed unlikely. It would've been impossible to fit another chair at the tiny table.

Malizia begged off. "I have my responsibilities," he said. "Maybe you saw what happened last night?"

"The drunk?" Larry said.

"*Sì,* an argument, an insult over *il calcio*—soccer. People here are passionate about soccer. He was an *Inglese* . . . saying bad things about *La Viola*, the Florence team."

"I imagined that I saw you last night," Larry said. "But I wasn't sure—and then you disappeared."

"Ah, yes, but I saw you. Curious, eh? Always something is happening. People drink too much. Usually I'm not here."

"This is really your place, your business?" Larry asked.

Malizia nodded. "*Sì,* for several years," he said. "It was a restaurant, but no one was coming. They were bad managers. I helped them by buying the building. A friend manages *Chiasso Swing* for me, but sometimes I come and then my people know what I expect. Another investment, you see?"

Larry was struck by how different Malizia seemed. He was a new person. No longer the sullen figure at Santo Buscemi's apartment, he was still reserved, but now urbane and courteous. The belligerent negativity was gone.

The band was halfway through *Georgia Cabin* and the dance floor was actually crowded with people dancing to the slow melody.

"I have to go now," Malizia said. He bowed again, very slightly, to the women. "Thank you for coming."

48

The next morning the three of them were sipping *caffelatte* in a *pasticceria* across the Ponte Vecchio in the Oltrarno. The room was in late 19th Century style with crystal chandeliers and red plush chairs.

"I could start every day like this," Josh said, glancing at himself in the mirrored wall next to the table. He stuck out his tongue and made a face. "I could be totally relaxed forever. Are you up for it, Claire?"

"This is what he was like in high-school," Larry laughed. "No, before high-school—maybe in fifth grade."

"Yeah, yeah," Josh said. "You were always the serious one. But, we did squeeze in some good times."

"I want to hear about Signor Malizia," Claire said. "How do you know him?"

"That was a real stunner last night," said Larry. "A complete surprise to me. He and I were co-investors in something—a deal already completed. I knew nothing about his nightclub."

He told them about the Ugo di Paolo painting. "A very special work of art, and we had a very special arrangement, too. Satisfactory all around."

"How do you know about a painting?" Josh asked. "I mean, aren't there fakes?"

"Absolutely. Buying art isn't risk-free, but, then, neither is any investment."

Josh dripped some honey on a piece of bread and popped it in his mouth. "Is it more risky here in Italy?" He chewed for a moment, swallowed, and then took a big slurp of coffee. "What do you really know about Mr. Malizia? How'd you meet him?"

"Through a dealer here in Florence," Larry replied. "It was at a meeting of potential investors at someone's apartment. I didn't like him at first. Compared to the other investors he barely spoke, and seemed kind of unfriendly. But then I figured, well, I don't need him to be my friend. We're all putting money in the pot to buy the painting, so as long as we sell it for a good price, that's enough."

"It worked out well?" Claire asked.

"Extremely well. We put our money in, and when the thing sold to a wealthy buyer the deal was finished. I didn't have to know much about Malizia or anyone else. It was very quick, very clean."

"Who bought it finally?" Josh asked.

"That's even more interesting," Larry said. "I was the one who actually found the buyer."

He described meeting Piero Gherardi by sheer chance over lunch one day. "That was the beginning," he said. "We talked about art, about my collecting, about my tastes. And then he introduced me to this very rare painting. I think he hoped I might be the buyer, but it was clear that even though I've got some wonderful pieces—I showed him photos of my collection—this was beyond my finances. It was in another class completely."

"So you all formed a group . . ."

"Right. We had to do it that way. And then I remembered a name I heard years ago from my father. It's a long story, but our buyer turned out to be the son of a man who was a Gerst family friend back before the war."

He described his phone call to Nathanson, his trip to Geneva, and Nathanson's passion for art.

"Alain Nathanson was the perfect buyer, and it made things a lot easier and quicker. He wanted the painting immediately, and he was prepared to do a little extra to make certain he would end up owning it."

"He paid more than others would?" Josh asked.

"Not precisely. It was more a matter of making sure that he would have greater leverage."

"Greater than whom?"

"Greater than other possible buyers."

"How'd he manage that?"

Larry laughed. "I don't want to give away all my secrets," he said. "But you might say that he enlisted my help."

"Paid you something?"

"Right."

"And you were able to do him the favor?"

"Well, he ended up with a wonderful painting. So, as I said, there was satisfaction all around."

"Amazing, my friend," said Josh. "You are amazing."

"I want you to see my apartment," Larry said. "Then we can go over to Piero's gallery. He's probably there, and he can show you his things. It'll be interesting for you."

They walked along the street facing the imposing extended façade of the Palazzo Pitti, and Larry talked about local history.

"This palazzo was commissioned in 1458 by the Florentine banker Luca Pitti, a friend of Cosimo de' Medici. A hundred years later the Medici family itself began living there and had a private corridor built along the top of the Ponte Vecchio that connected the palazzo with the office of Florence's government across the river. The Medici ran things in Florence for three hundred years. There was no Secret Service in those days, so the corridor gave them protection and allowed their feet to stay dry on their way to work."

They turned into a narrow sloping alley, crossed a busy street, and came out into Piazza Santo Spirito where Larry lived.

From his apartment they looked down at the quiet pleasant space with its trees and stone fountain. Larry pointed toward the large church at the end, its façade an unadorned light sand stucco.

"It was designed by Filippo Brunelleschi, the same architect who figured out how to put the dome on the Duomo."

"It reminds me a little of those Spanish mission churches in California," said Josh.

"Inside it's huge and spare, but there are quite a few good paintings, and in one room there's a small carved wood crucified Christ done by Michelangelo when he was about seventeen years old. Right around the time of Columbus."

He walked them through his rooms. They were decorated in a typically older Italian apartment style, with heavy furniture and an absence of anything modern or laborsaving, but here and there were personal touches. A rustic table with a pile of art books; a small, non-religious unpainted 17th century terra cotta sculpture of a peasant mother cradling an infant on her lap with an older child looking on at her knee.

"That's meant to be Mary, Jesus, and a young John the Baptist," Larry said. "But to me it's more like a normal family."

Josh smiled at the thought—a normal family.

"Oh, I love it," said Claire. "The tenderness. And the natural draping of the long dress and her shawl. Everything seems so soft and flowing."

"I can see why you're comfortable here," Josh said. "I can see it very easily."

"It's a small, uncomplicated apartment, and easy to take care of," Larry said. "I can lock the door, fly to New York, and forget about it."

They left, walked a few streets beyond the piazza, and came to another church with a simple brick façade.

"This is Santa Maria del Carmine," Larry said. "It has the famous frescos by Masaccio."

"Oh, we have to come back here," said Claire "I want Josh to see those."

"After we visit Piero I'll leave you to yourselves," said Larry. "The Brancacci Chapel is open all day."

They went down a narrow street that ended at the river and crossed over on the next bridge into an area that seemed devoted to antique shops and art galleries.

"Piero's place is half a block ahead," Larry said, slowing down. "I need to say one other thing. What I told you about my part in the sale of that painting is just for your ears. Piero knows nothing of any special arrangement that I have with the buyer. So, please don't allude to that."

"No," said Claire. "Of course not."

The marble bust of St. John the Baptist was no longer in the gallery's window, and in its place, on a very plain old walnut table Piero had placed the early 15th Century painted wood sculpture of the grieving Madonna. Larry rang the bell and looked up at a small window.

"Piero has his office up there."

They saw a hand wave, and in a moment saw Piero bustling down the iron spiral staircase into the front room. He opened the door to let them in.

"Hello, come in, come in. Welcome to Florence," he greeted Claire and Josh. "You are Larry's friends, I know. I am glad to meet you."

He didn't look well. The tanned face seemed almost sickly, and his expression was somber and anxious.

"Everything okay?" Larry asked.

"*Sì, si . . . tutto bene.*"

"We've been strolling around trying to see everything," Larry told him.

"It's not possible," Piero shook his head. "Even we Florentines haven't seen everything. But, please—look around, ask me any questions you have. There are many beautiful things."

Josh and Claire smiled and began to move about in the small room.

"There's more back there," Piero said, pointing to a doorway. "A larger room, more to see. Please, feel free."

He watched as they headed for the doorway. "Yes, take your time," he added.

He flashed a worried expression at Larry and motioned to him to move back toward the street door.

"We have a problem," he said. "It's good that you're here."

Larry waited for an explanation. Piero looked over his shoulder toward the doorway through which Josh and Claire had disappeared. Then he turned, hesitated, and went on. "A big problem."

"What?"

"Something unpleasant. I had a visit from the Guardia di Finanza. Our friend in Arezzo mentioned our arrangement to an acquaintance. Somehow the Guardia di Finanza heard about it."

"What does that mean?"

"They're—how do you say it—snooping."

Larry knew about the Guardia di Finanza, a department of military-style police whose mission was maintaining order and security in the economic and financial sectors. It ran the customs division; fought tax evasion, forgery, and counterfeiting; and controlled the export of currency and, especially, cultural items.

"They've been here?"

"Yesterday, a brief visit, but they'll be back."

"What do they know?"

"I'm afraid quite a lot. They demanded a photo of the painting, my financial records . . ."

"My God, that's terrible."

"More than terrible. It could be big trouble."

Josh and Claire came back into the room.

"I love your things," Claire said. "How fortunate we are to see them."

"But we're not actually shopping," Josh assured Piero.

"No, no. It gives me pleasure that you enjoy looking."

Claire smiled at Larry. “I think we’ll go on,” she said. “Back to see the Masaccio paintings. Then we’ll wander around. Will we see you this evening?”

“I could come by your hotel. Perhaps a nightcap after dinner. Then you’re on an early train for Torino in the morning.”

Josh and Claire agreed. “Okay, perfect. Then we’ll see you later. Now off to see the rest of Florence.”

Piero Gherardi held the door as they stepped out on to the sidewalk.

“*Arrivederci*,” Claire said. “*Grazie*.”

“*A voi. Arrivederci*.”

Piero watched them disappear down the street. “Nice people,” he said sadly.

“Look, what do we need to do?”

“Ah, you think there is something we can do? I’ll have to wait until the Guardia lets me know more.”

“Have we done something illegal?”

Piero sketched out the essence of the problem. The painting by Ugo di Paolo Menchini was very likely one that would be considered part of Italy’s artistic patrimony. Letting it go out of the country, even to neighboring Switzerland, was a crime. Of course, one never knew how assiduous the Guardia di Finanza would be in their snooping. The commandeering of Piero’s bank records was a bad sign. They would very likely ask for help from the Swiss police. The Guardia would be mostly interested in whether Piero, an authorized dealer in art, had avoided paying taxes on a sale, but if the question of illegally selling a cultural treasure came up, the Carabinieri would become involved.

“There is a possibility that the authorities could interpret the sale in another way,” Piero said. “And that is if they could be convinced that it was a private sale between Ercole Miglio and your friend Nathanson.”

“How likely is that?”

“I don’t know.”

“If we paid something to someone?”

"Yes, that's what I meant by *convinced.* It depends on whether I am made aware that there is an opening for that possibility."

"You mean they'll come to you and hint there is such an opening."

"Exactly."

Larry felt his heart pounding. What a mess! And Nathanson would be in the middle of it.

"What about the Swiss end of it?" he asked.

Piero explained that because of the strong Swiss concern for banking secrecy and personal privacy, it was very likely that the authorities there would simply ignore the demand for repatriation of the painting. If pressed, they would refuse to cooperate. Ultimately, the painting would remain with Nathanson.

Italy would not be lenient. The Guardia could impose fines against all involved parties. For Nathanson, there would be a demand, which he would be able to ignore. It would never be paid. Italian officialdom understood that quite well, and they wouldn't pursue it because they knew they had no effective way of enforcing the demand.

For Piero Gherardi and his group of investors things would be completely different. Assuming that the police couldn't be convinced about the truth of a "private sale", there would then be only two questions. How much? And how?

The amount of a fine would only be known at the time of the demand, but the mode of handing over the money could be either official, or unofficial. Fines, of course, could be duly registered in Guardia di Finanza records, but a more likely scenario might be money changing hands as simple bribes.

"It will be a very direct request," Piero Gherardi said sadly. "The Guardia controls the book of rules, and will tell us what they expect."

There was also the awkward matter that Nathanson had in his possession a paper from Piero Gherardi certifying a false and grossly understated value.

"If the Carabinieri get involved it will be much worse," Piero said. "Then the main issue is allowing a cultural treasure out of Italy. I could go to jail."

"Oh, my God." Larry had to sit down.

Piero shook his head. There were tears in his eyes.

"When will you know something?"

Piero shrugged his shoulders and looked away.

"Can the Guardia be paid something?"

"That's what I don't know. It's possible. I'll have to wait and see."

"You'll keep me up to date, of course? We'll stay in touch?"

Piero Gherardi was looking at the floor. "*Sì*," he nodded. "We'll stay in touch."

Larry hastened along the streets. He knew only one thing. He needed to get back to his apartment. He pushed on, stunned, legs stepping automatically with no direction from his thoughts; walking, yet completely unaware of everything around—store windows, people moving aside to avoid him, a truck making a delivery.

Just get back to the apartment.

49

Josh and Claire retraced their route back to the Piazza del Carmine.

"Larry looked different," she said.

"When we came back into the room?"

"Yes—pale, and awkward."

"I noticed it. They were talking while we were in the other room, but when we came back I thought the two of them seemed nervous, like they wanted us to leave. I was kind of glad to get out of there."

"I think your old friend has a secret life."

"Such as?"

"I find it hard to imagine what he's really up to. What is he after? Is it just money?"

"Not completely . . . he's got another side. But money's certainly what Larry has always wanted."

"Can you see yourself making deals where you get an extra cut that you have to keep secret from others in your group?"

"You already know the answer to that. People make choices. I once made a bad one; I hope Larry hasn't."

"Thinking about it gives me goose bumps."

"I envy his spirit of adventure. But it does make his life uncertain."

"What about *dangerous*?"

"Could be. Anyway, I'm not totally surprised by it. Ever since we were in school together, he was looking to the future, planning things long term, positioning himself to come out ahead."

"Ahead of other people?"

"Maybe ahead of his father. There was competition there."

"Remember my telling you once that I didn't really like him?"

"Have you changed your mind?"

"I've opened it. He has his complexities."

"What are you thinking?"

"For one thing, that it's odd to be here and we haven't met his lady friend."

"I didn't want to ask. I figured it's up to him."

"And what about his family in the Philippines?"

"He hasn't brought it up. Maybe we haven't given him a chance."

"You can sight-see and talk about other stuff, too. We haven't monopolized the conversation."

"We should ask him about that tonight."

They entered the church's cloister and walked along its arcades to a staircase that led up to the Brancacci chapel. Other visitors were viewing the frescos, but the place seemed to command reverence and silence. One could barely hear the footsteps as they moved slowly back and forth, looking at scenes from the life of Saint Peter, but especially at Masaccio's Adam and Eve being driven from Eden by a sword-brandishing, red-robed angel.

"I had to come back here," Claire whispered. "Just look at their faces—the two forebears of our human race."

"Incredible," Josh agreed. "I've seen it so many times in magazines or art books, but it's not the same."

"No, it couldn't be. This is the first time in Western painting that such profound emotion was shown. Fear, psychic pain, devastation—all that, and more, too."

They had lunch at Casalinga, a down-to-earth Tuscan trattoria recommended by Larry, sharing a salad of *finocchio in pinzimonio*, then a delicious *spaghetti al pesto*, and finally *sorbetto al limone* served in the peel of a hollowed-out lemon so cold to the touch that Claire thought holding it might give her frostbite.

Afterwards they wandered upstream along the river on the Oltrarno side and sat for a while relaxing in the small park that faced across to the Uffizi and the Palazzo Vecchio.

At three o'clock they arrived back at the Alberti Hotel and the clerk handed them an envelope.

Sorry I won't be able to make it tonight. Have a safe trip to Torino and enjoy the rest of the tour. I hope to see you soon, perhaps in California.

Larry

50

Larry knew exactly what he had to do—and right away. It would be stupid to keep so much money in his Italian account. If he had to pay a fine, so be it. But there was no reason to expose his affluence unnecessarily. It would be harder for them to get money out of his New York bank, so it was only prudent to send a sizable amount to his American account.

Thirty minutes before closing time he walked into his bank and filled out the necessary forms for an immediate transfer to New York of the deposit Nathanson had made plus an additional amount. Enough remained in the Italian account for two more months of living in Florence. The cash in his apartment was in a secure place. He couldn't exactly relax, but he felt a little more confident that things would be all right.

All he could do now was wait, but once back in the apartment he was assailed again by everything Gherardi had told him. He couldn't stop thinking about it and paced around the room, unable to sit still. They could come and find him easily enough, but it would be much worse for Piero Gherardi, and maybe for Nathanson, too.

What did it mean to be an investor in this? He wasn't responsible for the sale of the painting. Could he lose the return on his original investment? What about Ercole Miglio? How dangerous and utterly stupid to have mentioned the sale to anyone at all! Was that old man in Arezzo culpable, too? No, the painting had been in his family for a long time. It was a private sale . . . or was it?

If he only had to pay a fine he could live with that, but the thought of Gherardi going to jail was terrifying. And how immune from that horrible eventuality was he himself? He had no one to consult, no one to advise him. How long would he have to deal with this tension? In his entire business career, Larry had never felt so exposed.

As he thought back to that first chance meeting with Gherardi a feeling of queasiness came over him. He was in a trap, but he knew he had put himself there. He should've been more careful.

There had been clues. Gherardi was too smooth a salesman, and his willingness to mislead Ercole Miglio ought to have been a red flag. Why hadn't that acted as a brake?

Why? Because he'd been too recklessly wonderstruck by the whole deal and had failed to consider all possibilities. He'd been captivated by the adventure of it. And then there had been walking into that posh apartment in the Palazzo Guglielmini, and meeting the Italians in their business suits who did a good job of pretending that everything would be a simple matter of intelligent planning and calculation leading to a handsome profit.

No, he hadn't been diligent.

Over the next twenty-four hours he stayed in the apartment, going out only to buy food. He'd expected to hear from Piero Gherardi, but the phone never rang. He tried calling, but there was no answer.

Except for Alain Nathanson, no one knew about the finder's fee. That had nothing to do with any of the others and was completely apart from the whole mess. Maybe he could salvage that.

The following day he walked across the bridge and stood in front of Gherardi's gallery. The door was locked. People passed him on the sidewalk. The world hadn't changed. He waited a few minutes, and then retreated to his place.

At 8 o'clock the next morning, his buzzer sounded.

"Guardia di Finanza! Open, please."

Two men in gray uniforms stood at the door. One was lanky and fair; the other was shorter and impressively muscular. Both wore holstered revolvers.

"You are Lester Edwin Gerst?"

"Yes."

They stepped forward, edging Larry back into the apartment, and then closed the door behind them.

"Wait a minute—what are you doing? What do you want?"

"Passport, please."

"What? Why are you here?"

"Passport, please."

"What is this about?"

"You must show us your passport."

He went into the bedroom and brought it to them. They looked at the photo, checked it against him, and the shorter one slipped it into his inside coat pocket.

"You can't take my passport," Larry protested.

"We will return it."

"No, you have no right to take it."

"Yes, we have the right. You withdrew money and transferred it to America . . . a lot of money. Can you explain, please?"

"What are you asking?"

"You helped to export a painting to Switzerland? Is that correct?"

"I didn't export it. I did nothing wrong. A group of us . . ."

"Yes, yes. We know all about that, but you were one of them. Correct?"

"As an investor, yes."

"The painting was very valuable, yes?"

"Expensive, yes," Larry nodded.

"How old was it?"

"How old?"

"Yes, how old?"

"I don't know. I'm not an art historian."

The taller man muttered something incomprehensible to the other.

Then he said, "You will remain in Florence. You must not leave here until we authorize. You understand?"

"I'm an American citizen. I've done nothing wrong."

"You must remain in Florence."

"What does that mean?"

"Do not leave Florence."

"I can't go out?"

"You can go out, but you must not leave the city. We will contact you."

With trembling fingers he immediately dialed Luisa.

"Luisa!"

"What's wrong? Something in your voice . . ."

"Oh, God . . . the painting I told you about. You remember? An investment?"

"Yes, I do. What's happened?"

"I'm shaking. I can hardly talk."

"Please, tell me."

"The Guardia di Finanza . . . they've taken my passport. I can't leave the city."

"Wait, wait . . . you're not making any sense. Go back . . . begin at the beginning."

He stumbled and stammered back to Alain Nathanson—the family connection, the visit to Geneva, and the sale of the painting—and then went on to the Guardia di Finanza's alarming visit to Gherardi.

"His gallery is shut now," he said. "I've called him, but there's no answer. I went over, and it's locked."

Finally, he told her about the men who came to his apartment.

"They gave me no choice. I feel naked . . . lost without my passport."

"*Dio santo*! And they told you they'd come back?"

"Yes, but not when. What can I do? What about getting a lawyer? I didn't do anything illegal."

"*Sì*, but if they accuse you it would be a very long process. Here in Italy you're innocent until proven guilty, but it wouldn't be speedy."

"What should I do? I'm sick about it."

"I'll come over. Enrico's away . . . I can be there in an hour. We can talk . . ."

"I don't know . . ."

"Let me come. I'll make some dinner. I'll cook something you like. We'll just talk. We'll have some wine. And then I'll go home."

"I'm feeling so unsettled."

"It's up to you."

"Enrico's away?"

"Yes, he'll be home in a day or two."

"I feel helpless. I don't know what to do."

"When he gets home I'll talk to him."

"Do you think he can help? What can he do?"

"I'm not sure, but you understand how things are here. He knows people. There are ways. Let me talk to him."

"That would be awkward, wouldn't it?"

"Enrico and I are beyond that."

"Luisa . . ."

"Look, I'm free. I'll come to you. It'll be quiet. I'll give you some comfort. You'll relax a bit."

"Okay, I feel better talking to you."

"Try to relax."

"I will."

"*Ciao, amore*. Give me an hour."

"*Ciao. E grazie*."

Her visit did give him some comfort, although it didn't last long. Luisa was an exceptional woman—wise, loving, and pragmatic—and she stayed for three hours. They ate *risotto ai funghi porcini* and drank red wine, but Larry was anxious the whole time. When she left, the sound of her footsteps descending the stairs was the saddest thing he'd ever heard and he was close to tears. Alone again in the apartment, fear and frustration returned.

She had assured him that Enrico would probably know what to do and that was fine as far as it went, but there were no guarantees. Angry thoughts about Piero Gherardi and about Italy itself ran through his mind against a background of diffuse apprehension and doubt. The idea that Enrico Orlando might be able to pay someone off to retrieve the confiscated passport seemed less than plausible—an empty dream. He couldn't count on it. Something else was bound to happen, but he could only imagine worse. Jail for Gherardi? Jail for himself?

The distress and worry he'd felt right after Piero Gherardi told him about the Guardia di Finanza was nothing compared with what he faced now. Without a passport he was isolated and helpless. The few stray thoughts he'd had about possibly renting a car and leaving Italy—through France, or through Trieste and into Yugoslavia, or by ship to Tunisia—were now, he knew, pitifully futile. A flight home was impossible. A ship? What ship? Where to? No, he was a prisoner.

He remained holed up, trying unsuccessfully again and again to call Gherardi. A few times he went out for what he hoped were inconspicuous strolls to the gallery just to see if it was still locked. It was, and without a *Chiuso per ferie* sign. Just shut.

It was as if the entire world had given him the cold shoulder. Cold, and threatening.

It startled him to realize how little he knew about Gherardi. Was he married? Where was his home? The only number listed in the phone directory was the one for the gallery. And the other investors? He knew where Santo Buscemi lived, but Buscemi wasn't a friend. He barely knew the man, and certainly wasn't inclined to search him out to lament the web of issues that now jeopardized the whole group.

51

Four days after their first visit the two Guardia officers returned. It was mid-afternoon and Larry was about to go down to Tiberio's for an *espresso* when the buzzer sounded. This time the men were in plain clothes and they flashed their badges.

"Today you must come with us," said the shorter, muscular man.

The explanation was perfunctory, but understandable. The painting had been taken out of Italy without permission. It was a part of the Italian cultural heritage. Did Signor Gerst understand that? He said he wasn't sure what it meant.

"You have been a part of an illegal transaction," the lanky man said. "It is a serious crime." His insincere and abruptly withdrawn smile was chillingly sinister.

"But I did nothing wrong."

"You participated in a crime against the Italian state. You will have to pay a fine."

The officers' faces were sober, but their expressions and body language seemed to indicate a willingness to grant a few minutes for reality to sink in.

"What is the fine?"

"First, we take you to our *stazione*."

"Where is it?"

"Very near," said the taller one.

"You're arresting me?"

"Ah, no. This is just a procedure. You must write some papers, sign some papers."

"I should have a lawyer."

"No, you won't need one," said the muscular one.

"When can I leave?"

"Perhaps in two hours."

"It takes that long?"

"Please, just come with us now. It's no problem."

"Maybe it's not a problem for you, but it is for me."

"Yes, just now it is a problem for you," the tall one acknowledged. "Please, we go now."

He walked between the two men to the far end of Piazza Santo Spirito and continued into a narrow street where a four door black Fiat sedan was parked.

"Get in," the muscular one ordered. The terror Larry was feeling quickly intensified. Crimes of exporting cultural treasures were supposed to be handled by the Carabinieri. These were men from the Guardia di Finanza. Why were they out of uniform? Why were they using a civilian car?

He stood looking at them.

"I am not going with you."

He turned abruptly and took several rapid strides back in the direction of the piazza.

They were quicker and grabbed his arms.

"Get into the car."

They shoved him into the back seat and the shorter man followed. The tall one got into the driver's seat and started the engine, heading out of the city in the direction of the broad boulevards that encircle Florence just outside the old walls. Larry knew the area. They passed

Porta Romana and headed up Via Ugo Foscolo toward Bellosguardo. In five minutes they were out in the countryside and the driver pulled off the road into a grassy field where he stopped and turned off the motor.

"We're not going to hurt you," he said. "We just need to discuss the best way for you to survive this problem."

There was no one around. An occasional Vespa sped along the road without paying attention to the black car that was now twenty yards off the pavement.

"Let's talk about the fine you will have to pay," the shorter man said. "It could be very large."

"I take it that this isn't an official visit," Larry said quietly.

"We would like to make sure that you survive a bad problem that you created for yourself."

"I'm much obliged. What is it you expect of me?"

"We can be of great help to you," the taller man said quietly. He took Larry's passport out of his shirt pocket, waved it for a moment, and then put it back.

"What is the fine I have to pay?"

"We will go with you to your bank. You will take out some money. If you give that to us, we will make sure that no one troubles you. You will be able to return to America. No questions asked."

"That appeals to me," Larry said. "I'm looking forward to returning to America. How do I know you'll honor an agreement? I don't know either of you."

"Yes, you know us now. We will help each other. You will get what you need; we will receive the fine, and the problem—your problem—will go away."

"How much are we talking about?"

"Fifty thousand U.S. dollars."

"My God, how do you expect me to get that for you?"

"There are two possible ways, Signor Gerst. Withdraw it from your local account. We know quite well that you have that. Or, perhaps, even a better way would be simply to let us have it in cash . . . cash that you received from Mr. Nathanson. I think you know what we mean."

He chose the no-nonsense practical route. It was easier than he'd feared. Weeks later he was still reimagining the sequence: the drive back to his apartment; going upstairs alone while they waited below for him on the sidewalk; then the walk together through some back streets until there was no one around; and finally the rapid handoff of a small paper bag containing 50 one thousand dollar notes.

In return, he received brief smiles that now seemed genuine, briefer handshakes, and finally his passport. The men indicated that he was free to go, but that he should continue to the next corner and walk around the block until he reached his building. They would go the opposite way. Nothing more was said. They went their separate ways and in a few minutes he was back in front of his building. The piazza was quiet. Pigeons waddled, and then suddenly a whole flock of them lifted and flew off toward the church. A group of young mothers with toddlers stood talking near the fountain. Three teenage boys kicked a ball around.

The air in the apartment was hot and stale and he opened two windows. If he felt any easing of tension once he closed the door behind him it wasn't much. A little breeze stirred and it felt cool on his clammy skin. Touching his shirt he realized how much he'd been sweating. He let the tap run and drank two large glasses of cold water. The afternoon light was fading and he sat down in the dim gloom of the living room. Right away he felt anxious, got up, and began pacing the room.

Everything churned in his mind. Anger at being fingered. Extortion by a couple of thugs. Jesus! And he knew handing over 50K to those two didn't guarantee a thing. They might even have been impersonating Guardia officers.

No, that couldn't be. That first time when they were in uniform . . . no one in his right mind would take that chance. They were just crooks, like everyone else around here. He had to get out of Italy. They could still come after him. And what about the Carabinieri? Just looking at one of them you knew. They were hard. Never smiled. And for all he knew Piero Gherardi might even be in jail already. What a country! How does anything get done here with all this corruption?

No, he had to leave. Maybe there was a chance he'd be able to return some time in the future, but he might have to live with the possibility that his Italian time was over. That was okay—he could cope. Right now New York seemed the epitome of a calm, secure, relaxed place. Thank God, the world was huge.

52

At eight o'clock he remembered he hadn't eaten anything since early morning. Sitting in a restaurant would have been impossible for him. He picked up the phone to order a pizza to take out.

"What kind you want?"

"Napoli."

"*Va bene. Nome?*"

"Larry."

"*Va bene*, Larry. *Venti minuti. Ciao, ciao.*"

The place was crowded and he had to stand, squeezed in at the entrance amidst a group of young people who were waiting for a table. Finally, he heard his name called and he took the warm cardboard box smelling of oregano, capers, and anchovies.

The alleys were dark and he had to step carefully along the cobblestones. At the edge of the sidewalk before he reached the front of his building a man moved out of the shadows.

"Signor Gerst."

He stopped.

"Who is it?"

"I am Malizia."

"Oh, my God. Why don't you come out here in the light? I didn't recognize you."

The tall, broad-shouldered man with the unusually small head was pale and unsmiling.

"I need to talk to you."

"About what?"

"Let's go upstairs."

Larry hesitated, but the deadly serious look on Malizia's face told him he had to submit. They began the ascent, but at the top of the first flight Larry stopped to catch his breath.

"Are you okay?" Malizia asked.

"Yes, I'm okay. I just wish we had an elevator."

"*Sì, sì*. Take your time."

Once in the apartment, Larry put the pizza in the kitchen and filled a pitcher with cold water. He handed a glass to Malizia.

"*Grazie. Molto gentile.*"

They sat opposite each other at the table.

"You know about Piero Gherardi?" Malizia asked.

"I know his place is closed. Where has he gone?"

"They took him to jail."

"Oh, my God."

"For illegal export. You understand?"

"I do," Larry nodded. "Piero told me there was a possibility."

"Yes, it's terrible, but I want also to warn you. Santo Buscemi is very angry. He knows everything."

"What do you mean?"

"Buscemi is a gentleman, but he has a lot of friends. He is connected with the government, with important people, and with the banks. It is easy for him to find out secrets, and he makes people pay for double-crossing him."

Larry shifted uneasily. "What are you talking about?"

"He knows that you got an extra payment from Nathanson."

"That's not true. I got my share just like all of you."

"No, don't lie to me. I am here only because when I met you I could see that you are an intelligent, sensitive man. You love Italy, you love art. I felt you are *simpatico*. I liked your nice friends the other night at my club. I like you. I don't want you to get hurt."

Larry waited, but said nothing.

"Santo Buscemi knows people at your bank. It was very easy for him to look at your account. He saw that you had a big deposit on September 20. It came from an account in Geneva. He knows you are a friend of Nathanson. He is not a stupid man. He is powerful. And he is dangerous."

Larry stood up and went to the window. Except for circles of light on the pavement from street lamps, the piazza was completely dark. He could barely make out a little group of young people smoking and talking outside a *trattoria* across the way. Their voices rose and fell, with occasional emphatic exclamations followed by short bursts of laughter.

"I met Nathanson only a month ago. My father knew his father. We're not really friends."

"Larry—may I call you Larry?"

"Sure."

"The money—it was for doing Nathanson a favor? For helping him? For leading him to the Ugo di Paolo painting?"

Larry took a deep breath. "Look, just because Mr. Buscemi can bribe someone to have access to my bank account . . ."

"No, he doesn't bribe. People do favors for him. You are offended of course. Bank accounts should be confidential. No one should be able to look at what is private."

"You're damn right. That money came to me from my own investments. I have business interests in America, in Asia, in Europe. The fact that it came from a Geneva bank has nothing to do with anything or anyone. What a nerve!"

"He knows that the money came from Nathanson."

"How the hell does he know? How could he?"

"This isn't America. It's different here, but not only in Italy. Even Switzerland. I don't want you to get hurt. Believe me, Santo Buscemi knows."

Larry couldn't sit still. He paced around the room.

"You came looking for me, just to tell me that?"

"And I didn't think you knew about Piero Gherardi."

"I didn't know he was in jail. And what about you, and Zampini? What about Buscemi and me?"

"If you're asking if we're going to jail, forget it. That's not going to happen. Gherardi is an authorized dealer in art. He has a particular vulnerability. He made a big mistake."

"How long will he be in jail?"

"Probably just a few months. There are ways, you know."

"In this country there seem to be ways for everything. And what about the cash we received? Are they going to go after that?"

"Each of us needs to attend to that in our own ways."

"What's that supposed to mean?"

"It means that cash is easy to hide."

"Some people seem to know about it, too."

"What do you mean?"

"I had a couple of visitors who knew." He told Malizia about the two men from the Guardia di Finanza.

"And you paid them?"

"They were police. They were armed. I had no choice."

"Ah, it's because you're American. They just scared you."

"Yes . . . scared enough so that I agreed to pay them."

"How much did they take?"

"Fifty thousand dollars."

"*Madonna*!"

"Will they leave me alone now?"

"I don't know."

"But they won't come after you and the others?"

"No, it's just because you're American. I'm not worried. They know who I am. They wouldn't dare to bother me. They are afraid of me, and they don't want to risk losing their jobs."

"So, what should I do about Buscemi?"

"Do? You are naïve, Larry. You should go away. It's not just that he's furious about your receiving an extra payment. He's also angry with Piero Gherardi for doing a stupid thing. He doesn't tolerate that. When Gherardi gets out of jail, you can be sure that Buscemi will want to talk to him, too."

"So . . ."

"You should go back to America. You don't really know how things operate here. You should live quietly and keep in mind that Buscemi has friends everywhere. I'll say it again—he is a dangerous man. If he thinks someone double-crossed him, he won't forget it."

"Oh, Jesus."

"I'm sorry. I don't expect you to thank me, but, yes, you should leave Italy."

53

He dialed Luisa's number. She had to know.

"*Caro mio*, what's wrong?" she said.

"I have to return to New York."

"No!"

"It's about that painting."

"What happened?"

"The Guardia came back. I had to pay them, but they returned my passport."

"Thank God!"

"But there are other problems. Gherardi's in jail. Santo Buscemi is angry with me. I have to get out of here."

"*Oh Dio!*"

"The painting was very valuable. The Carabinieri found out. They say it was exported out of the country illegally."

"Was it?"

"Probably."

"Did you know?"

"That was Gherardi's department."

"But why do you have to leave?"

"Oh, my God, so many things have happened since I saw you."

"Tell me."

He started with his trip to Geneva, and then the connection between the Nathanson and Gerst families. "Nathanson really wanted the painting. He paid me extra for making sure that he would be the preferred buyer."

"There's nothing unusual in that. It's expected in arrangements like this."

"That maybe true, but Santo Buscemi found out about it, and he's not willing to forgive and forget. That's why I'm leaving."

"I don't understand."

"You were right about him being well connected. Someone he knows at my bank let him search my account records. He saw the deposit from Nathanson's Geneva bank. It was a big amount and he's furious. He feels he was double-crossed. I don't trust anyone around here. That's why I'm going."

"When are you leaving?"

"I'll try to get a flight tomorrow."

"You'll write or call?"

"I'll call from New York."

"Be careful."

"Will you do me one favor? Do you think you could pack up my stuff for me, or have it packed up for me? You have a key, right?"

"Yes, of course I have a key. But pack up what?"

"My books. Some little pieces of sculpture."

"*Mamma mia*!"

"I know. It's a lot to ask."

"No, what I meant was . . . you're thinking of . . ."

"Yes, not coming back."

"*Oh mio Dio*!"

"At least, not for a while. Maybe a couple of years."

She said nothing.

"Luisa, I think it's better. I don't feel comfortable . . ."

"I know. I know. You're right. I'll pack them. I can do that, and I'll come to New York, but when . . . I don't know."

"Thank you."

"You'll call me? Soon? I'm very nervous."

"I will. *Ciao, Luisa. Un bacio.*"

"*Un bacio, carissimo. Un bacio a te.*"

PART TEN

1985
Manhattan

54

It wasn't easy—New York was far from the calm, secure, and relaxed place he'd invented. An entire week after his abrupt departure from Italy he was still looking over his shoulder. He slept fitfully. His appetite was gone. Instead of feeling pride and pleasure in his carefully nurtured collection of paintings, they only triggered hellish and disfigured images of his life in Florence. And what kind of life had that really been? It was impossible to say. Those months seemed lost forever, smothered under a miasmic blanket of anxiety and dread. The glories of art and of history that had sustained him were extinguished. Life was shrunken. Only survival mattered.

There were entire days when he sat alone in his dim rooms, trying to put those last weeks out of his mind, but nonetheless insistently compelled to relive them. That first lunch when he met Piero Gherardi—had it really been pleasant? The tanned, intelligent face and the aureole of white hair that he remembered now had only a malevolent meaning. Hadn't he seen something menacing there? The way the man held his knife in one hand, his fork in another? Then it had seemed natural. Now it seemed aggressive. How could he, Larry Gerst, an agile, yet circumspect investor, not have detected obvious disquieting notes? The hawk-like nose coming down and approaching the pointed chin? Or the small piercing eyes? And the persuasive salesmanship?

Had Gherardi immediately seen him as an easy mark? Were the others, his fellow investors, all in on it together? What if he hadn't discovered Nathanson for them? Would he then have been dragged into some even more duplicitous plot?

Yet it wasn't Piero Gherardi who loomed . . . he'd been straight with Larry. What appalled was his own inept judgment of people. How unexpectedly odd it was to feel grateful to Orfeo Malizia for going out of his way to warn him. Any worries he'd had about the tall man with the disproportionately small head and the semi-belligerent attitude had disappeared, but the snuffed out, positive memory of Santo Buscemi—tall and distinguished in his fine apartment, pouring vintage Chianti for his visitors—was now replaced by an image of vengeful contempt. How long would this panic go on? Never in his life had he been so stricken by fear. His earlier vague and amorphous forebodings had eased, but now there was a narrowing down. His peril lurked in a specific quarter.

It took all his concentration and will to force himself to go out, but some things were unavoidable. He was alone and had to fend for himself. There was shopping for food, and there were more than a few business details that had been neglected during his time away from New York. Somehow he overcame his inclination to hide and managed brief forays into the neighborhood, but he was scrupulously vigilant, even during the day. He searched faces, alert to peculiarities, and he studied individuals in ways that weren't his custom. Any face could hide a threat; any figure standing quietly could be a challenger.

Days went by and nothing changed. It didn't take long for him to catch up with the details of his business affairs, but he had trouble mustering interest in the things that had always appealed to him in New York. He went out only from necessity. Every day he read *The Times* thoroughly, but whatever was going on in theatres and museums seemed bland, if not actually dull.

Recently there had been a small earthquake in Westchester County and, despite the fact that no major damage had occurred, articles and letters to the editor about seismic activity continued to appear almost daily. References to California were frequent, and it made him wonder about Josh and Claire. After his terse apology to them for not saying goodbye in person, they had disappeared from his thoughts and his life, but now he suffered moments of embarrassment when he remembered his abrupt note.

He'd enjoyed showing them around Florence, and he was certain they'd found it interesting. Both Claire and Josh were receptive, but he saw that between him and the two them there was a barrier. The friendship was ancient. The intimacies of boyhood belonged to the past, and there was no bringing them back. There had been old frictions, but there had also been a fundamental caring about each other. Josh's closeness had meant a great deal to him during his parents' divorce, but he knew very well that he'd also been a good friend at the time of Josh's expulsion from Bartlett College.

Maybe there had been competition, but it didn't seem likely that it had continued. Or had it? How could a comparison be made? They were so different. Was he envious now? He didn't think so.

I helped Josh, he remembered. I got him a nice little investment in Danville years ago. He made out all right in that.

After lunch Larry lay down on the sofa, closed his eyes, and slept for two hours. It was three-thirty when he awoke. He looked around the room. All the paintings he'd collected hung in their proper places. Books and art auction catalogs filled the shelves, but he wondered about the ones he'd left in Florence.

He'd promised to call Luisa. She would be worried and angry. It was nine-thirty there. He got up and dialed her number.

"*Pronto.*"

"Luisa . . ."

"*Finalmente*! Where have you been, Larry? I don't know whether to be angry or worried."

"I'm sorry."

"You don't sound okay. What is it?"

"I'm a nervous wreck . . . not my usual calm self. It's hard to relax if you think someone is after you. And it all happened so suddenly."

"*Oh Dio*! Larry, I am sorry, too. I couldn't do anything about your books."

"No?"

"Please don't be upset about this . . . I had to talk to Enrico."

"About . . ."

"About you. He has no secrets from me, and I have none from him. You know that."

"Of course. What did he say?"

"The main thing is that he knows all about Santo Buscemi. Enrico is very connected, too. He knows things about a lot of people. It's his business to know."

"That doesn't surprise me."

"He said I must stay far away from the situation, and that means away from your apartment. He said Buscemi knows more important people than almost anyone else. He is incredibly powerful and dangerous. Someone to avoid."

"Why are you telling me this? I'm aware of it."

"Because Enrico doesn't want me to go to your apartment. He says I must stay out of it."

"All right. I certainly don't want you to put yourself in danger. So be it."

"It's just that those people don't forget or forgive."

"I understand."

"You should forget about your books. I'm sorry."

"Okay, I'm sure Enrico is right. As of this moment I've already forgotten them. You mustn't get involved. I'm sorry I even suggested it."

"I want to see you. I'll come to New York. I don't know when."

He missed her terribly. The world was an unfair place. Why couldn't they be together? Would it ever be possible again?

"I want to see you, too," he told her. "But it's not a good idea, not now anyway. Later . . . some other place."

"You'll call me again?"

"Of course."

"Soon."

"I promise."

PART ELEVEN

1985
Thanksgiving

55

Josh and Claire saw her parents fairly frequently, and always for Thanksgiving. In the early years Eve and Lou Johnson had prepared the dinner at their own home, but they were both in their early eighties now and pleased that Claire had taken on the responsibility. Josh's parents were a few years older and living in Arizona. They often came for Thanksgiving, but this time had decided to spend a month in Guadalajara.

It was a cold, overcast day, and Josh crouched at the fireplace making sure that the little flames in the kindling were spreading to the oak logs. Finally, he stood.

"Now we're talking," he said, satisfied that a good crackling blaze had begun.

The Johnsons sat quietly, sipping martinis and luxuriating in the mellow mood of the day.

"You're pretty damn good at that, Josh," said Lou. "I could have done it, you know, but the old knees won't squat any more."

Holly, in her third year of medical school and just home for the weekend, came in from the kitchen with a tray of chopped liver on crackers and placed it on the coffee table. The Johnsons doted on their accomplished granddaughter, but they were always especially comforted and reassured when they could see at first hand that Claire and Josh had made a good marriage. They liked their son-in-law—his sense of humor, his music, and his genial and undemanding good nature—and on a family occasion like Thanksgiving they counted their blessings.

Claire came in and sat with them. "Dinner's almost ready," she said. "Maybe another twenty minutes."

The warm and savory aroma emanating from the kitchen was making them all hungry. She had taken the roasted turkey from the oven, and was letting it cool a bit so that Josh could start carving.

Holly was in the mood to talk.

"Tell us more about the trip," she said. "I'm so jealous."

"Oh, it was great," said Claire, looking to Josh for verification.

"Wonderful," he agreed. "We loved each place. Florence was my favorite. And the band did really well. We could be invited back."

Lou asked if it was a night club.

"Sure, I guess you could call it a night club. Similar to the places I play here. They seemed to like the band a lot. Claire actually met the owner of the club. He was very courteous."

"Maybe a little too courteous," Claire said. "Sinister for sure."

"I didn't actually get to meet him," Josh said. "I was playing."

"And you met up with an old friend?" Eve said. "How was that?"

"Very nice," Josh said. "Larry was our Florence tour guide."

"I remember he came to dinner here when I was ten," Holly said. "He gave me a little purse. I don't have it anymore. What was it like seeing him?"

Josh and Claire looked at each other. She had gently probed Josh's childhood remembrances and they had spent hours going over the details of their visit. Larry's succinct message remained as an unsatisfying end to their time in Florence. Had they done something wrong? Was he so emotionally involved that he couldn't bear to say goodbye? That wasn't in keeping with his personality, but who knew? Or maybe something more interesting for him had come up in which he saw another opportunity for himself. Would that have been in keeping?

"An interesting, complicated man," Claire said. "He spent a lot of time showing and explaining things to us that most tourists will miss, but he's very private. I guess it's not that unusual . . . maybe Josh feels differently . . . but I felt he was pretty guarded."

"How so?" Eve asked.

"We know he has a lady friend there, but we didn't meet her."

"Wait," Josh said. "He did have us up to his apartment. His lady friend—Luisa—is married. The two of them don't live together. He explained that."

"Very true," Claire agreed. "And that particular situation makes him protective, but I still feel he has a bit of a wall around him."

A timer in the kitchen went off and she got up to check on their dinner.

"Let's give it another ten minutes," she said, coming back.

"Just being in Europe must've been nice," said Eve. "We had some wonderful trips when we were still traveling."

"When we were first planning the trip I had my doubts," Josh admitted. "But I would love to go back . . . to play music, but even just being a tourist would be fine. I want to see more—more places, more cultures."

"That's the first time you've said that," Claire said.

"No, I mean it. I'll talk it up with the other guys, but even if there's no gig, let's plan another trip. Not now, but maybe next year."

"Oooh, that would be so cool!" Holly said. Her two years in the Peace Corps had led directly to her decision to apply to medical school, but it also aroused a strong desire to see the world. In Honduras she had worked in the area of women's health, even assisting in the delivery of babies. She had planned lectures to village women on birth control, and had given talks on the importance of clean water in the prevention of infantile diarrhea. But it was seeing the wrinkled and exhausted women who, by the age of thirty-five, had had fifteen children—only half of them surviving—that made her know immediately what her specialty would be.

"There's an Ob-Gyn clerkship for a medical student to go to Guatemala for a month," she said. "I'm going to apply for it."

"When is it?" Josh asked.

"It would be next year. I'll have electives then and it will be great to do it just before my internship."

Josh watched her and smiled. He exchanged looks with Claire, Eve, and Lou. Were they all thinking the same thing? A wonderful kid . . . smart, poised, confident, great values . . . medical school. Long ago that had been his half-formed plan, but it hadn't been in the cards.

"Okay, I want to hear more," Holly said. "You went to his apartment. What was it like?"

They described the neighborhood, the living room overlooking the piazza, and the shelves filled with art books and catalogs.

"Larry was pretty happy about a deal he and some others had just completed," Josh said. "They'd purchased an important painting, and then sold it to a really wealthy collector."

"So, is that what he does?" Lou asked.

"He's always been interested in art," Josh said. "But this was apparently kind of special."

"That's part of what I meant saying he's complicated," Claire said. "I don't think it was a totally above-board kind of deal. He got paid extra for finding the wealthy collector, but the other investors were not included in that. I don't know . . . it sounded strange and a little scary to me."

"Well, we don't know all the details," Josh put in. "It's peculiar."

"No," said Lou. "He's smart, that's all. It's a business, isn't it? There's nothing wrong with getting a bonus for exerting yourself."

"That's one way of looking at it," Josh said. "But as a friend . . . and we were pretty close growing up, although not so much in recent years . . . I've always been puzzled by his two completely separate motivations. He has a real passion for art. You know that immediately just hearing him talk about it. But, then there's this approach to it—as you say—as a business."

"Well," Eve said. "It's a mark of intelligence to be able to keep two disparate things in mind simultaneously."

"Maybe that's it," Josh laughed. "Larry certainly qualifies there. Anyway, even though he and I grew up together, our lives went separate ways. People have their quirks. We're all different. There are things we can never know about another."

"Are you sad about that?" Holly asked.

"Not really. Just interested . . . and, maybe wary."

"You grew up together, but it was pure chance," Claire said.

"What was chance?" he asked.

"I mean that you probably always were pretty different. You had some common experiences, but the two of you . . . just boys . . . isn't it possible you never really had basic values in common?"

"We grew up close, we were close for a long time. We shared a lot. I don't think it's surprising that we stayed friends."

"Could be, but just think of all the kids you knew when you were in third or fourth grade, and try to remember them now. Most of them fade out of consciousness. Maintaining a friendship based on childhood is rare."

"Okay, but we were friends all through high school, and we kept in touch during college, too."

Claire nodded, but she wasn't buying. "It's unusual," she said.

"You've always had your doubts about him," he reminded her. "But you began to like him, didn't you?"

"I detected some sadness there," she said.

"You detected right," he replied. "Both he and I have had our trials. And we've both had to deal with them and then go on in life. We've improvised."

"I know, I know. Anyway—go carve the turkey."

PART TWELVE

1988
The Cormorant

56

On the first Tuesday night of December 1988, Josh was playing at The Cormorant. A group of local characters sat drinking at the carved mahogany bar in the front room, but a lively crowd was listening to the music. For Josh, it was one of those happy evenings when he knew he was playing beautifully.

Sitting at the piano he watched what was going on around the room. It was almost closing time and he had just finished an up-tempo *'Deed I Do*. A quiet ripple of applause floated up from the tables nearby, and then he noticed that a couple of cops had come in. They were probably getting off duty and would have a beer listening to him play, just like everyone else in that crowd, before heading home.

His next tune would be his final one for the night and he decided to play some funky blues in G. That would end the evening quietly. He threw everybody a smile, waved, and settled into it.

What a good night, he thought. He felt great. He was getting closer to *fine*. He modulated from G into E flat, and then into C. Music—a work in progress.

It was eleven-thirty when he finished. He closed the keyboard, picked up his music bag, waved to the bartender and headed for the exit. Some people were behind him and he turned back to hold the door open for them.

It was the two cops.

"Josh Lowen?"

It wasn't the first time a cop wanted to talk to him, but it had been many years and he didn't like thinking back to that time.

"What can I do for you officers?"

"We'd like to ask you a few questions—down at headquarters."

"You kidding me?"

"No, we're not kidding. Just come with us," one of them said, reaching for his arm and gently moving him toward a patrol car sitting a few yards away.

"Wait," he stalled. "What's it about? You can't just . . ."

"Do you know Lester Edwin Gerst?"

"Larry Gerst? He's an old friend. A real old friend."

"Yeah, he was," the other officer said. His nametag read '*O'Meara*.'

"What are you talking about?"

"That's what we need to discuss."

"Wait a second. I think you're harassing me."

"No, Sir—we're not."

"Grabbing me? Threatening me? Coming here where I'm working, like I'm a criminal?"

"Nobody said anything about being a criminal."

"How'd you know I was here?"

"Sir, these are routine questions. You know him, or you knew him, isn't that right?"

"What do you mean *knew*?"

"I'm afraid he's dead."

They let him call Claire.

"Hello?" He knew she was reading in bed.

"I'm going to be late."

"What's wrong?"

"Oh, God!"

"Josh, what is it?"

"It's about . . . Larry."

"What about Larry?"

"I'm still at the Cormorant. The police are here."

"What?"

"They say Larry's dead. That's all I know. They want to question me."

"I'll come right away."

"No, they're not going to keep me. They say it'll be a couple of hours, but then I can go home. They just want to know how I know him . . . stuff like that."

"I think I should come down."

"No, please. I'll be fine."

"Aren't you exhausted?"

"Not really. This kind of thing wakes you up."

"Drink some coffee before you drive home."

"Yeah, I'm sure the police can provide that."

"I can't believe it."

"I know. I can't either."

"I'm sure I'll be awake when you get home."

"Sure, we can have a nice long chat."

"Start at the beginning—how you knew him."

"Oh, Christ—you got about an hour?"

It was more than an hour, and only the beginning of a very long night for Josh. At the police station the questions went on until four in the morning. But they got his story and they showed him documents from down on the Peninsula in San Mateo County so he'd understand why they'd picked him and how the case was developing.

The first item was a copy of a small page full of names and phone numbers. It was from an address book and had the letter '*L*' at the top. Half way down he saw "*Lowen, Josh.*"

"We check everything," one of the officers said. "The address book was in the Redwood City motel room where he'd been staying."

"Redwood City?"

"Correct. So, once we had your name and a local phone number, it wasn't difficult."

Josh tried to recall the motels south of the airport along Bayshore Freeway. You caught glimpses of them as you went by at 70 mph, but the only impression he had was that they all looked sleazy. Where were they? San Mateo? Redwood City? San Carlos? Not at all the kind of place that Larry would select. Incredible that he'd been in the Bay Area and hadn't called. How odd, considering their history. Nonetheless, the shock he was suffering left no room for feeling offended.

"Thanks for letting me know," he said.

The other documents were longer.

San Mateo County
Sheriff's Office

Transcription of Interview Tape

Discovery of Body
Witness: Ernst K_____

I row alone and it makes me happy. The sky wasn't completely dark. There was that very early light from the sun just beginning to come up. I had my sweatshirt on. It has a hood, you know. It was a little cold, but I like that. I got in the shell and waited for a few minutes, just enjoying the stillness of the air. You know, it's kind of a religious feeling I get. I feel connected to the world, all that space out there. It's awesome. Maybe that's what got me back to rowing again. And I'm pretty self-disciplined. I was on the crew in college, but that was forty years ago. Still, my neck muscles and my back, and my shoulders and arms seem to have precise memories of exactly how it's done. So, there were these puffs of mild wind from the east that pushed water against the bow. You hear these gentle little slapping sounds. Finally, I pulled, and I slipped out from the slough into open water. I felt great. Off to the north I saw the lights of one fishing boat heading up the bay toward San Francisco, but that was all. I got into a steady rhythm. You know, you feel that smooth surge forward with each stroke; and you see the little eddies of your wake going back and back until you can't see them, especially at that hour.

I kept moving parallel to the shore, about thirty yards out, but I could make out the border of sedge grass. I was pulling along. You know stroke . . . hover . . . stroke . . . hover . . Then I let it glide, just listening for other sounds. I didn't hear anything. I felt totally alone. But I like that.

Then there was a new breeze from the north and I pulled harder. I hadn't checked the tide tables. I thought maybe I was fighting an incoming tide. I was rocking a little, and I saw that I'd inadvertently allowed myself to be pushed closer to the shore. The sky was getting lighter and to check my bearings I turned to face the bow. A large bird rose up from the sedge. The shell glided closer and another flew up; then, a third. And I wondered if they were vultures, but I thought—well, there are no deer out here. Maybe a dead fish, or a rat.

But then I saw something white, and I knew.

San Mateo County
Sheriff's Office

First Report of Crime Scene

Caucasian male, appearing between 60 – 70 years old, found in marsh off Redwood City by a recreational rower. Body nude with scratches on face and dark bruises around eyes. Height: 73 inches; Weight: 220 lbs; Eyes: brown; Hair: brown with gray; thin at temples and crown.

Marks: 2 cm. flat light brown mole on right hip.

Wounds: bullet hole in center of forehead with exit at posterior base of skull

Other possible identifying facts: segmented ivory bracelet (African?) on wrist; laminated plastic tag fastened to ankle with braided picture-hanging wire; message inside with letters cut from slick magazines pasted on cardboard (Latin? Italian?)

a r s   l o n g a   v i t a   b r e v i s
n u l l a   d i m e n t i c a t a

October 3, 1988 The Peninsula Times

Body found in Bay not yet identified

Authorities have not identified the body of a man found in the bay off Redwood City on September 20. The circumstances surrounding his death are unclear at this time. The San Mateo County Sheriff's Department has issued a brief statement saying that investigations are taking place.

When Josh finished reading he stood up, but immediately felt woozy, and he dropped back into his chair. His hands were trembling. It was too much to take in—the whole thing. He was more tired than he could ever remember feeling. Exhausted. He believed what they were telling him, but kept shaking his head. No, it was impossible. And yet . . ?

"His body was found two months ago?"

"That's correct."

"How long was he staying in that motel?"

"He lived there for six weeks."

"Six weeks! He never called us."

"He moved around a lot. Before Redwood City he lived in St. Louis for close to a year. Before that, in Tulsa for four months, and before that in Miami for another four months. We know he lived originally in New York, but there are several gaps in our knowledge when he just disappeared."

"Oh, my God."

"Yes, we're still trying to piece everything together. When was the last time you and he saw each other?"

"My wife and I saw him in Italy. He lived over there part of the time."

"Italy? When was that?"

"Three years ago—October, 1985. Our band was playing and Larry came to hear us."

"Do you know if he had any enemies?"

"No, he was a business guy. He'd made a fair amount of money. He loved art. We grew up together."

"You saw that Latin phrase in the Sheriff's report? Know what it means?"

"*Ars longa vita brevis* means art is long, life is short."

"Mean anything to you?"

"It's just a saying."

"What about *nulla dimenticata*?"

"I don't know. Sounds Italian."

"It is—means "nothing is forgotten." What about that? We think someone was getting even with him. Can you recall back to whether he ever told you anything that made you think he might have had enemies?"

Josh stood up again and began pacing the few steps he could take in the small interrogation room. He shook his head. Those conversations he and Claire had had about Larry's matter-of-fact assertions about the painting? About being diligent and clever when it came to any sort of financial dealing? About being smart? About not being cheated by others? Oh, my God—the horror!

"He had an investment in a painting," Josh began.

"Okay, go on," one of the officers said.

"He was in a group that bought the painting and then they sold it to a wealthy buyer."

It took another thirty minutes, but Josh sketched out what he remembered. "That's all I know," he said finally.

"Thank you. We'll check into it," the officer told him. "And you can go now. We appreciate your coming down. We appreciate your help."

"I'm sure."

"Sir, just like you, we have our jobs."

"Tell me one thing," Josh said. "When you figure it out, will you let me know? I mean, whatever you discover?"

"That depends," the officer said. "With homicide, some things we can do, some we can't; but if it's possible we'll try to let you know."

They returned him to the Cormorant so that he could pick up his car and go home. He went into a phone both and called Claire.

"They turned me loose," he said. "I'm through. I can come home." It was almost five.

"I haven't slept a wink," she said. "Was it awful?"

"Yeah . . . worse. I'm coming home."

"Are you awake enough to drive?"

"I'm wide awake, Claire. I'll be okay. I don't know much more than I did yesterday . . . but I know he was murdered."

"Oh, God."

"He was moving everywhere, running from whoever finally got him. Miami, Tulsa, St. Louis. Jesus!"

"Oh, Josh."

He began sobbing. "It's so awful, Claire."

"Honey . . ."

"I know . . . and you know . . . that he wasn't perfect. Flawed . . ." He had to stop for a moment.

"Josh?"

"I mean . . . no matter what he might have done . . . this can't be . . ."

"No, of course not."

"I'm sorry," he said. He took a deep breath. "I'll be okay."

"Please take it easy coming home. The traffic should be pretty light."

"I know. I'll take it easy."

All the way home he kept thinking about how the police had pinpointed his location playing at the Cormorant. At the same time he brooded about how Larry had been killed just two months before . . . and not very far away. Living in Mill Valley, Josh and Claire would never have seen *The Peninsula Times*. And anyway, there were reports of violence like that all the time. When he read a newspaper he wanted to know what was going on in Washington, or Europe, or the Middle East—not local stuff. He knew about the Vice-Presidential debate just a few weeks ago when Lloyd Bentsen told Dan Quayle, "Senator, you are no Jack Kennedy." He knew that George H.W. Bush had defeated Michael Dukakis. He knew that the USSR was withdrawing from Afghanistan, and he knew fires had destroyed over a million acres of Yellowstone National Park. Those were what he read about, and he skipped lots of things—sports, society doings, and, for sure, police reports.

Images of figuring out whose body it was went spinning through his mind. They had their ways, the police did—dental records, maybe even DNA—and just routine checking led them to the motel in Redwood City where Larry had been staying in mid-September.

But it was the transcontinental trail of changing addresses that Josh found most disturbing, especially visualizing it alongside all his other memories of Larry Gerst. Only an unimaginable terror would have forced Larry into that.

The contrast between the genial tour leader who had guided them around Florence three years ago, and a hunted man, whose face Josh couldn't even invent, was unspeakably dreadful.

I've done these deals before. To be a winner you always have keep at least a few steps ahead of others.

Oh, my God!

He drove up the familiar street and saw his home.

The neighborhood was dark, but Claire had left their light on.

THANKS

To Debbie Gould, Laurie Palmer, Nicole Goldstein, Madaline Goldstein, Beth Gould, and Diana Panconesi for helpful thoughts about my story as it grew and developed.

To Peter Benson, Tom Frankel, and Paul Resnick who elegantly satisfied my curiosity about police departments, real estate developments, and the world of finance.

To Gianluca Salvatori for *gentil' incoraggiamento* of my investigations into the complexities of the art market, and who put into my head the idea of layers of dishonesty.

To Diana Panconesi and Margherita Panconesi for their friendship, their love of the Italian language, and for their insights into Italian life.

To all of my musician friends who have provided me with another kind of education, and who know very well the challenge and the joy of the note played next.

Above all, to Sue, for her patience, her willingness to listen, her acute perceptions, and her love.

ABOUT THE AUTHOR

William M. Gould, a creature of habit with a short attention span, is still to be found in Northern California practicing medicine, playing jazz, and messing around with words.